Pandora Reborn

First published by Samak Press 2018

Cover design by 100 Covers

First edition

ISBN: 978-1-73-248711-6

This book was professionally typeset on Reedsy.
Find out more at reedsy.com

1

First day at a new high school and Ron sensed he already had a fight on his hands.

"Soccer isn't a sport. Real men play football."

A barrel-chested teen, roughly the same age, planted himself in front of Ron and his locker. His eyes shifted into a menacing glare. Mimicking a nightclub bouncer, this unwanted antagonist made every effort to tower over Ron. He owned a perfect frame for an outside linebacker and did not hesitate to use it to his advantage.

A smattering of laughs and high fives rippled through the small group of football players flanking Ron and the other teen.

Ron rolled his eyes and smirked.

"I'll bet a hayseed like you doesn't even know what a soccer ball looks like," he said.

"Who the hell cares what it looks like?"

"Enjoy all of your concussions and knee injuries while I'm playing pro ball."

"Pro ball? Only thing you're ever going pro in is being a pussy."

This new retort earned another smattering of laughs and hoots. One of the other football players fist bumped Ron's antagonist.

"Way to go, Trevor. Burn!"

Ron drew a sharp breath and clenched his teeth. His face and ears grew hot, as if an invisible hand plucked coals from embers of a fire and wedged them right under his skin. Going to a different high school seemed bad enough. Being stuck out here in the sticks among a bunch of no-good soccer hating hicks felt like pure torture.

"Guess what? I'm going pro in kicking your ass."

Ron dropped a textbook and notebook by his feet and then slammed the locker door shut with his other hand. He locked eyes with Trevor. Every muscle in his arms and chest tightened like ropes stretched out by pulleys.

Trevor cocked his fist.

"Time to shut your mouth."

A quick jab sent Ron stumbling backward into his locker. His cheek rippled around Trevor's knuckles and pushed his lips toward the other side of his face. Blood escaped between Ron's teeth and trickled over his tongue with the same speed as fizz escaping from a freshly opened soda can. He ran his tongue across his lower lip to catch dribbling blood and saliva trickling down his chin.

"There's one injury you don't have to fake."

Trevor's teammates roared with approval at his latest one-liner. Ron charged forward, mirroring the speed of an agitated bull trying to take down a matador. He sized up Trevor's jaw and let a pair of haymakers fly. Trevor weaved out of the path of the first blow. Ron's other fist didn't miss. His knuckles connected with the top of Trevor's jawbone and his left ear.

Trevor let out a grunt and latched onto Ron. He drove him backward again like a tackling dummy and slammed him down on rough carpet. The two teens became a jumble of punches and kicks. One blow here. Another there. Blood mingled with sweat started to trickle down both sides of Ron's face.

"STOP IT! STOP IT NOW!"

A loud whistle pierced the air. A hand grabbed Ron's shoulders and wrenched him backward. He found himself peering up into the face of a scowling bald man who owned the whistle. As he hunched over him, Ron practically inhaled the coffee stains checkering his thick mustache. His tight polo shirt, complete with a school logo emblazoned over the left breast, didn't leave enough of the man's flabby pecs and gradually advancing gut to the imagination.

Ron squinted and turned away. He glanced straight ahead and saw another man clad in a long-sleeved dress shirt and tie restraining Trevor. Pulling him away must have been a chore. The man's glasses were a bit askew on his nose and his carefully slicked down hair now sprang free in multiple directions, giving greater prominence to his receding hairline.

The mustached man grabbed Ron by the shirt collar and yanked him to his feet.

"Do you want your first day of school to also be your last day?"

Before Ron said a word, Trevor beat him to the punch.

"He started everything, Coach Barker. Took a swing at me. I had to defend myself."

All of Trevor's teammates nodded vigorously. A couple chimed in with shouts of "He's right." and "The new kid is a total psycho."

Ron's mouth dropped open.

"He's a lying son of a —"

Coach Barker held up his hand to silence them.

"I don't care who started it. I'm finishing it."

Without another word, Ron found himself being marched down to the principal's office. First day at school and already he felt like a soldier captured behind enemy lines. The principal wasted no time doling out a punishment. Detention. Ron had it for one hour after school for the entire week.

This outcome didn't sit well with Ron. He stared hard at the principal's nameplate, tracing the words "Principal Reynolds" with his eyes, and frowning.

"I can't spend an hour holed up inside the school."

Images popped into his head of a wooden bench with his name stamped on it. Missing soccer practice ahead of the season opener offered a sure formula to not be included in the first XI going forward. Ron knew he possessed good enough attacking skills to get the lion's share of playing time at forward, but he also needed a chance to prove himself to a new coach at a new school.

"Should have thought about that before getting into a brawl out in the hall," Principal Reynolds replied.

"He threw the first punch." Ron whipped out his wrist and gestured to Trevor standing on the opposite side of him. "Am I not allowed to defend myself?"

"Let me give you a free piece of advice, Mr. Olson. Fighting doesn't solve anything. You can't get rid of your problems in life by punching them away."

Ron squinted at her and scrunched up his nose in disbelief. Did his new principal swallow a self-help book? Where did she come up with this nonsense?

"You're absolutely right, ma'am," Trevor said. "I've seen the light. I'm turning over a new leaf."

Ron snapped his head toward Trevor. The smirk plastered across his face offered a true reading on his actual thoughts. He obviously didn't give a damn about detention or what the principal had to say.

Principal Reynolds apparently could not see the same facade Ron saw. Her eyes instantly lit up and she slapped a hand down on her desk as she rose from the chair.

"That's a highly mature attitude, Mr. Judd," She turned to Ron. Principal Reynolds pushed her glasses higher on the bridge of her nose with her index finger. "You could learn a thing or two by embracing the same philosophy, Mr. Olson."

Ron was already learning one lesson.

Spending his junior year at Deer Falls High would turn out to be a bigger pain in the ass than he first imagined.

* * *

“Nice shiner. Who’d you piss off?”

Ron instinctively brushed his fingers over his black eye. It lingered as a souvenir of his earlier fight with Trevor and offered a tender reminder of what put him in this stupid classroom. He looked up from his smartphone and saw a freckled red-haired teen with braces leaning over his desk. The other teen thrust his hand forward.

“I’m Casey. I noticed you’re new at this school, so I thought I’d introduce myself.”

Ron scowled. The detention crowd wasn’t a social circle he felt compelled to join. Hanging out and training with other soccer players offered a much healthier option for his social life.

“Hey, I feel you.” Casey remained cheerfully oblivious to Ron’s reluctance to engage in small talk. “Not a fan of Trevor either. He figures he can get away with anything because he’s a star linebacker.”

“Yeah, well, that’s how football players everywhere roll. ...”

Ron trailed off as he glanced away toward the window. He couldn’t see the soccer practice field from his current location. It only added to a sinking feeling that he had been effectively exiled from the rest of his team. Being stuck inside tore him up.

What tore him up even worse was the fact Trevor wasn’t trapped inside the detention room with him. He hadn’t even bothered to show up. Ron got the impression that one of his football coaches found a way to bail their star athlete out of trouble.

“If it were up to me, I’d give him a taste of justice just like an Avenger would dish out.”

A loud laugh answered Casey from the back corner of the classroom.

Ron turned and saw a teen with spiked brown hair dressed in baggy jeans like a wannabe rapper. He leaned back in his chair and propped up both feet on an adjacent desk.

"Dude, Trevor could make you his prison bitch in a heartbeat if he felt like doing it."

Casey frowned. A slight shudder ran through his frame as he took in the full meaning of those words.

"Thanks a lot, Nick. I didn't need that visual."

Nick laughed again and gave him a thumbs up.

"Props to standing your ground," He turned to Ron and gave him a quick nod. "Better to show you're a real man than a tough-talking geeky chicken shit — even if it gets you a black eye."

"You should see how he looks," Ron replied.

"Yeah, I saw him." Nick leaned further back in his chair and locked his hands behind his head. "Let's just say, I wouldn't declare you the winner."

Ron scowled and buried his face deep in his smartphone again. An hour inside this room with these clowns already began to feel like an entire day.

"Trevor is the least of your worries living in this place," Casey said.

Ron looked up at him and sighed.

"Tell me about it. I'm stuck here in some backwoods hole away from my friends, my club team and my life."

"That's not what I meant."

"What do you mean, then?"

"Deer Falls is a nexus of supernatural weirdness."

Nick laughed again, dropped his feet on the floor and jumped out of his seat.

"God, it never ends with you, does it?"

"You can't deny the things that go on around here," Casey said.

"Which things is it this time?"

1

"What about that subterranean reptilian monster that attacked a couple of years ago? Pulled like a dozen people into the ground and fed on them before being exterminated."

"What the hell?"

Ron heard some nonsensical stories in his life. This one topped them all by a mile.

"It gets better," Nick said. "Trust me."

"How do you explain that cursed section of the Arapaho Forest?" Casey threw his hands out and gestured like a politician making an impassioned campaign speech. "You know for a fact our mayor sent a search and rescue team into that place last summer. They went in there to find and extract a lost group of hikers. Barely anyone made it back out alive."

"Wild animal attacks. Exposure to the elements. Falls from extreme heights." Nick counted off on his fingers as he went through the list. "There are tons of more reasonable explanations for all of it."

"You're just like all the other people in Deer Falls." Casey replied. "Pretend nothing happens. It's all cool to see this stuff in movies and TV shows. But then everyone is too afraid to accept the real thing."

Ron glanced at the teacher sitting in the front of the classroom. She had buried her face in a tablet. If the teacher eavesdropped on their conversation, and heard anything Casey said, she didn't care enough to respond.

"I gotta admit I'm feeling skeptical," Ron said, turning back to Casey. "I'd have to see it before I believe it."

Casey's lips curled tight. His expression turned grim.

"Once you do, you're gonna wish you hadn't seen anything."

2

Nick always heard people say Dean was no ordinary vagrant. He personally didn't see what made his brand of oddness so special.

Dean camped in the exact same spot under the same giant willow tree every day. At least it seemed that way to Nick. Images of his heavy green jacket with a frayed collar and sleeves, coupled with jeans that had holes torn in both knees, became tattooed on Nick's brain. He wondered if this dude ever left long enough to grab a bite to eat or go to the bathroom.

A small camping trailer parked a short distance from the tree offered convenient shelter. Still, the door remained closed, and Dean stayed fixed to his favorite spot like a grubby statue whenever Nick walked or drove past the lot. He really wished the bum would do something — anything, really — to change up his daily routine.

"You suppose the rumors about him are true?"

Nick glanced over his shoulder. Trevor stood behind him and shielded his eyes with his hand. Nick smiled. Did he own a pair of sunglasses?

"Beats me," he said. "He's got a weird vibe, but no different than your typical drifter."

"How many drifters sit there and guard a tree like their life depends on it?"

Nick shrugged.

"Is this a trick question?"

"I'd like to know why he hangs out under that tree." Trevor said. "Maybe he buried a dead body there."

"Dead body?"

"That's what Alex Moss claims."

"The stoner from your English class?"

"Moss claims Crazy Dean chased him and a couple of other guys off with a huge stick when they came out here to huff on some weed."

Thinking about Dean tearing after some stoners made Nick laugh. Given how weathered and disheveled he looked, he didn't feel convinced the old bum could even pursue a tortoise and catch up to it.

"The best part is, Moss claimed the old man rambled the whole time about how this was for their own good," Trevor continued. "Told them he had to protect them or some other retarded thing."

Nick shook his head. He had a good idea where this train would travel. The same stories spread through Deer Falls over and over again like a late summer brushfire. Hidden dead bodies. Monsters attacking people. Demons arising and walking the Earth again. Deer Falls, of course, always ended up as ground zero in each tale.

All those stories made no sense to Nick. Simple nonsense from bored people in a town no one cared about.

"It's a bunch of horse shit," Nick said. "People in this fucking town always end up believing all the same garbage. No one has an original thought."

"What's your theory?"

"I don't know. Buried treasure?"

Trevor laughed and slapped him on the back.

"Buried treasure! Why in the hell doesn't he dig it up? Dude could build himself giant houses and bang a bunch of hotties with big tits."

"You got a better idea?"

"Give anyone five minutes and I'm sure they'll all come up with a bunch of better ideas."

Nick frowned and started walking away. Trevor ran after him.

"Where are you going?"

"I'm coming back later tonight."

Nick had figured it all out in his head. He'd bring along a metal detector to help pinpoint whatever was buried there, a sturdy shovel, and a crowbar.

"Tell me if you find any gold," Trevor scoffed.

He turned and walked away. Nick flipped him off and fished his car keys out of his pocket. Once he finally discovered whatever Dean was hiding, Trevor definitely wasn't getting a share.

* * *

Light from a nearby streetlamp reflected off the metal detector lying against the passenger seat of Nick's car. He peered at Dean through a pair of binoculars. Once again, he found the old vagrant curled up in the same exact spot under the large willow tree where he kept a vigil during the day.

Damn, Nick thought. *That old man never moves an inch. What's so special about this spot?*

Nick opened the car door and pulled out the metal detector, a shovel, and a crowbar. He tugged the hood of his wind breaker tight around his head. Flipping on the metal detector, Nick fanned out from the edge of the sidewalk toward the tree. He carried the shovel and crowbar in his other hand.

A steady hum emanated from the metal detector as he climbed a slope leading from the sidewalk to the willow tree. Nick couldn't be sure if the metal detector still worked right. It sat unused in his dad's closet for longer than he could remember. He always laid out his plans to Nick about going prospecting in the Rockies. The only problem? His dad didn't have the slightest clue where to even start looking for a mine near Deer Falls. Hell, he couldn't find his own truck keys half of the time. Nick or his mom usually retrieved them from a different room each day whenever he was in town.

Leaves crunched under Nick's sneakers as he zeroed in on the willow tree. Combined noise from the metal detector and his sneakers did not rouse Dean from his slumber. That wasn't a terrible thing. If he didn't crowd the spot where Nick needed to dig anyway.

Only a few feet from where Dean slept, beeps grew more forceful from the metal detector. A smile crept across Nick's lips. He set down the metal detector and started digging just arm's length from the old bum. Random sprays of leaves shot past him as a breeze kicked up near the tree.

"Now let's see what you've got hidden here, old man," Nick muttered.

"No! Get away from the tree!"

Nick turned and faced the hoarse voice barking out commands. Dean's eyes were wide open now. He scrambled to his feet.

"Leave this place right now, you damn fool," Dean said. "You're in serious danger!"

Nick swung the shovel blade upward and pointed the tip straight at the vagrant.

"You're not keeping me away from whatever treasure you're trying to hide here. Go back to sleep."

Dean lurched forward and stabbed his hands at the shovel. Nick swung the handle backward to keep it away from his grasp. With the same motion, he brought the back of the shovel head down and planted it in the middle of Dean's forehead.

The old vagrant crumpled to the ground and flopped over on his side. Nick reached down with an index finger and felt his neck. Dean still had a pulse. Good. No need to kill him. But Nick also didn't want him in his way either.

A brownish plume of dust wafted upward. Nick scattered loose dirt and chunks of rock around him as he attacked the soil with his shovel. Carving out a hole near the willow tree required much more effort than he expected. Wooden finger roots reached out from the tree and plunged through the soil. Beads of sweat dotted Nick's forehead like clear freckles as he dug around one root after another. His shoulder muscles hardened into a bundle of knots with each shovelful of dirt and rock he tossed to either side of the deepening hole.

Nick lost track of how long he had been digging before a loud clank greeted his shovel blade. The hole climbed to his hips. He let go of the shovel and shined a flashlight on the dirt. Beneath the beam lay a large, blackened object. It had the wrong color for a boulder. Only one other remaining option made sense to Nick.

This had to be a box or a chest.

He dropped onto his hands and knees and brushed aside loose dirt. It took a minute or two to find the edge of the object. Once he did, Nick plunged one end of the crowbar into the surrounding soil and wedged it underneath the object. With repeated tugs and pulls, he jerked it loose from the soil. The crowbar raised the bottom of the object up in the air. Nick got his hands underneath it and pulled the object forward until the other side finally popped out of the dirt.

It resembled a small square chest with an arched lid. Nick could easily carry it in his arms. A wave of disappointment splashed over him once that realization sunk into his head. How could a chest so small hold much treasure at all?

Nick touched the chest and instantly smiled. A chain wrapped around the outside like a metallic snake. He glanced down and noticed a lock holding the lid in place. No one would go to such great pains to seal and bury this chest if the contents weren't extremely valuable. This would definitely be worth the effort.

Nick glanced over at Dean. That crazy vagrant was still out cold. Good. It meant he had enough time to gather up his tools, along with the chest, and take everything back to the car without meeting more resistance. He needed to find a better spot away from prying eyes where he could crack open the chest and get a look inside.

* * *

Sneaking upstairs past his parents proved a simpler task than Nick expected. Both were engrossed in watching some new Netflix series in the den. Neither one popped their head out, or said a word, when he raised the garage door or walked into the kitchen. Nick lugged the chest, along with a pair of bolt cutters, upstairs to his bedroom.

He swept random junk off a dresser with his forearm and placed the chest on top of it. Now illuminated under a bright fluorescent bulb in his bedroom, Nick noticed unusual patterns crisscrossing the chest lid for the first time. The patterns formed circles, triangles, squares, and other shapes. He had no idea what any of these designs meant, but they sure looked cool.

A sturdy iron chain wrapped around the chest and sealed the lid tight enough to prevent the smallest visible crack. An iron lock kept the chain bolted in place against the clasp and lock plate. Nick's eyes lit up when he saw these things. Dean had really gone to great lengths to conceal the chest's contents from the outside world.

Once he opened it, he felt certain he would be filthy rich. Nick could finally do whatever he wanted. To hell with school. He could buy himself a mansion and spend his days laying down hip hop tracks. When not making music, he could hang out in his personal hot tub with hotties of his choice.

Nick brushed loose dirt off his shirt. He propped up the lock and snipped the bolt in half with bolt cutters. The lock dropped to the floor in two separate pieces. Nick elevated the chest with one hand and unwrapped the chain from around it with the other. Images of treasure heaped inside danced behind his eyes as he set the chest down again and flipped the clasp up from the lock plate.

Nick raised the lid.

Darkness greeted him.

No gold coins. No jewelry. Nothing. Not even a visible bottom.

How was that possible?

Nick scowled. What a huge waste of time! Trevor and the rest of the football players would never let him hear the end of it once they found out. Hell, the whole school would get a good laugh out of his misfortune. He had to get rid of this useless chest before anyone else found out what happened.

Nick tried to slam the lid shut again. It didn't budge. The wooden lid seemed to be frozen. He tugged on it again. It resisted his hand like a tightly sealed jar lid.

At once, darkness inside the chest took on a reddish hue. It grew into a crimson glow and formed small billowing clouds. Nick backpedaled toward the middle of his room. These clouds crept over the edge of the chest and down the dresser.

Red mist.

Flooding the room.

Everywhere.

It settled across the floor. The mist climbed Nick's dresser, his bed, and his desk. A tingling crept from his feet up to his knees. Nick looked down.

Red mist engulfed his legs and rapidly crawled toward his torso. Only one idea dominated Nick's mind now.

Run.

Nick tried to bolt toward the door. Neither leg moved an inch. His bedroom carpet acted like cement, binding both feet to the floor as if he were a living statue.

"Mom! Dad! Help!"

Nick's hoarse calls to his parents were seemingly held in place by the mist as well. It billowed upward toward the ceiling and did not slow its march across the rest of his body. He waved his arms back and forth, frantically trying to dissipate it. The mist clung to his clothes and blanketed his skin.

Wisps of red mist gathered near the open chest. They took the shape of a human-like figure. Barely more than a shadow to start. It didn't stay in that state for long. The figure grew more distinct. Lines and colors hardened and solidified. Flesh, bone, and flowing clothing filled the empty spaces.

"What's going on up here?"

Nick wrenched his head toward his bedroom door. His mother stood in the doorway.

"Mom," Nick's voice devolved into a terrified whimper. "I can't move. Help me!"

The bedroom light above him shattered and hurled shards of glass into the mist. An ear-piercing scream escaped her lips.

"Call 911!" she shouted down the hall. "Nick's in trouble."

Nick's lips trembled and his eyes widened. His mother suddenly lurched forward as if an unseen hand yanked on her shirt. From the corner of his eye, Nick saw the still materializing figure stretch out an arm. It pulled his mother straight into the bedroom against her will.

Suddenly, the figure thrust their hand forward. Nick's mother screamed and tumbled backward. She flew back through the doorway and slammed into the opposite wall with the force of a crashing car. Nick pinched his eyes shut as her body slumped to the floor. A wide streak of fresh blood trailed down the wall behind her.

Nick's father appeared and called out his wife's name. He opened his eyes again. Nick saw his father cradle his mother's hand tenderly for a moment. Then, turning to the bedroom, he fixed his eyes on the figure near the dresser. His father brandished a large boning knife and charged inside the room.

The figure thrust an arm toward him and closed its fingers into a tight ball. Nick could not make out any distinct facial features, but it resembled a woman. It owned long flowing hair and wore a matching cloak and black gown. Nick's father rose off the ground until he became suspended in mid-air. His knife turned inward while he struggled to push it away with his other hand.

His efforts to resist were futile. The blade cut through any obstacle in its path and plunged into a spot right underneath his father's rib cage. Nick's father gasped. The figure raised her hand toward the ceiling. Its upward motion matched by the knife. The blade cut through his entire sternum as he moaned and gagged up blood before he finally dropped into the mist.

Red mist now covered all but Nick's eyes, nose, and mouth. An ethereal voice echoed in his ears. It seemed to belong to both the figure in the mist and the mist itself.

"Thank you for releasing me."

Red mist finally enveloped the rest of his face. A tingling sensation washed over every inch. Suddenly, Nick cried out and clawed at the mist anew.

It burned. All of it burned.

His skin. His bones. His blood.

Right up until Nick drew his last breath.

3

"We aren't ever gonna see him again. You can mark it down."

Ron swung back his locker door to see Casey standing on the other side. He sported a black Star Wars t-shirt and a pair of cargo pants with as many rips as pockets.

"Who?"

"Nick."

Ron gave him a blank stare.

"The other guy who's supposed to be stuck in detention with us?"

"So he hasn't been at school for three days?" Ron offered up an indifferent shrug. "What's the big deal?"

"He's history."

Ron couldn't suppress the smile forming on his lips. Ever since meeting Casey in detention, a distinct image of him formed in his mind. He pictured Casey sitting alone in a darkened basement in front of a laptop. There, surrounded by empty pop bottles, he feverishly typed up a new blog post or posted a YouTube video warning the world about Armageddon.

"Let me guess." Ron put his fingers to his temple and pinched his eyes shut. "Aliens abducted him, so they could bond over a group probing activity."

Casey sighed.

"You're obviously not a believer. But I have proof."

"Proof of what?"

"Proof that Nick is dead."

Ron glanced down at his smartphone and shook his head. Casey needed a new hobby that didn't involve tinfoil hats and paranoia. The dude was only a half-step away from digging out his own backyard bomb shelter and hoarding tons of supplies.

If he hadn't done it already.

"I gotta get to class." Ron waved his hand dismissively and then shut the locker door. "Have fun hanging out in the X-Files."

"I'm not making this up," Casey insisted as Ron walked away. "This is legit scary shit."

By the middle of his English class, Ron wished he hadn't bumped into Casey. It didn't matter how hard he tried to focus on the lesson. Ron just couldn't wrap his mind around figuring out what to do with dangling participles. His thoughts kept wandering back to Casey's words. What did he mean no one was ever going to see Nick again? Did he secretly kill him or something?

I have to make some actual friends in this stupid place quick. Ron thought. *I don't want to get stuck talking to this freak show for the entire trimester.*

Another day of detention guaranteed Ron would get a detailed breakdown of Casey's crackpot theory whether he wanted to hear it or not. He made every effort to slip into the detention room unnoticed. Ron nudged the door open with his toe. His eyes scanned the room, and he claimed a seat at a pace more suited to a hunter doing their best not to scare off a trophy buck into the surrounding bushes.

An awful aroma blending markers, bleach, and hidden cigarettes greeted him once inside. Ron avoided eye contact with the teacher and slipped into a seat behind a desk near the door. Maybe Casey didn't see him, and he'd survive the hour in peace. Those hopes faded as soon as a shoe squeaked against the linoleum. Ron just knew the wrong someone would be standing behind him when he turned around.

"Save your breath. I don't really want to hear it."

"I just came over to say hi. No need to be rude."

Ron raised his eyebrows. That voice definitely didn't belong to Casey. He didn't recognize who it belonged to at all. This voice sounded softer yet more forceful. No hint of eager chattiness.

When he turned around, Ron discovered the voice belonged to a girl. He counted his good fortune. She had brown wavy hair, almost approaching a black hue, gathered into a ponytail away from her olive face and hazel eyes. The girl wore a black tank top with a lace border and a pair of dark blue jeans.

"I'm sorry. I thought you were someone else for a moment. I'm Ron."

"I'm Christina."

Ron smiled.

"You don't resemble someone who identifies with the detention crowd. What brings you here?"

Christina laughed. Ron at once felt enchanted by it. She had the sort of laughter that came not just from a mouth, but also drew in the eyes. Christina took a seat on the desk in front of him and rested her feet on the chair in between their two desks.

"You must be new to Deer Falls. I'm always getting in trouble." She glanced over her shoulder and then back at Ron again. "No one understands me around here."

"I know how that goes. Only my first week here and I've already spent more time stuck in detention than I did both years combined at my last school."

"Where did you come from?"

"We lived in Commerce City. Wish I was still back there to be honest."

Christina's eyes lit up.

"I love Denver. I seriously want to move there once I've graduated and can put this town in my rear view mirror."

Ron folded his arms behind his head and leaned back.

"Cool. That means we have something in common."

"So you like to practice witchcraft too?"

Ron and Christina whipped their heads toward the back of the room at the same time. Casey sprang up from his chair with a smartphone in hand and walked toward their desks.

"What are you talking about, bruh?"

Ron raised an eyebrow and his lips melted into a bemused half-smile. The longer he hung around Casey, the stranger his personality grew.

"Why don't you tell him about it?"

Christina shot Casey an icy stare.

"Can you go five whole minutes without trying to embarrass me?"

"Embarrass you? I think it's cool. It's like you're a real-life part of the X-Men!"

Ron glanced over at Christina. Her cheeks flushed a slight crimson. She avoided eye contact with everything except the round clock hanging on the wall at the other end of the classroom.

"Witchcraft?" he asked. "What's he talking about?"

"He's just being a dork. As usual."

"Seems like a sensitive topic."

Christina transferred her icy stare to Ron.

"Let's just drop it. Is that okay with you?"

Ron raised his hands to signal surrender.

"Fine with me. I don't want to go down this rabbit hole anyway."

Casey plopped down on a desk behind him and Christina. He tapped his phone's screen twice and clicked on an app. A few seconds later, a video appeared on the screen, cued up and ready to play.

"Here's my proof for what happened to Nick. Judge for yourself."

Casey pressed the play button and handed the video clip to Ron. Images appeared a bit grainy and out-of-focus in spots at first. Soon it shook off the potato quality and came into better focus. The video revealed a random bungalow with a weathered sedan parked in the driveway. Orange and yellow splashed across the sky as the sun dipped behind distant mountains. Only scattered traces of sunlight lingered around the car and house. Nothing out of the ordinary stood out to Ron beyond a lack of lighting. No one had turned on the porch light or floodlights hanging over the garage door. Just a simple outline of flickering candlelight showed beyond the blinds.

"What's this supposed to mean?"

"Look at the car. It hasn't moved for several days."

Ron looked closer. On second glance, his eyes caught a bunch of leaves in the gray shadows. Christina leaned over his shoulder to also get a better look. On the roof. In the windshield wipers. On the trunk. Leaves overran the car, claiming fresh territory after falling from their home tree. The sedan looked like it hadn't budged from that spot for at least a few days.

Ron didn't see the same things Casey seemed to be seeing here.

"Most people have more than one car. How does a car parked in a driveway offer proof of anything?"

"Nick drives that car all the time." Casey tapped on the same spot it occupied on the screen. "I always see it out in the school parking lot."

"Maybe he had car trouble?"

"So why isn't it in the auto shop downtown?"

Ron handed the phone back to Casey.

"Why don't you go ask his folks that question?"

A laugh greeted him from the other side of the detention room. Ron turned to see a kid with curly hair, ratty jeans, and a t-shirt with the words *It's 4:20 somewhere* printed on the front.

"My school day wouldn't be complete without another patented Casey Duggan conspiracy theory," he said.

Casey glanced at him and frowned.

"Shut up, Alex."

Alex made himself at home on a desk directly across from Ron. A wide grin was already plastered on his face.

"So what is it this time, Casey? A ghost? A monster? A flying lawn mower? All of the above?"

Ron couldn't help cracking a grin as well. Casey didn't show appreciation for the humor at his expense.

"Does everyone around here have to be a skeptic? Can anyone accept that Nick disappeared without a trace?"

"You ever stop to think that maybe his mom ran off to Golden and brought him along for the ride? Wouldn't be the first time."

Ron cast his eyes skyward, then glanced back at Casey and nodded.

"That actually seems like a reasonable theory to me."

"Why did he leave his car behind?" Casey asked. "You don't up and move without taking something like that with you."

"Maybe his mom was in a hurry because she finally had enough. Everyone knows Nick's old man works as a trucker. My mom used to work with Nick's mom in Golden. She said you could always tell when Nick's dad was back in town by the number of bruises his old lady sported."

Ron frowned as he connected the dots. Alex's speculations hit a little too close to home for him. He stared at the background photo on his smartphone. More than a year had passed since his family gathered for that portrait. It was guaranteed to be the last one.

"Why are you guys so quick to dismiss Casey?"

Christina's eyes darted between Ron and Alex. She sucked in part of her lower lip under her upper lip. It looked like she had an added thought she wanted to express but couldn't find the right words.

"You believe him, don't you?"

Ron took a stab at what he figured was on her mind.

"Lots of strange things happen around here," she said.

"Okay, let's say someone or something killed Nick like Casey seems to think. What am I supposed to do about it? What are we supposed to do about it?"

Christina and Casey glanced at each other and then back at Ron again. Their blank expressions told him that doing anything beyond sharing idle theories had not really occurred to them.

"Maybe we should go check out the house." Casey offered up his idea in a tone suggesting he craved Ron's approval. "We can find out what happened for ourselves. Be like detectives solving a mystery."

Alex laughed and slapped his knee.

"Detectives! Hell yeah! I'm sure Nick's family will be eager to have you all poking around their house."

Casey glared at Alex. Ron decided on a more diplomatic approach.

"Isn't checking out the house something that the police should handle?" he asked.

Casey let out a loud laugh that devolved into a brief snort at the end. Ron answered with a hard stare that made Casey's smile disappear as quickly as it appeared.

"Oh wait, you're serious. The sheriff's office here in Deer Falls is pretty worthless when it comes to dealing with the supernatural."

Ron sighed and buried his face in his hands. He rubbed them down the length of his nose and looked back at Casey again.

"Let me put it another way. I only care about one thing: keeping my soccer career alive while I'm stuck here. Four schools are recruiting me and the last thing I want to do is disappear off their radar."

"Probably shouldn't be in Deer Falls in that case."

Ron shot Alex a cold look. His obvious statement wasn't helpful or needed.

"Keeping my name out there, soccer-wise, is a definite concern in this stupid town. So how about we let someone else deal with this situation?"

Christina pressed her lips tightly together. Her unblinking eyes barely concealed the annoyance bubbling up inside. It seemed ready to burst out from her with a force comparable to soda escaping a shaken pop can.

When Ron looked at her, mixed emotions washed over him. One part of his brain told him to play along. Christina looked cute and it never hurt to score points with a pretty girl in a new place. Even if they entertained some crazy ideas.

The other part of his brain told him to stick to soccer. He couldn't let a bunch of nonsense distract from his training. An entire week already lost to detention. He couldn't afford to let more time slip away and create more ground for him to make up.

That's the one thing which truly mattered to Ron right now. He spent so many hours training and playing with his old club team to elevate his skills to their current level. Now he faced a real danger of falling behind. The competition he would face here did not measure up to what he had grown used to seeing. Small town high school teams like Deer Falls didn't possess top-level coaching or skilled athletes comparable to even lesser clubs in Denver.

Still, watching Christina's body language convinced Ron he should play a little nicer with their conspiracy theories. It offered his only sure ticket to interacting with her again outside the detention room.

"I'm sorry," Ron said, touching her forearm. "I shouldn't be so blunt about it. I guess I just don't deal in supernatural things. It's all so foreign to me."

"With all I've experienced, it's impossible not to believe," Christina replied. "Spend enough time here and you'll feel the same way."

Ron wanted her to be wrong. He honestly hoped there wasn't anything more to this situation with Nick. Adjusting to a new school and a new town already put enough stuff to deal with on his plate.

4

Dean clenched his hands together and traced an invisible circle as he paced back and forth in front of a desk. His squinting eyes barely concealed the frustration welling up within him while waiting inside the sheriff's office.

How many times had he tried to warn these people over the years? No one in this town ever bothered to listen to him.

Even now.

"Do you want to file a police report on your stolen property or not?" a deputy asked.

"We're wasting time." Dean's tone became equal parts abrupt and urgent. "You need to track it down immediately. Every new day that passes while the chest remains out of my possession only puts this town in greater danger."

Now his worst nightmare had begun anew. Dean wondered if someone had already reopened the chest. An unspeakable evil dwelt inside. Now Deer Falls would feel its wrath a second time. This evil would strike them down in ways they could not conjure up inside their worst nightmares. Dean knew it because he had seen it all firsthand.

Burnt flesh. Dean could almost smell it even now. Contorted and screaming faces. Mangled bodies everywhere. In the gymnasium and in the hall. All of it sprang from the darkened cellar of his mind whenever he closed his eyes. Dean tried to shelve those images away and lock the door behind him. It only took the wrong sight or sound to push everything back into the light.

"Look, I can't do anything unless you give me more concrete details." The deputy slid a paper over to Dean. "I told you this the last time you came in here. Fill the report out and tell me exactly what happened."

Dean stopped and stared at the form for the police report. He had no idea where to start. He didn't know the teen who stole his chest. He had no idea where he had come from or where he went. On top of that, his head still throbbed from being hit with a shovel a few days earlier.

The deputy glanced at the clock on the wall and then tapped the paper with his finger.

"If you're not going to file a report, then get the hell out of here. I'm not in the mood for this Dean."

"Please. We need to find her before it's too late."

"Her? I thought you said a teenage boy stole your property."

"No. I'm talking about that awful monster. If she's free, we're all in serious trouble."

Only death and destruction came from inside that chest. Dean saw it. He lived through it. And it ate at him that he did not do more to stop what transpired before he sealed the chest up again.

"Let me put this in clear terms for you, Dean." The deputy rose from his chair and walked over to Dean's side. "There are no such things as witches, monsters, demons or whatever else your imagination is trying to cook up."

His firm eyes and stony expression made it clear their chat was destined to meet an abrupt end. Dean felt dismayed at the deputy's stubbornness. After every sacrifice he made to keep Deer Falls safe, he had become a joke and an afterthought to this entire town. How many more times did he need to come in here before they took his warnings seriously?

"You have to know what will happen if that chest isn't sealed and buried again."

"I only deal in the real world," the deputy replied. "Catching real criminals. Stopping real crimes."

"I'm not some random lunatic. I guarded that tree with my life for a good reason. You must listen to me."

"Go get yourself cleaned up. See a psychiatrist. They'll give you some meds and counseling. It will make a world of difference for you. Trust me."

Tears brimmed in Dean's eyes. His chin dipped to his chest. He buried his mouth in his hands for a moment, before glancing back up at the deputy.

"Why would I lie about this, Deputy Palmer? What do I have to gain? All I want is to stop this monster from destroying other lives the way it destroyed mine."

Deputy Palmer grabbed Dean's left arm and motioned to the door with his other hand.

"Leave. Now."

"Go check out my lot," Dean insisted. "That little thug stole the chest right out from under me. See the hole he left behind for yourself. He's in danger. His family is in danger. This whole town is in danger."

Dean dragged his feet for a bit, trying to impede his impending departure. Deputy Palmer's fingertips pressed deeper into Dean's tattered green coat. Each finger latched onto his skin and clamped down with the strength of five little vise grips.

Dean soon found himself standing on the steps outside the sheriff's office again. Every muscle, from his shoulders to his legs, tightened like guitar strings. He pinched his eyes shut and tried to take deeper breaths. His worst nightmare sprang to life again. Not a single soul who mattered wanted to believe him. It took every ounce of energy his body owned to keep from screaming until his lungs gave out.

Perhaps the worst part of this nightmare is he failed Valerie. He promised her this wouldn't happen again. Each word he spoke to her while he gently held her in his arms for the last time played an endless loop in his mind.

"I'll protect all of them," he said. "You have my word."

Dean's lips trembled and his hands shook as he latched onto that thought. This whole ordeal had been a burden from the start, but he really had no choice. He had to do it. For her. For Adam. All who had fallen counted on him. No one else could make the necessary sacrifices. Dean put it on his shoulders alone because he found nobody else who he trusted to be strong enough to handle the burden.

Yet, 55 years later, Dean had not been strong enough. He did not keep the chest from falling into the wrong hands.

Dean sniffed and cleared his throat. He wiped away tears from his eyes and started walking down Main Street. With each step he took, a sharp burst of pain spread through his right knee. It throbbed as though a hundred small needles jabbed each ligament. Age caught up to him, no doubt. How could he face this alone? He needed to find help. But who could he trust?

Trees, houses, and fences all meshed into a blur. Dean paid no attention to where he walked. He had no destination in mind. All his eyes and ears latched onto were sounds and images from a distant past. Valerie's deep blue eyes, golden blonde locks and infectious smile flashed before him. Her favorite blue cardigan sweater and plaid skirt were as fresh in his mind as if she stood before his eyes again.

A picture unfolded in his mind with the clarity of a photo developing in a dark room. They sat in a booth at the old malt shop, talking and laughing. It felt so real, right down to a checkered tablecloth under his arm and sounds of *Mack the Knife* playing on a jukebox in the corner.

Dean didn't need a mirror to know his thin disheveled gray hair had vanished. He ran his fingers through the short, brown flat top adorning his head again. His old letterman's jacket, paired with new dark blue jeans, took the place of tattered clothes that had been a part of him for such a long time now.

"Where do you come up with these clever jokes?"

Valerie sipped on her soda. The straw kept her from laughing just a little bit more. Whatever suppressed laughter lingered behind, her eyes soaked up.

Dean cracked a broad smile and leaned forward.

"I've been doing my daily funny bone exercises."

Valerie giggled and playfully shoved his shoulder. Her eyes trailed over to the clear window next to their booth.

"What am going I do when it's time to head off to college at the end of the summer?" she asked.

"Come with me?"

"You know I can't. I've already been accepted to DU. Toured the campus. Picked out my dorm. Everything is all ready to go."

Dean held out hope at the time her answer would change. He so desperately wanted Valerie to go to Greeley with him. Playing football wouldn't be the same without her cheering him on from the sidelines. Her presence always gave him an extra boost whenever he got a first down or plowed into the end zone for a touchdown.

Fate wouldn't allow it. Their paths already started to diverge. It began with going to different colleges. Would it stop there? His smile vanished for a moment before he forced it back into place.

This football scholarship had gradually turned into more of a burden than an opportunity. If only Denver hadn't dropped their football team a few months back. Dean could have taken his chances as a walk-on and won a roster spot with the Pioneers.

"I don't have to play football. I can be with you."

Perhaps sensing his hidden concern, Valerie reached out and gently caressed his forearm. Dean knew it would be the last thing she wanted.

Valerie did not want him to sacrifice his own dreams just to make her happy.

"Semesters don't last forever," she said. "We can still write letters and, you know, we'll see each other again when the holidays roll around."

A loud horn blared at Dean. He looked up and saw a small pickup truck headed straight for their booth. At once, Valerie, the booth and the malt shop melted away. Cracked asphalt marked by white and yellow paint assumed their spot.

"Look out!" a voice behind him shouted.

A pair of hands yanked Dean backward by the shoulders. He fell to the ground and out of the truck's path. The driver laid on his horn and shouted a string of curse words while continuing down the street past Dean.

"Do you have a death wish?"

Dean turned and saw a boy dressed in cargo shorts and a t-shirt scrambling to his feet behind him. The boy shook his head as he stood up and brushed off the front of his shorts.

"You can't wander out into traffic like that," he said.

Dean nodded and mumbled a hasty "thank you" to the boy. What he said counted as sound advice under most circumstances. Then again, death offered a promise of a release from his current burden. He could be with Valerie again. His arms would encircle her, and their lips would meet while tears flowed as they experienced such a happy reunion. Thoughts of Valerie were often the only thing that kept Dean pressing forward on those especially cold nights in the lot.

It wasn't a thought Dean could cling to right now. His heart pounded and each breath he took grew shallower as he undertook the long walk back to the lot. No doubt lingered in his mind that awful monster had gotten loose once more.

Now it fell on his shoulders to stop her all over again.

5

Ron couldn't help himself. His wandering eyes locked onto her as soon as she descended the carpeted steps leading into the cafeteria. The girl owned blonde locks that danced above her shoulders as she turned her head. Her lacy top and tight pants invited every boy who laid eyes on her to let their gaze linger a little longer.

"Dude, that's the last girl you want to hook up with."

Casey's words were as pleasant as sandpaper rubbing across Ron's ears. Unbelievable. He popped up all over the place.

"I can get whatever girl I want."

"Not Lisa. That's Trevor's girlfriend."

A sly smirk crawled onto Ron's lips.

"Even better."

He stood up from the table and walked straight toward Lisa. A couple of other girls joined her at the bottom of the steps. The trio laughed and chatted about random things. Ron focused on their conversation as he drew closer, hoping to discover a quick way to insert himself organically into their group.

"You know that he's after only one thing, right?" one of the girls said to Lisa.

Her lips curled into a smile.

"What makes you think I don't want it too?"

"Whoever he is, you can do better."

All three girls turned. Their eyes zeroed in on Ron like three distinct pairs of lasers. His words didn't sound as cool aloud as he thought they would sound when they first popped into his head.

"And who's this better option?"

"You're looking at him."

Both of Lisa's friends responded with barely restrained giggles. Lisa held up a hand to silence them. She circled Ron, her eyes trailing him up and down as if he were a department store mannequin sporting the hottest new fall outfit.

"You do look like an athlete. I only date athletes, you know. But I don't know you."

"We can fix that. The name is Ron. Ron Olson."

"Ron ..."

Her voice trailed off while she shut her eyes and rolled his name over her tongue. For a moment, Ron wondered if she was picturing him naked or some other such thing.

"You play a sport, right?" she asked, opening her eyes again. "You wouldn't waste my time if you didn't, right?"

"I'm a soccer star in the making."

"I guess that qualifies," Lisa scoffed. "Never been with a soccer player before. Guess there's a first time for everything."

A hand jerked his shoulder backward. Ron spun around and came face to face with Trevor. The linebacker greeted him with a stare that could have melted ice. His cheeks reddened to match the rage already present in his clenched jaw.

"Stay away from her!"

"Why should I? I don't see your name tattooed on her anywhere."

"You're just begging for another beating."

Ron ripped Trevor's hand off his shoulder and pushed it back toward his chest.

"You aren't dropping me with a lucky sucker punch this time."

His knuckles clenched into a ball. A well-placed haymaker would send Trevor the right message. Ron propelled his fist forward with the velocity of a stone launching from a slingshot.

That same fist plowed into a hard leather surface. Ron glanced down to see he made contact with the broadside of a medium-sized briefcase. Principal Reynolds lowered her briefcase while staring down Ron. He got the message and dropped his arm back down to his side.

"Congratulations, Mr. Olson," she said, shaking her head. "You just bought yourself a return trip to the detention room."

Trevor cracked a smile behind the principal and made a quick throat slash gesture at Ron. It only made Ron's face burn hotter with anger. How in the hell could Trevor get away with saying and doing whatever he wanted all the time? Ron wanted to do nothing more than tackle that punk and pummel him into the hall carpet. He promised himself he would find a way to make that idiot linebacker pay for this latest stint in detention.

* * *

Ron wondered why he never noticed her before now. Two whole weeks in English class and this marked the first time this particular girl caught his attention.

She had a striking appearance. Icy blue eyes. Deep brown hair that formed spiraled curls resting on her shoulders. Smooth light skin. Her outfit consisted of a crew neck sleeveless blouse and a pair of hip hugger jeans that totally flattered her slender body.

Ron couldn't peel his eyes away from her once the door creaked open and she entered the classroom. The teacher glanced at the clock on the wall and back at the girl. Her brows knitted together, and her lips formed into a scowl.

"Can I help you?"

The girl countered the teacher's grumpy expression with a smile. It crept onto her face with the subtlety of an object casting a shadow while passing a sunlit window. Much like those types of shadows, the smile retreated from her lips as quickly as it appeared.

She handed the teacher a note.

"I'm sorry. I think I'm supposed to be in this class."

"You think you're supposed to be here?"

"This is my first day. I just moved here and I'm still trying to get my bearings."

The English teacher stared at the new girl for a moment, her eyes forming a half-squint. She glanced down at the small note and mumbled some words as she gave it the once-over. The teacher then quietly nodded and gestured toward the desks.

"Please be aware that class starts when the second bell rings at 9:35," she said. "I don't tolerate tardiness, Miss Hightower. See to it you're on time next time."

The new girl claimed an empty desk right across the aisle from Ron. His eyes trailed her as she took a seat. Immediately, she turned toward him and met his gaze. Ron's cheeks grew a little flushed. His first instinct was to turn away and pretend he hadn't been looking in her direction. Too late to do that now. She obviously noticed him staring at her.

"I'm new here too."

The words barely wriggled through his lips. Ron did not want to draw his teacher's attention at any cost.

"I guess we're in the same boat. I'm Cassandra."

Cassandra flashed a smile again and brushed back a lock of hair that had fallen to her cheek. A measure of relief swept over Ron. If she thought he had been acting creepy toward her, she hid it well.

"I'm Ron. Good to meet you."

"It's good to meet you too."

5

Cassandra's eyes suddenly darted away, and she gazed past Ron's shoulder. He didn't need to turn around and look to know his English teacher stood behind him.

"Is it okay with you two if I continue my lesson uninterrupted?"

"My bad." Ron turned to the teacher. "Just being —"

"A distraction? God, don't I know it! Save your socializing for after class."

Ron glared at her and shook his head at her backside as she returned to the front of the room. He glanced over at Cassandra again and noticed she bore a similar agitated frown as he did. Her smile emerged a second time though as soon as she noticed Ron looking at her again. Ron's smile also returned. Another cute girl who liked him? Maybe his short stay in this backwater town would have a few highlights after all.

When the bell rang again, Ron made a point to strike up a conversation with Cassandra before he headed off to his next class. Even if it was a brief one.

"English teachers, am I right? Can't live with them. Can't graduate without them."

Ron cringed inside a split second after those words escaped his lips. Another line that sounded so much cleverer inside his head than it did aloud. Cassandra didn't seem to mind. She offered up a small laugh that felt more real than polite.

"Teachers are drunk on whatever power they can get," Cassandra said. "It's a fact of life."

"Isn't that the truth?"

"Hey, who's the newbie?"

Ron closed his eyes and sighed. An unwelcome third voice had joined their duo. Casey seemed to possess a homing beacon that drew him to whatever spot in the hall Ron occupied.

He opened his eyes again and turned toward Casey. This time around, Christina walked beside him. They approached from the opposite direction. Ron introduced Cassandra to both teens. Casey presented his fist for a fist bump. Cassandra glanced down at his knuckles and then up at him.

"You don't do fist bumps?" he asked.

"Fist bumps?"

Cassandra's question caught Ron by surprise. Her tone made it seem like she was unfamiliar with the term or gesture. That seemed a bit odd. He gave her a funny look. Sensing the uncomfortable stares building around her, Cassandra quickly thrust out her hand.

"Sorry, I didn't mean to be rude. I usually just shake hands when I greet people."

Casey smiled, quickly loosened his fingers, and shook her hand. Christina followed suit.

"Ignore it," she said to Cassandra. "It's just Casey's way of trying to look cool."

A sharp laugh greeted Christina's words.

"He needs to try harder. His geek is showing."

Ron turned and saw Lisa and her friends approaching their group. She zeroed in on them like a lioness or tigress sizing up some fresh prey. Lisa made her first pounce. Now she moved in to complete the verbal kill.

"So sad. I had such high hopes for you, Ron. But now I find you hanging with a geek and a wannabe witch freak."

"Wannabe witch freak?"

Christina wheeled around and marched right up to her. Ron had a feeling this wouldn't end well.

"Get out of my face," Lisa said. "Go play with your cauldron and broomstick."

Christina grabbed a shoulder strap on Lisa's top and suddenly yanked her forward a couple of steps.

"I'm not in the mood to put up with your garbage today. Just leave me alone."

Lisa leaned in closer to her and flashed a broad smirk at Christina. "Why? You gonna put a spell on me if I don't?"

Christina let go of the shoulder strap and gave Lisa a hard shove. She stumbled backward a couple of steps. Anticipating a fight, a few students started gathering around the group. Lisa did not let the newfound attention slide by unnoticed.

"You all saw it. She attacked me." Lisa's voice grew louder to draw in even more onlookers. "Our little resident witch has a big problem controlling her anger."

Christina's lower lip trembled until she bit down on it. Cassandra gave her a concerned look. She pivoted toward Lisa. Her icy blue eyes flashed a subzero chill.

"You heard her. Leave her alone."

Lisa turned and looked Cassandra up and down. She snickered and focused her attention on Christina again.

"How cute! You got a little fashion reject to stick up for you."

She glanced at Cassandra a second time. A self-satisfied grin now adorned Lisa's face.

"Did you raid your grandmother's closet, or does she just handle all of your shopping for you?"

Cassandra pinched her lips together. Her hand instinctively formed into a fist for a second or two before she quickly relaxed it and cast her eyes to the ground. Lisa glanced down at the hand in question and leaned forward as if daring her to strike.

"You think you're going to hit me? I rule this school. Touch me and I'll make your life a living hell."

Ron didn't like where this situation was headed and figured, somehow, it would end with him ending yet another day stuck in detention. He had to put a stop to it now. Carefully, he wedged himself between the three girls and faced Lisa.

"Do yourself a favor and walk away."

Lisa clucked her tongue. A slight grin reappeared on her face, and she turned to depart as requested.

"Looks like you've chosen your side, Ron. Too bad. Enjoy being branded a loser."

6

A loud whistle pierced the air and reverberated throughout the gym.

"Let's bring it in, girls."

Lisa gathered with several other girls in the middle of the basketball court. They formed a circle around a short blonde woman dressed in a polo shirt and khaki shorts. One thing became clear to Lisa after seeing the squad mess up their finishing routine yet again. They all needed to incorporate more jump drills into warm-ups. Some of the newer squad members struggled to get enough lift in their jumps. It threw off the timing on the routine and ended up making the whole thing look sloppy.

"We need to get this right," Lisa said, putting her hands on her hips. "This isn't just about Friday's game. If we want to finally get a state title, we have to take it to the next level."

They came painfully close a year ago. Only one other cheerleader squad finished ahead of them in the whole classification. From the moment she took over as head cheerleader, Lisa wanted nothing more than to cement her legacy by adding another trophy to the school's trophy case.

"I love your enthusiasm," their cheerleader coach said. "If you all try to mirror Lisa's attitude and work ethic, we'll get there. We want this year to be unforgettable."

She rattled off a few more instructions and then dismissed the squad for the day. Lisa headed straight to her locker. She couldn't help feeling a little torn as she entered the locker room. A twinge of guilt washed over her for not sticking around and getting in some extra conditioning before leaving for the weekend. She worked to squash those feelings soon after they emerged. Not today. It had to wait until Monday. More important things needed to be done.

"Ready for a girls' night out?"

Lisa poked her head out from behind her open locker door and frowned.

"I can't do it Jenny. I'm sorry."

"You've got to come with us. Adam and his band are playing a set in Golden tonight."

Lisa grabbed a towel, a small bottle of shampoo and another small bottle of body wash. She shrugged and sat down on the bench. It had all the right elements for a perfect Friday night activity, but there was no way she could join in on the fun.

"Sounds so tempting. But I promised my parents I'd stay home and watch Nate. They're celebrating their anniversary."

"Can't they just get a babysitter this time?"

Lisa didn't need a crystal ball to know how that scenario would unfold. She stayed awake until sunrise the last time they hired one, taking turns with her parents while they tried to coax her hysterical brother out of his bedroom closet. His sobs became almost unbearable as they struggled to soothe him.

Neither of her parents blamed the babysitter. Lisa figured she deserved some blame. When her dad flipped on the TV before leaving for work the next morning, he discovered it cued to a music channel with the volume set twice as high as normal. In her mind, Nate's breakdown wasn't an accident. Sacrifices needed to be made to keep it from happening again.

"Nate doesn't deal well with strangers. You know how freaked he gets by loud noises and unfamiliar faces."

Jenny gave an understanding nod.

"Being autistic sucks."

"It does. But I love that kid so much. If he can't count on his big sister to be there for him when it matters, who can he count on?"

"He's lucky to have you as a sister."

Lisa gave her an appreciative smile. She felt equally lucky to have understanding friends. Jenny cracked a smile in return and held up her smartphone.

"I'll text you some pics. It's gonna be lit."

As soon as Jenny rounded the corner, Lisa finished taking off the rest of her practice garb and hit the shower. Steamy water droplets danced across her skin. It felt so good on her tense, tired muscles. Lisa lathered herself up with scented body wash and shampoo and let the water cascade over her repeatedly like mountain rapids. Other squad members filtered in and out as Lisa showered. When she finally turned off the water, wrapped the towel around her naked body and stepped out of the shower area, the smattering of voices had vanished.

Must have taken a longer shower than I realized, Lisa thought. *I better hurry up and get dressed and get out of here.*

Lisa unwrapped the towel and rubbed it over her legs, arms, and torso with the speed of a mid-distance runner generating a kick on the final lap. As she slipped into her panties, a whispering voice drifted into her ears.

It sounded odd and unsettling. Almost like a breeze blasting through chimes combined with a low guttural tone. Lisa held the damp towel against her still bare chest and tiptoed to the end of the wooden bench.

"Hello? Who's there?"

She glanced toward the shower on one end and the coach's office on the other end. No one seemed to be inside the locker room except her. Lisa shook her head and returned to her locker. Nothing more than a random noise in a random spot. She only noticed it because she was in here alone. Certainly, nothing to get worked up about. Lisa tossed the towel on the bench and put on her bra, blouse, pants, and shoes. She grabbed her purse and her backpack out of the locker and slammed the door shut. As she walked toward the sink, the same low whispering voice echoed through the locker room again.

Lisa glanced side to side and then behind her.

"Is someone else in here?"

No answer.

Lisa closed her eyes for a moment and sighed. She dropped her backpack next to her feet and set the purse on the counter. Lisa pulled out a brush and ran it through her hair to tame some post-shower wildness. Then, she brought out a mascara tube and started applying it to her eyelashes.

The whispers returned. This time, the faint voice bordered on evolving into a shriek. Lisa whipped her head around in the direction where she thought the voice originated. Only wet floors and rows of empty lockers greeted her eyes.

She had enough.

"This isn't funny! Whoever the hell is screwing with me better knock it off."

Lisa turned back to face the mirror. She jumped.

Her mascara tube fell out of her hand and clattered against the tile floor. A short burst of labored breaths escaped from her lips. A reflection of a woman had appeared out of nowhere in the mirror.

This woman was clad in flowing black gown mingled with dark red hues. A hooded cloak adorned her head while a matching veil covered her face. Her eyes and her hair, which peeked out from the inside borders of the cloak and flowed just past her shoulders, bore the same coloring as her attire.

6

"It's not nice to sneak up on a person like that," Lisa said, turning to face this mysterious woman. "What do you want?"

The woman in black extended her left arm. Her fingers cupped the palm of her hand, concealing some substance from Lisa's view.

"Power. Vengeance. Justice."

Lisa backed up against the counter and reached into her purse. She blindly fished through the contents for a few seconds, before finally wrapping her fingers around her smartphone.

"I don't know who you are, but you better leave me alone. I'm half a second away from calling for help."

The woman in black opened her hand to reveal a small mound of dark red dust. Lisa's eyes widened into a blank stare as they focused on the woman's hand and then trailed back to her face. Who carries a handful of dust around with them?

A second later, the woman in black spoke again. She recited some unfamiliar words. Lisa couldn't make heads or tails of the language she spoke. Latin? Maybe. It certainly wasn't English.

Red dust burst out of the woman in black's hand. It shot straight at Lisa with the velocity of a bullet. Before she could even think to step out of the way, a legion of dust particles swarmed her and rushed inside her nose and mouth.

A dry sensation crept down her throat. Lisa coughed. Her throat suddenly felt scratchy. Lisa coughed again. This time she saw it.

Dust.

A plume of dust burst from between her lips.

The woman in black responded with a low laugh.

More coughs followed. More dust. Lisa looked down at her hands. Skin grew dry and leathery before her eyes. Her fingernails began to crack and splinter. Tremors now gripped both hands.

She spun around to face the mirror. Lisa screamed. Hair and skin began peeling off her head at an alarming rate. She yanked on the cold-water knob connected to the faucet and splashed water into her face. Puddles formed around the sink. Once that precious liquid hit Lisa's skin, though, it vanished with the same suddenness as a mirage in a thirsty desert.

Lisa broke down into sobs and snatched up her phone from inside her purse. The woman in black pressed her fingertips together and pulled her hand backward. At once, Lisa's phone flew out of her hand and zipped through the air. Then, as it neared the woman in black, she threw her hand forward again and slammed the phone back into the mirror.

Shards of mirror mingled with broken pieces of phone exploded from the wall. It all fell in a heap into the sink.

Lisa's body continued discarding layers of dried skin like a shedding snake. Only no fresh skin lay underneath to replace it. Muscle tissue withered. Blood bubbled to the surface and evaporated at the same speed.

The woman in black faded out of the locker room when the red dust completed its assigned task. Only a decomposing shell of a body, now crumpled to the floor, remained of what used to be a healthy and vibrant girl.

7

Ron turned the knob and pushed open the kitchen door with the care of a person trying to diffuse a bomb. All he wanted to do was to make it upstairs to his bedroom without drawing any unwanted attention. He hoped his mom would be too absorbed with her usual nonsense to have noticed his car pull into the driveway or have seen the garage door open.

"You're so screwed."

Ron stopped in the middle of the stairs and turned. The mischievous grin plastered on his brother's face told him one thing. And it wasn't a good thing.

"Go find something useful to do, Eric."

Eric shrugged.

"Okay, I'll just go let Mom know you're home."

Ron thrust up his hand in front of him like a crossing guard trying to slow an oncoming car.

"Wait a minute. You don't want to do that."

"Yeah ... I do."

"What will it take for you to not do it?"

"That's not an easy answer. This sort of request carries a hefty price tag."

Ron pinched his eyes shut and pressed his fingers against his forehead. Eric had stretched him over a barrel this time.

"Fine. Name your price."

Eric closed his eyes and stroked his chin.

"Hmm … I could use an upgraded mountain bike. My current one is beat up from the last trail I rode."

"Not a chance."

Ron had to draw a line somewhere. He wasn't getting Eric a new bike for any reason. If their mom wanted to buy his love, she could knock herself out loading him up with gifts. It felt like she already did it most of the time anyway.

"Deal's off." Eric turned and held his hand to the side of his mouth. "Hey, Mom! Ron's home."

Ron's eyes darted back and forth looking for something to throw at the little snitch. Eric bolted away from the stairs, laughing. A second later, their mother emerged from her downstairs office. When she laid eyes on Ron, her face scrunched up and released into a deep frown. He already had a good idea which thoughts occupied her mind.

"You promised me you wouldn't get into any more trouble."

"Who says I got into trouble?"

"So, I guess the principal made it all up when she told me you were sent to detention again today?"

Ron tilted his head to the ceiling and let out a sigh.

"I was targeted by the same stupid football player that harassed me before. What ever happened to sticking up for myself?"

"So turn him in. Tell a teacher or the principal —"

"Tell them what? They don't believe me. I'm an outsider. He's the star linebacker. I'm guilty from the word go."

Ron's mother folded her arms. A mixture of concern and annoyance radiated from her narrowed eyes.

"I know you don't like going to this school, Ron, but you really need to make the best of this situation."

"Make the best of this situation?" Ron's voice cranked up a decibel or two. "I get pulled away from my friends and my club team to come to this backwater town. For what? So you can work on another stupid novel? My college soccer dreams are dying. I have to start over everywhere and you don't seem to care."

"That's not fair." Her eyes burned hot with anger. "Your father put me in this position. I had to do this to give us a better life."

"My life was plenty good before you divorced him."

"Do you even understand what kind of hell he put me through?" Ron's mother slapped her hand down on the banister. Tears started to trickle down each cheek. "Maybe I don't possess any visible bruises. My wounds aren't ones you can see or touch. But, believe me, they're very real."

"So you're taking it out on me? Good call … Emily."

She pinched her eyelids shut and rubbed her temples. Ron knew he crossed a forbidden line by addressing his mother by her first name. He stood there as motionless as a statue.

"Go to your room and stay there." her voice descended into a low whisper, seething with rage. "NOW!"

Ron stomped up the stairs away from his mother and slammed his bedroom door behind him. It isn't fair. Staying with his father had been his first choice. But his mom earned full custody rights and that sealed Ron's fate. Ron spent several days begging his mother to at least let him stay with a host family during the club season. She refused to consider any other options.

So typical of her as a parent.

He slammed his backpack onto the floor. The vibration caused a soccer ball to bounce out of his open closet. Ron glanced at the ball and then at his window and finally at the ball again. Wheels started turning in his head. He had plenty of time for homework later. Right now, he needed to go somewhere else and cool off.

Ron snatched up the soccer ball and cradled it like a football in his arm. He opened the window and dropped the ball into the grass below. A rope connected the window to a small tree house. It sat on the middle branches of a willow tree standing in the middle of their backyard. Ron counted it as a stroke of good fortune that the house's previous owners built a tree house for their children. The thick rope suspended between the two places gave him a clean, quick escape route from his mother's eyes.

He hopped onto the windowsill and wrapped his hands around the thick rope. Going from his bedroom to the tree house required a bit more effort than he expected. His biceps and triceps burned as Ron pulled himself across the rope. Upper body work needed to take a higher priority in future weight training sessions.

Once he reached the willow tree, Ron dropped onto the largest branch supporting the tree house. He crawled through the open window and opened a small door built into the floor. Ron dropped through the door and climbed down the tree trunk. He retrieved his soccer ball and left the yard.

Ron checked his text messages as he walked. He could use a reassuring word from his dad. No new messages. Nearly a week had passed since the most recent one.

His face couldn't mask the letdown consuming him. It seemed like his father's consulting work kept him hopping from one city to another. Airports and hotels had practically turned into his first home now.

I'd much rather be in whatever place Dad is at right now than stuck here, Ron thought.

Virtually every destination held more appeal than Deer Falls.

Ron followed the sidewalk as it wound north. He remembered passing a small park in that direction — within walking distance — on his way home from school. Hopefully, it housed a wide enough field and a decent soccer net, so he had enough space to do some footwork and shooting drills.

7

No one appeared to be hanging out inside the park as Ron approached. Too bad. Showing off his skills to a captive audience brought him enjoyment. Ron saw no children laughing and shouting while climbing the jungle gym or taking turns in the swings. No parents hung around chattering and watching their children from a distance. A few ducks crowded the shore of a pond near the park entrance. Their contented quacks drew Ron's attention and he decided to take a detour over to the pond's edge.

"I didn't expect to see you hanging out over here. Do you live in this neighborhood too?"

Maybe Ron would have a captive audience after all. He stopped in his tracks and turned around. Ron came face-to-face with Christina. She walked up to the park entrance from the opposite direction he had traveled.

"Yeah, just a half-mile down the street. I thought I'd come out here. I needed to find a place to clear my head."

Christina glanced down at the soccer ball nestled in Ron's arm and smiled.

"You have the right idea. I can't get enough of soccer."

Ron's ears perked up. Finally, he found someone in Deer Falls who spoke his language.

"Do you play?"

"For fun. My game isn't polished. I tried out for our high school team last year but didn't make the cut."

"The girls' soccer team makes cuts?"

This nugget of information caught Ron by surprise. He assumed anyone who tried out for a sports team at Deer Falls made the roster. Nothing he saw from the boys' soccer team made him feel like his new coach had selectively culled that group from a larger herd of wannabe soccer players. Ron hadn't seen so many missed passes or sloppy footwork since his U-12 days.

"You're only cut if your last name, your family's net worth or your social status doesn't preclude it from happening."

"Small town politics?"

"You got it."

Ron shook his head as he pondered her misfortune.

"That really sucks. I'm sorry. Did you give it a shot again this year?"

"I thought about it, but I don't really have a good coach to work with out here."

Ron dropped the ball at her feet.

"I can fix that," he said, smiling.

Christina matched it with a grin of her own.

"Wait a second, hot shot. How do I know if you're any good?"

"Let me prove it to you."

Ron latched onto the ball with his left foot. He pivoted around her left side and sprinted through the park entrance. Christina gave chase, laughing. They made their way over to a short grassy field. It didn't offer an ideal spot for serious training. The field sloped in a couple of spots and didn't appear to be regulation length. Such aesthetics didn't matter as much to Ron though when given a chance to hang out with a girl like Christina.

They kicked the ball back and forth and Ron offered up a snapshot on various possession and attacking techniques he favored. Mostly, they just talked about soccer. Ron grew increasingly impressed with her passion for the game and soccer knowledge as their conversation progressed.

"I'm not seeing why you shouldn't be on that team," Ron said. "You have enough potential to do well."

"It's nice to hear somebody tell me that," Christina replied. "Maybe I'll give it another shot. I know my dad would love to see me pick up the sport."

"He's a soccer fan too, I take it."

7

"Definitely. He bought us tickets for the MLS Cup final when the Rapids won it all. We had seats right down near the field. Such an amazing experience."

"My whole club team went to the match. I don't think I sat down the whole 90-plus minutes."

They soon settled into casually kicking the ball back and forth as they walked down the field. Ron couldn't understand why she wasn't popular at this school. Christina certainly owned a winning blend of looks and personality.

It didn't add up.

"I don't mean any offense by this, but there's something I don't get," Ron said. "How is it that you and Casey are friends? You seem like polar opposites. He's into all this geeky stuff and you're into cool stuff."

Christina stopped running. She picked up the ball and gazed at Ron. He had seen that expression from her before, the one revealing thoughts swarming her mind that she didn't necessarily want to share with him.

"Casey understands me. He's never been scared of who I am."

Ron scrunched up his face. Her response puzzled him.

"Why would anyone be scared of you?"

"People are always scared of what they can't explain."

"That's completely cryptic. What do you mean?"

A slight frown emerged on Christina's face. Her eyes could not conceal her worried thoughts any longer.

"I can show you what I mean."

"Lay it on me."

Christina quickly held up her index finger.

"Only if you promise me one thing."

"What's that?"

"You won't make fun of me, or fear me, once I share my secret."

Ron nodded.

"You have my word. I promise."

Christina dropped the soccer ball on the ground again. She turned and faced a large cottonwood tree looming over the edge of the field. At the same time, Christina extended her arm toward the tree.

One of the lower branches started to shake. A small number of leaves exploded into the air like kernels inside a popcorn popper. Christina moved her hand in a circular motion. Every leaf changed direction and moved toward her. The leaves suddenly halted above her head.

Christina spun her index finger in a swirling pattern. Each individual leaf mirrored the same motion. She caused them to form different shapes — a square, a circle, and a diamond. Then, finally, she dropped her hand to her side and all the leaves simultaneously fell from the sky to the ground.

Every ounce of color drained from Ron's face. His eyes widened and he licked his lips. His heart raced with the same intensity as a little kid worrying about a monster hiding under their bed or inside their closet. Casey had not exaggerated his claims. Lisa's insults held a grain of truth.

Christina was a real-life witch.

When she witnessed his reaction, Christina showed tangible disappointment. She looked down at the fallen leaves scattered across the ground.

"You're afraid of me."

She kicked the soccer ball off to the side and barged past him. Ron pinched his eyes shut and rubbed his hand down the bridge of his nose. Why was he so afraid? Sure, he didn't understand the first thing about magic and couldn't explain how Christina could do any of this. Still, she opened up to him and shared something special about herself. She didn't do anything to hurt him. But he quickly figured out how to hurt her in a different way.

"Wait. Christina. Just wait a minute."

7

Ron sprinted after her. Christina turned back to him. Tears had already started to well up in her eyes.

"I'm sorry. I've never seen anything like that before. I didn't know what to think or how to react."

Christina looked at him stone-faced. Ron realized he needed to do better than that.

"I know this might sound dumb but hear me out. Until a few minutes ago, I didn't think magic existed. It's so much for me to take in all at once. But I promise I'm not afraid of you. I don't want you to feel like I am."

Christina quickly wiped away the tears with her hand and walked back toward him.

"I didn't ask for the ability to use magic. It's just a part of who I am."

"So how do all these people at school seem to know about it?"

"I showed it to someone who I once thought was my friend. I thought I could confide in them. I ended up being wrong."

Ron felt raw pain dripping from her words. Discovering she was different would be hard enough. Being betrayed and rejected by a friend left behind some obvious scars.

"I can't believe they would betray your trust like that," he said. "That's not what a real friend does."

Christina drew a sharp breath and kicked at some fallen leaves near her feet.

"I hesitated to even open up to anybody about my magic in the beginning. It scared me at first when I discovered what I could do."

"I can only imagine."

"Now it seems to inspire fear in everyone else."

"Maybe you could do something to show them they don't need to feel so afraid?"

Christina frowned and looked away.

"I'm not the one who needs to change, Ron."

"I'm sorry. That came out all wrong. That's not what I meant."

"Then what do you mean?"

Ron touched her shoulder, and she turned back to face him again.

"I guess I just want to help you, so you don't keep feeling this pain. I want you to feel safe about being yourself — magic and all."

A smile finally broke through and spread across Christina's face.

"That's sweet of you."

"If you want, we can keep coming here to the park," Ron suggested. "I still have a bunch more soccer tips I can share while we talk."

Christina threw her arms around Ron and embraced him. He soaked in the softness of her hair and warmth of her cheek.

"I'd like that very much," she said.

8

A somber mood gripped the whole classroom after Principal Reynolds addressed the school over the loudspeaker. She broke the news of Lisa's death at the end of morning announcements. It explained flushed faces and bleary eyes Ron noticed from several teachers he passed in the hall on the way to his first class.

Ron could not deny it any longer. Something about this whole picture didn't sit right with him. Maybe he shouldn't have been so quick to dismiss Casey's claims about Nick after all. Lisa's death followed only a few days after Nick and his parents vanished into thin air. It made Ron wonder if the two events were somehow connected.

When he ran into Casey again at lunchtime, Ron voiced those same suspicions to him. Casey answered him with a wary nod.

"What happened to the skeptical Ron I've grown used to seeing? What have you done with him?"

"I deserve that," Ron replied. "I really do. Let's just say, I've seen some things recently that opened my mind to new ideas."

"Christina showed you her magic, didn't she?"

Ron's eyes darted back and forth, and he put his finger to his lips. This wasn't a suitable time and place for this sort of discussion. Christina certainly wouldn't appreciate it.

"Oh please." Casey shrugged and offered up a dismissive hand wave. "Everyone around here knows, or suspects, Christina can do that stuff.

You can't keep secrets in a small town."

"So what's your theory?"

Ron wanted to steer the conversation away from Christina and her magic. Ever since he learned how much of an emotional toll the parade of fear, ridicule and gossip had taken on her, Ron felt a growing urge to be protective of Christina. He really didn't want Casey to inadvertently start trouble for her.

"Honestly, I think that someone or something murdered both Nick and Lisa."

"You really think Lisa was murdered?"

Ron had not given this idea much serious thought. Everything he heard from other students in his first-period class made it sound like an accident. They claimed the heating system malfunctioned, overheating the girl's locker room, and knocking Lisa unconscious. She lay there over the entire weekend until a janitor stumbled upon her dried-out corpse when the school opened again on Monday.

Casey evidently heard the same rumor, and he didn't buy it for a second.

"Do you know just how hot a locker room would have to get for a person's body to get sucked dry?"

"So what do you think really happened?"

"I don't know. My guess is there's some sort of monster on the loose. Things like what happened to Lisa just aren't explainable any other way."

"Why attack a random cheerleader?"

Casey threw up his arms.

"You got me. Maybe our mystery killer hates cheerleaders. Or she was just in the wrong place at the wrong time. Who knows?"

Ron and Casey walked down into the atrium and spotted Christina sitting on the carpeted steps. Her nose was buried in a textbook resting in her lap. She jotted down notes in a small notebook sitting on top of one of the open pages.

"Mind if we join you?" Ron asked.

Christina glanced up at him and her eyes lit up.

"Saved you a seat." She patted the ground next to her. "I'm getting a head start on a history report, so we have plenty of time for soccer in the park later."

The two boys parked themselves on either side of her.

"Soccer in the park?" Casey grinned and playfully tapped her arm. "So is that a secret code phrase for what you're really doing?"

Christina fiddled with her pen and refused to look him in the eye. "Yeah ... it's code for playing soccer in the park."

The hesitation in her voice made it sound like Christina hadn't quite convinced herself that soccer lessons were all there was to it. It didn't cross Ron's mind to make a bigger deal out of them spending time alone outside of school until now. His thoughts kept drifting back to the morning announcements.

"Something feels strange about Lisa's death." Ron said. "Casey doesn't think it's an accident. I'm starting to feel the same way."

Christina put down her pen and set down her textbook in front of her. She gazed at the main doors, for a moment, lost in thought.

"These sorts of things happen more often than they should here in Deer Falls," she finally said.

"What sorts of things?"

All three teens turned to see Cassandra standing behind the group. She sported a dark red crop top that hovered just above her belly button and a black skirt that made her eyes appear even more striking than the first time Ron saw her. Cassandra walked down the steps and stopped on the bottom stair directly in front of the group.

"What sorts of things?" she repeated.

Casey cracked a grin.

"Crazy small-town end-of-the-world things."

"I can relate."

"I thought you were new here," Ron said.

"Of course, I'm new here. But I grew up in another small town. We dealt with our share of unexpected problems there too."

Casey raised his hand.

"Did you deal with monsters attacking and killing people sort of problems?"

He added a little laugh after the question. Ron rolled his eyes. Casey's attempts to hit on Cassandra as soon as he got around her were painfully obvious. Still, she seemed to enjoy it. Cassandra returned his laugh and made a point to sit down right in front of him.

"What do you think?"

"Probably not. No place is as strange as Deer Falls."

Christina glanced at Cassandra's outfit. Her hazel eyes did nothing to conceal a twinge of jealousy caused by Casey's gawking. Ron did his best not to follow suit. Then again, the bare midriff Cassandra teased didn't make it a simple task.

"Looks like you gave your wardrobe a makeover," Christina said.

"I didn't like what that other girl said to me the other day, but I guess she had a point," Cassandra replied. "I decided to make a change. Hopefully, this is more in style around here."

Casey leaned forward and nodded.

"I got no complaints."

She winked and her lips parted into a small smile.

"That's always good news."

"I guess you don't have to worry about what Lisa says any longer," Christina said.

Cassandra leaned back and looked up at the ceiling. A moment later, her eyes returned to Christina again.

"Is she the girl who just died? Wow, I didn't make the connection. That's a tragedy."

Ron gave her a sideways glance. Something in her tone didn't match her words. For the briefest moment, he sensed a hint of contempt from Cassandra.

"She wasn't one of my favorite people either, but it's always sad when anyone dies unexpectedly like that," Christina replied. "Gotta be tough on her whole family."

"Stop acting like you gave a shit about her."

Christina pressed her lips into a slight frown. Ron didn't need to turn around to identify the source of those words. The voice of that sneering dumb ass Trevor had practically become tattooed on his brain at this point.

"This is a private conversation," Ron said. "We didn't invite you to join it."

"Then maybe you shouldn't be putting my dead girlfriend's name in your mouth."

"Hey, I'm sorry for your loss," Christina said. "Everyone feels bad about what happened to her."

"Yeah, I'm sure you're really broken up about it."

"What's that supposed to mean?" Christina's voice climbed a note higher in pitch. "Look, I know you're hurting and I'm trying to sympathize."

"How do I know you're not responsible?"

Ron tilted his head at Trevor and creased his brow.

"Are you serious?"

Trevor stomped his foot into the carpet, making both Casey and Christina shrink back an inch or two from him.

"They said they found Lisa in a state of 'unnatural decay.' I don't even know what the fuck that means!"

"How dare you accuse me of killing your girlfriend!" Christina sprang to her feet and stabbed her index finger straight at Trevor. "I've never done a thing to hurt anyone in this town."

"I know what I've heard. I don't buy your act for a minute."

"You shouldn't believe everything you hear."

"You did some sort of witch curse on her. I'd bet my life on it."

Trevor's clenched jaw and narrowed eyes told Ron the moment had arrived for him to step in before this spiraled out of control.

"Leave her alone."

Trevor swung around to face Ron. Tears threatened to seep out from the corners of his hardened eyes. Both fists clenched tight.

"Stay out of this for your own good, Olson."

"Or what?"

Trevor raised a fist.

"Do you really want to find out?"

Ron's arms and shoulders tensed up. His pulse quickened while anticipating Trevor's impending explosion. Trevor hesitated. He did not narrow the gap between him and Ron. Instead, the linebacker did the exact opposite of what Ron expected him to do. He dropped his fist and took a couple of steps backward.

"I know your damn magic is behind this." Trevor sidestepped Ron and stared at Christina. "I can't prove it yet, but when I do, you're gonna wish you never met me."

"I've already reached that point," Christina said.

Trevor rushed forward like he intended to grab her and strike her. Christina backpedaled across the same step where she had been standing. Before he could reach her, Ron and Cassandra cut between the two teens.

"Stop harassing her," Cassandra said. "You need to go cool off somewhere else."

Trevor scowled at Cassandra and then gave her a hard shove. She lost her footing and fell onto the steps. Cassandra let out a little moan and gave him a dirty look.

Ron grabbed a fistful of Trevor's shirt collar.

"Walk away. Right now."

Trevor pushed his hand away. He straightened out his purple shirt and pointed his finger at Christina again.

"You'll get what's coming to you. That's a promise."

With those words, Trevor turned and stormed down an adjacent hall. Ron clasped his hands over his head. He turned and looked back at Christina. Visible signs of fear gripped her body. Eyes wide as plates. Quickened breathing. She had stiffened in place like a wooden beam. Casey and Cassandra both mirrored her body language. They did not budge an inch from their spots on the steps. All three teens kept staring at Trevor until he finally moved out of their sight.

Ron walked down the steps and helped Cassandra to her feet. Cassandra straightened out her skirt.

"Does he make a habit of intimidating and threatening people?"

"He's nothing more than a loud-mouthed bully," Ron replied, glancing back down the hall where Trevor went.

"I can't stand bullies." Cassandra said. "Someone needs to do something about him."

Ron seconded that idea. After this latest encounter, he started to fear for Christina's safety. Ron couldn't see what Trevor saw. When he gazed at her face, he didn't see a cold-blooded murderer. Now, for the first time, he wondered how many classmates shared Trevor's judgment of Christina.

9

Each plank wobbled as Eric scaled the trunk to reach the tree house. Rain and snow pelted the wood long enough over many seasons to warp the planks to a point where rusted nails barely held each piece of wood in place against the thick bark. Another boy stood motionless at the base of the trunk. His eyes darted up and down, bouncing between Eric and the lowest plank.

"It's safe," Eric said, glancing back down at the bottom of the tree as he climbed. "The wood won't break."

"You sure about that?"

"Trust me, Max. You aren't gonna fall off."

Max took a deep breath and closed his eyes for a moment. After opening them again, he clamped onto the plank directly above his head with both hands. Max hoisted himself up and gingerly set his feet on the lowest plank. He followed Eric's path up the trunk and didn't start breathing normally again until after climbing through the trap door in the tree house floor.

Eric had turned the tree house into his own personal lair. Two sleeping bags spread across the floor on one side. Comic books lay tossed in a loose stack against one wall. A flat screen TV was mounted on the opposite wall across from the sleeping bags. Cords connected the TV to a video game console. Both devices were plugged into a surge protector. This surge protector, in turn, connected to an orange extension cord running down the side of the tree house and over to an electrical outlet on an outside wall of the house.

"Cool." Max plopped down in front of the video game console and picked up a controller. "How did you get the TV up here?"

"My brother Ron helped me put it up here," Eric replied. "I handed it to him on a ladder. He pulled the TV in through the open window and then we mounted it on the wall."

"This is awesome. I wish I could get my dad to build a tree house like this, but he can't even nail a board straight. We always hire other people to build things."

"Hey, at least you can hang out at this one."

Eric turned on the video game console and the two boys started playing a shooter game. Max got the upper hand after a few minutes. His zombie kill count exceeded Eric's two-to-one. It soon grew even worse when Eric rounded a blind corner straight into a hungry horde.

Eric scowled and tossed the controller onto the floor when his last life bar melted off the screen.

"Damn. I never make it past this level."

Max smirked. He continued blasting zombies with the reckless abandon of a trigger-happy survivalist testing out new weaponry at a gun range. It quickly grew obvious to Eric that he'd end up watching Max dominate zombies more than doing it himself. He had zero interest in spending his afternoon being an observer.

"Hey, I've got something kind of fun and dangerous we can do," Eric said. "If you're up for it."

Max paused the game and turned to Eric.

"How fun and dangerous are we talking here?"

"There's a rumor going around school about a family who disappeared a while ago. No one knows what happened to them or where they went."

"Everybody's heard that story. What about it?"

"I've heard their house isn't actually abandoned. Cody Pugmire told me he rode his bicycle past it yesterday and claims he saw someone moving around behind the living room blinds."

Max pitched his controller back on the floor in front of the console and stood up. A smile crept onto his face as he considered the implications of this latest rumor.

"We should totally go and see who's lurking around."

"That's what I think too," Eric said. "We explore it like detectives. Look for clues. Solve a mystery. It'll be fun."

The two boys climbed out of the tree house and scaled down the trunk. They sprinted around to the front of the house and through the front door. Eric grabbed a heavy-duty flashlight from his bedroom, and they raced back down the stairs.

Before they reached the front door again, Emily poked her head out from her home office. Eric and Max slammed on the brakes as soon as they saw her face.

"What's with the ruckus out here? I can't get much writing done with all the running around and doors slamming."

"We're headed to the park."

His mother glanced down at the flashlight poking out from his hand and then back up at Eric. She looked at him like an attorney preparing to cross-examine a witness on the stand.

"With a flashlight? Just how late do you think you're going to be out there? I don't want you off running around after dark."

"No worries, Mom. We'll be back for dinner. Just found something cool we want to investigate over there."

Eric's voice carried a higher pitch, and he blurted his words out faster than normal. He had a bad habit of doing those sorts of things when trying to hide something from her. Telling the truth was out of the question. Eric knew he wouldn't make it past the front door.

"Hmm." She put her hand on her chin and looked at Eric through half-closed eyes. "Whatever you're doing, stay out of trouble. Text me or call me once you get to the park and again when you start for home."

"We'll do that, Mom."

His mom turned and walked back into her office. That went easier than Eric expected. She had been pushing to meet a manuscript deadline for her latest novel. Letting him and Max go with barely an argument meant she must have fallen seriously behind schedule.

Eric didn't dwell on it too long. They had to get going. He and Max only had a couple of hours before dinner, so they didn't have a ton of time to poke around the house. They went out to the garage, grabbed their bicycles, and pedaled off into the street.

Max punched in the address on his smartphone and balanced it on his handlebars while he acted as a self-appointed navigator. Their route took them a mile past the Deer Falls Recreation Center and into a small subdivision. When they turned down the second street and pedaled toward a cul-de-sac, their destination came into view.

Leaves peppered the front lawn and a car parked in the driveway. To Eric, it looked like the car hadn't budged from that spot for at least a couple of weeks. They rode up the driveway and parked their bicycles behind the car. Max glanced over at the mailbox. The door sat partially ajar. An assortment of mail peeked out from inside. It threatened to spring out of the mailbox and spill out across the sidewalk.

"You'd think that somebody at the post office would eventually figure out no one is home," Max said.

"They have to actually file a change of address to stop mail delivery," Eric replied. "That's what my mom had to do when we moved here. I'm guessing they didn't actually move somewhere else."

He opened the mailbox and pulled out the stack of envelopes and ads stuffed inside. Eric started thumbing through the mail. Bills. Junk mail. Coupons. Nothing terribly exciting. Still, it offered solid evidence no one planned to leave. One big question popped into his mind. What happened to the family who used to live here?

"Do you think it's a good idea to go through their mail?"

Max's eyes darted from window to window and door to door in the cul-de-sac.Eric shrugged. He didn't bother to look up. If the neighbors really cared about what they were doing, someone would have popped out of a front door by now and started interrogating them.

"I think we'll be alright."

"My mom says it's illegal to open other people's mail."

"I haven't opened anything yet. Besides, aren't you curious to find out what happened here?"

"Of course. I'm just nervous about neighbors spying on us and then tattling on us."

Eric grinned and pointed to the bicycles.

"We can outrun them."

He stuffed mail back into the mailbox. Eric hopped up on the sidewalk and started across the front lawn. When he reached the porch steps, he turned back and noticed Max hadn't moved an inch from his spot near the mailbox.

"What are you waiting for?" Eric signaled for him to walk forward. "This is why we came over here."

Max hesitated. He glanced up and down the street a second time and a third time. Then, taking a deep breath, he followed Eric's path across the lawn and joined him by the porch steps.

"If we get in trouble, I'm blaming you."

Eric frowned.

"Don't be a snitch."

They walked up the porch steps. Eric lifted a copper knocker on the front door and rapped it against the wood. A few seconds passed while the two boys stood there in silence. No answer. Eric didn't expect to get one, but it didn't hurt to give it a shot.

Max slid over to the window and put his face up against the glass.

Seeing what lay beyond it proved impossible. Horizontal blinds were drawn shut. Cracks between each plastic slat allowed for traces of sunlight to sneak inside, but those slats obstructed eyes wanting to peek inside the house.

Eric twisted the doorknob to see if the front door was locked. To his surprise, the knob turned.

"Huh. This is our lucky day."

"You're not going in there, are you?"

"That's the plan." Eric said, turning to Max. "You can stay here on the porch if you want. Act as a lookout while I check things out."

Max bit down on his lip. A satisfied grin crept over Eric's face. Staying outside alone under the potential observation of unseen cul-de-sac residents didn't appeal to Max and he knew it.

"Fine. I'll go in too."

Eric turned the doorknob again and pushed the door open. Max followed a couple of steps behind him. A rich aroma greeted his nose when Eric stepped inside. It reminded him of an herb garden. An assortment of plants adorned various tables or occupied pots hooked to chains suspended from the ceiling. Candles lined the mantle behind the living room fireplace.

"Someone here loves gardening," Max said. "I swear there's more plants here than at the park."

"I wonder if the other rooms are like this one."

"Maybe the plants ate the family that lived here."

Eric raised his arms above his head and made exaggerated growls. He lumbered forward, mimicking a killer plant devouring a defenseless human. Both boys broke down into laughter. Max suddenly stopped after a few seconds.

"Did you ever text your Mom?"

"Uh oh. I forgot," Eric whipped out his smartphone. "She's probably freaking out over it right about now."

Even though his mom spent almost every free minute in her office, she always seemed to have a sixth sense of when he was doing anything that didn't meet her seal of approval. A vision of her scolding words, in a matching tone, had already drifted into his head.

He wasted no time firing off a text, pretending to check in from the park. Eric stared at the screen for a couple of seconds after getting the reply from his mom. A crooked smile emerged deep from the corners of his lips and splashed across his mouth.

"What's the number for that pizza place downtown?"

"Pizza Wagon? 555-7499. Why do you ask?"

"Just got an idea for a wicked prank. It's gonna be lit."

Eric punched in the phone number and placed an order for a pair of sausage and pepperoni pizzas. His insistence in rattling off the order and street address in a pseudo-serious tone made it tough for Max to stifle his own laughter in the background. After Eric finally ended the call, Max let loose and howled until his sides hurt.

"They're gonna be so pissed off." He wiped away tears from both eyes. "This is savage."

"We gotta go find a place to hide outside before they get over here."

"Let's find a spot where we can still get a clear view of the front porch. I wanna post this on YouTube later."

Max and Eric walked back outside and left the front door open just a crack behind them. The two boys scaled a willow tree near a fence that divided the front yard from a neighboring property. They both crawled onto branches overlooking the front porch and the living room window. It put them high enough off the ground and far enough away from the house to reduce their odds of drawing any unwanted attention when the target of their prank showed up.

Only a few minutes passed before a car pulled up along the curb in front of the house. It displayed a Pizza Wagon sign on top of the roof. Eric and Max looked at each other and grinned. Max pulled out his smartphone and started recording. A teenage boy stepped out of the car with both pizzas in hand. He walked up to the front porch and rang the doorbell.

No one came to the door.

The pizza delivery boy shifted the pizzas in his arm and rang the doorbell a second time. Again, a minute or two passed without a response.

"Hello?" He gave it a third ring. "I have your pizzas. Two large sausage and pepperoni with extra cheese."

Eric pressed his hand against his lips to stifle a laugh. This was playing out exactly how he hoped.

The pizza delivery boy formed a fist and banged it against the door three times. It popped open a few inches. His eyes darted back and forth between the doorknob and his car. Finally, he pushed the door wide open with his free hand.

"I'm at the front door. Come out and get your pizzas."

Still, no one appeared at the door. He hesitated for a moment and, finally, took a few steps inside.

"This isn't funny! Whoever ordered these pizzas had better show their face. I'm not leaving until I get paid."

Max couldn't hold it in any longer. He let out a snicker before quickly cupping his free hand to his mouth. The pizza delivery boy spun around and glanced up at the tree. His eyes immediately zeroed in on Max's smartphone.

"You stupid little twits! You're paying for this order."

He started for the door again before suddenly stopping a few inches short of the doorway. Neither Eric nor Max could tell what he had seen or heard. The pizza delivery boy started to tremble as he slowly turned to see who or what was behind him.

"Hello?"

An awful shriek answered his question. He dropped both pizzas on the floor. At once, the front door slammed shut behind him. The doorknob shook as the pizza delivery boy tugged at it from the other side.

"Help! Help!" Pounding fists accompanied his pleas. "Somebody open the door!"

Max's grip tightened over his phone. He looked behind him and exposed widening eyes. Eric could feel his eyes doing the same. He backed up on the tree branch and started climbing down the trunk.

"Where are you going?"

"Someone's gotta help him."

About halfway down the trunk, Eric jumped free of the tree and landed on the grass. He sprinted toward the porch steps. A body pushed up against the blinds and mashed them into the glass. Fingers burrowed between the middle slats and clutched them in a death grip.

Eric stopped in his tracks on the bottom step.

Blood. On the fingers and now on the slats.

His breaths devolved into shorter, quicker bursts. Eric started backpedaling to the lawn. At once, the same hand ripped the blinds away from the window. They crashed to the floor in a heap.

An unseen force tossed the pizza delivery boy against the glass. Cracks formed at various collision points. Bubbling lacerations covered his face, throat, and forearms. His lips trembled. His mouth became fixed in a frozen scream.

In that moment, Eric realized his prank had gone awry in the worst way imaginable. His heart never pounded so forcefully inside his ribs until now.

Whatever they awakened inside the house probably wouldn't stay inside for long.

10

Eric took off on a dead run for his bicycle. One thought dominated his mind — putting as much distance between himself and this house as possible. He stopped halfway to his bike and snapped his head back to the tree. Max clung to the same tree branch as before, continuing to record everything playing out beyond the living room window on his smartphone camera. He remained frozen against the branch, seemingly unable to move.

"What are you doing?" Eric shouted. "We gotta get out of here."

"I'm safer up here."

"No, you're not!"

Something yanked the pizza delivery boy backward and out of their view. In his place, a hunched over old man appeared. At least, Eric thought it was a man. A flowing black cloak with a hood partially covered their head, making it tough to be 100 percent certain about their identity.

Thin gray strands of hair covered the temples and ears. Skin hung off his cheekbones and jaw like melted wax flash frozen in place. Liver spots and wrinkles dotted that flesh. One hand rested on a gnarled walking stick. Both were white as bone.

The old man's eyes first settled on Eric and then shot upward to Max. Each eye held a swirl of dark red and black in both iris and pupil. His mouth formed into a nightmarish sneer, revealing jagged incisors tinged with yellow and red hues.

"I think you're right."

Max shimmied down the trunk and caught up to Eric at the curb. The two boys hopped on their bicycles and pedaled down the street at blinding speed. Eric and Max pushed themselves through one intersection after another as if their lives depended on not stopping. After what they had seen at the house, Eric figured they couldn't afford to slow their pace. They couldn't let that old man —or whatever it was — catch up to them at any cost.

Eric tuned out a couple of car horns and a shout from an angry pedestrian. No stop signs, red lights, or yield signs obtained his obedience. Neither Eric nor Max bothered to tap their brakes until they laid eyes on Eric's safe, familiar house.

The first words from Eric to Ron burst out of his mouth at a spoken word version of light speed. Ron didn't get a clear read on what happened to his brother, but something obviously spooked him big time. Eric was a step away from hyperventilating into a paper bag. Ron pressed a hand down on his shoulder.

"Slow breaths, bro. Tell me again what happened."

Eric closed his eyes and drew as deep of a breath as possible. When he finally exhaled, tears started forging a trail down both cheeks.

"I saw a pizza delivery boy get killed. It's all my fault. I'm so sorry. I'm so sorry."

Ron's eyes widened into an unblinking stare.

"You saw somebody get killed? Where were you? What in the hell were you doing?"

"We were at an abandoned house. Just playing a prank. I made a fake pizza order. He showed up and … someone attacked him."

"What do you mean someone attacked him?"

"I don't know. Someone inside the house. They attacked him."

"Can you remember what they looked like?"

"A really old man?" Eric's breaths grew short and frantic a second time while dredging up the attacker's image again. "I don't know. Looked right at us. His teeth were so jagged. His eyes were such a weird color. Like a monster."

Ron glanced over at his brother's friend. Max hadn't joined them on the porch. He stood frozen in the middle of the driveway, still clutching both handlebars on his bicycle. His jaw was clenched tight. Tears also streamed down his cheeks.

"Did you see this 'old man' too?"

"Yeah. I tried not to look back though." High-speed tremors infected Max's voice. "I kept pedaling as hard as I could until we got here."

"Where did this happen?"

"Out in Willow Flats. We thought we were going to an abandoned house. Some people at school talked about how the family that lived there had vanished."

Ron's ears perked up at this little nugget of information. What Max said mirrored the tale Casey shared involving Nick and his family.

"Do you remember the address?"

"It's right here in my phone."

Max swiped the screen and read off the address.

"What are you gonna do?" Eric asked.

Ron whipped out his smartphone. His first instinct was to call the local sheriff's office and report the crime. But something didn't add up. This didn't sound like a random killing. Eric and Max were spooked like they laid eyes on a genuine monster. Ron didn't know what to do about it. He stared at the phone screen for a few seconds.

"You're not calling the police, are you?"

Ron looked up from the phone, glanced down at Eric, and nodded. "This is a situation they probably should handle."

"No! You can't do it." Eric reached out and seized his arm. "I don't want to get in any trouble."

"Yeah, if we don't report the murder, we'll be in worse trouble."

"They'll blame me. But I didn't mean for it to happen. I'm sorry. I'm really sorry."

"Relax, kid. You're not going to jail ... I think."

"That's not reassuring."

Ron dialed 911. He connected with a dispatcher a few seconds later. The dispatcher peppered him with questions that required dragging other details out of Eric and Max. Both boys remained in full panic mode, which turned getting answers into a huge chore. Ron wanted to swat them by the time the dispatcher ended the call.

"Good news," he said. "They sent a deputy over to check the house."

Max finally let the bicycle drop to the ground and ran over to Ron like a sprinter breaking the finish line tape.

"No! They can't do that. That thing will kill them too."

Ron stuck out his hand like a crossing guard before Max could reach him. The other boy skidded to a stop right in front of the porch steps.

"Calm down. They're the ones trained to handle these sorts of things."

Max frowned and his eyes slid over to Eric. Both boys seemed ready to run off and hide somewhere. Ron turned away and started up the porch steps. Before he reached the front door, a loud hum from an engine greeted his ears. He turned around again and saw a sheriff's truck with flashing lights approaching.

The vehicle pulled into their driveway.

"Oh no!" Eric shouted. "We're going to jail."

Eric sprinted up the steps and tried to run past his brother. Ron caught him by the arm and held him in place. A deputy stepped out of the truck and crossed the front lawn, walking toward the house.

"I'm Deputy Leeds. Are you the one who just reported a murder?"

"That was quick," Ron walked to the top of the steps. He still held onto Eric's arm and dragged him along. "What did you find out?"

"I'm already in the neighborhood on another case, so I came here to get a statement." Deputy Leeds parked himself at the bottom of the porch steps. He removed a small notebook from his pocket. "We sent another deputy over to check out the house."

"Well, I just called it in," Ron replied. "I didn't actually see anything. It was my brother and his friend here who witnessed it."

The deputy turned his attention to the two boys.

"What did you see?"

Eric lowered his head and stared at the deputy's scuffed black shoes.

"We were biking past a house in Willow Flats that everyone at school claimed was abandoned." A shaky voice betrayed twitchy nerves now gripping Eric's body. "We decided to check it out and came upon a Pizza Wagon delivery boy at the front door. Someone answered the door and pulled him inside."

"It was horrible," Max added. "Someone flung him up against the window. We saw cuts and blood all over his hands and face."

"Huh." Deputy Leeds furiously scribbled their words down in his notebook. "Did you get a good look at who pulled him inside?"

Eric finally glanced up at him and grimaced.

"He looked like a really old man. Skin hanging off his bones. Only he had some really jagged teeth."

"Approximately when did all of this happen?"

"Less than an hour ago."

Deputy Leeds turned and marched back to his truck. He hopped back inside and grabbed his police radio. It quickly grew clear the conversation wasn't progressing in a favorable direction. Ron didn't know how to read lips well enough to figure out exactly what the deputy said, but his body language told him it wasn't good. The deputy's shoulders stiffened, and a scowl became etched on his face. Even though sunglasses covered his eyes, Ron sensed a steely glare emanating from inside the truck.

When Deputy Leeds finally climbed out of the truck again, he slammed the door behind him. Beads of sweat started dotting Ron's forehead. What changed the deputy's demeanor so quickly? His eyes drifted over to Eric and Max. Did they do something at that house they didn't tell anyone about?

The deputy fixed his gaze on Ron.

"Son, are your parents home?" he asked.

"Yeah, my mom's in her office," Ron said. "I can go inside and bring her out here."

Deputy Leeds nodded and pointed at the house.

"Please do that. I need to have a discussion with her right now."

Ron glanced at Eric and Max again and shook his head at them on his way into the house. He returned a minute later with his mother. Concern filled her eyes upon seeing the deputy standing in front of their porch.

"What's going on?" Emily asked.

"Well, ma'am, your son and his friend here apparently think it's funny to pull pranks on the local sheriff's department."

"What are you talking about?" Eric shook his head vigorously and looked at his mom for support. "We didn't do anything."

"Oh yeah, smart guy? I just got done talking to the other deputy. She didn't find any evidence of the alleged murder. No dead body. No vehicle. Nothing."

"That's impossible!" Eric protested. "I saw the whole thing happen with my own eyes."

"You reported a phony murder to the police?" Emily grabbed Eric by the shoulder and spun him around to face her. "This has got to be the most foolish and irresponsible thing you've ever done."

"It really happened." Eric insisted. "Max recorded the whole thing on his phone."

All eyes fell on Max. He shrunk back like he wanted to crawl inside one of the rose bushes in front of the house and stay hidden until everyone decided to finally leave. He refused to make direct eye contact with either adult staring at him.

"I accidentally erased the video." His voice grew sheepish. "Sorry."

Eric frowned and he gazed up at his mom again. His eyes pleaded with her to believe what he said earlier. She wasn't having any of it.

Neither was Deputy Leeds.

"The other deputy actually called the pizza place where the alleged murder victim works," The deputy said. His sunglass-covered eyes were trained squarely on Eric and Max. "They told her that he called them a while ago from his cell phone and requested to take the rest of his shift off because he was feeling sick."

"I'm really sorry, deputy." Emily's expression matched her apologetic tone. "We recently went through a tough divorce as a family. He has a knack for pulling little pranks. This must be his way of acting out."

"I'll let him off with a warning this time," Deputy Leeds said. "But if he acts up like this again, I might not be so forgiving."

The deputy returned to his truck and peeled out of the driveway. Eric didn't get off so lucky with his mom. Before the truck vanished down the street, she threw the hammer down.

"Here's your warning: You're grounded until I say otherwise."

Eric's mouth dropped open.

"What? Mom you gotta believe me. I'm not lying."

"Just stop it and go inside. I don't want to hear another word." Emily turned to Ron and jabbed a finger back at Max. "Can you take his friend home?"

He nodded and fished his car keys out of his front pocket. Eric glanced back at Ron as their mother marched him through the front door. His eyes pleaded for his older brother to come to his defense.

Ron just shook his head.

"Bro, you gotta find yourself a better hobby than crying wolf."

11

Eric wouldn't let it go. He knew what he had seen, and he kept pestering Ron to do something about it. Closing his bedroom door and turning on some music only chased Eric away until the next afternoon arrived. Ron finally broke down and listened when he found his iPod had gone missing.

"What exactly do you want me to do about it?"

"I want someone to believe me." Eric showed none of the usual mischievous glint in his eyes or face while standing in the doorway. "I didn't make this stuff up."

Ron's eyes lit up. Christina might know what they should do about this situation. He fired off a text to her. Just a brief one.

Need your help. Come over to my place.

Ron sent his address in a second text. Christina had lived in Deer Falls long enough to have a solid idea of what they were dealing with here. Maybe she heard about this creepy old man monster or whatever the hell it was Eric thought he saw in Nick's house. One thing felt certain. Ron knew he was in over his head when it came to dealing with this stuff.

"You got your wish." Ron said, glancing back at the doorway. "My friend Christina is coming over here. We'll get to the bottom of this."

He turned away again and watched for her from the bedroom window. Once a car pulled into the driveway and Christina stepped out, Ron sprinted out from the bedroom and down the stairs. Eric followed close on his heels. Both wanted to reach the front door first before their mom did.

Ron flung open the door at the same time Christina raised her hand to knock. She jumped a little at his sudden appearance. A slight frown graced her face when she noticed concerned expressions from both brothers.

"What's wrong? Your text seemed urgent."

Eric started to blurt out everything he had told Ron earlier. Ron pressed his hand against his brother's mouth.

"Let me talk for a second."

Eric nodded and Ron pulled his hand away.

"My brother insists he saw a monster murder someone at Nick's house yesterday."

Christina raised her eyebrows.

"A monster? What sort of monster?"

"Looked like some really old man from the sound of it. Doesn't act like one from what I've been told."

"Who got murdered?"

Ron glanced down at his brother.

"Eric swears up and down that he saw a pizza delivery boy get ripped apart."

Christina cringed.

"That sounds gruesome."

"Yeah. He's freaked hardcore about it."

"We gotta call the sheriff."

"They sent a car over to check it out and didn't find any evidence of a murder," Ron explained. "The deputy who came here to get a statement from my brother was pretty pissed about it."

Christina fidgeted with a small silver ring adorning her right hand. Her eyes darted over to Eric and then back to Ron.

"Something awful really happened to Nick and his family, didn't it?"

"You believe my brother?"

Eric immediately shot Ron a hard stare when he posed that question.

"Seems like too much of a coincidence to me," she replied. "I don't care what that pothead in detention said. I really don't think Nick and his mom split for Golden."

Christina had a point, but Ron struggled to bring himself to agree with what she said. Like his mom told Deputy Leeds, Eric developed a habit of pulling pranks back in Commerce City. He had a tougher time believing anything his little brother said these days. On the other hand, he did promise he'd do something about this situation.

"I guess it wouldn't hurt to check it out."

"Who put you up to this?" Christina gave Ron a sideways glance with unblinking eyes. Going over to the house apparently hadn't crossed her mind. "Do you really think that's a good idea?"

Ron threw up his hands and shrugged.

"Probably not. But you and Casey wanted me to get involved. You got your wish."

"Are you insane?" Eric finally broke his silence. He shot a frantic look at the front door and then back at Ron. "Do you know what Mom's going to do once she finds out where you're going?"

Ron smiled and patted him on the shoulder.

"You really don't want to go down that rabbit hole, bro. Do you want me to fill her in on some of your other adventures that she doesn't know about?"

Threats of revealing hidden episodes of misbehavior to their mother shut Eric up in a hurry. Ron knew the last thing his brother wanted was to see his grounding extended from indefinite to until he graduated from high school. Eric shrunk back from him and stared at the porch in defeat.

"And when I get back, my iPod better be back in my bedroom where it belongs."

"What iPod?"

Eric instinctively tugged at his jeans pocket. Ron noticed a faint outline of the iPod hidden behind the outer fabric.

"I mean it, bro. On my desk when I get back."

Ron and Christina hopped into her car and drove away as Eric stood on the lawn watching them leave. Reaching Nick's house didn't take long. When they pulled into the driveway, the sun already began dipping behind jagged mountain peaks dotting the horizon.

Christina opened her trunk. Ron snatched up a flashlight and a lug wrench from inside. She looked over at the lug wrench in his hand and smiled.

"Planning on changing a tire?"

"Or beating up a monster. Whichever comes first."

She laughed and shut the trunk lid. They cut across the lawn toward the front door. Shadows from trees along the fence line swallowed up the lighter green of the lawn into darker hues. Ron's eyes slid over to the stationary car in the driveway. More leaves had piled up since he first saw the video. Tons of leaves now blanketed the lower half of the windshield. They also scattered across both roof and trunk.

When he and Christina reached the front porch, nothing seemed amiss. A closed front door. Drawn blinds behind a clear and clean window. No visible blood or dead body anywhere. Just like the deputy who stopped by earlier, Ron found no hard evidence of the alleged monster that sent Eric and Max into such a frenzy earlier.

Christina tried the doorknob. It turned in her hand and the door popped open.

"Wow. I didn't expect this house to be unlocked."

She pushed the door open. Ron followed her inside. He flipped on a light switch on the wall next to the door jamb. A light bulb flickered above their heads. Then, like a small meteor streaking across the night sky, the light suddenly vanished. Ron tried another switch controlling the living room lights.

The same scenario repeated in that room.

"Somebody forgot to change light bulbs around here."

Christina nodded.

"Good thing you brought a flashlight."

She held out her hand and Ron tossed the flashlight to her. Remnants of sunlight lingered outside the house, but drawn blinds blocked most of the light from seeping into the living room. Traces of light that slipped past the blinds grew progressively fainter heading up the stairs or down the hall leading to the backdoor.

Christina shined a beam on the living room walls and trailed it across the far wall. Random branches and vines popped up in the light's path from time to time. Where the light did not reach, a legion of plants made the room feel like a darkened jungle.

Ron grasped her arm with one hand. His other hand tightened around the lug wrench at his side. He didn't say anything, fearing his voice would betray what his nerves already told him. Something didn't feel right about this house. His instincts told him they should turn around, sprint out the front door, hop in the car, and drive away. Ron's curiosity wouldn't let him listen.

"Look at this."

Christina focused the flashlight beam on the mantle and trailed it upward toward the ceiling. Three heads hung high above the fireplace. Dried out skin like unwrapped mummies. No eyes filled the sockets. Mouths wide open, each one still possessing a full set of teeth.

Ron swallowed hard and took a step back. Christina's mouth dropped open. His eyes slid to the spot where she stared. One head looked familiar.

"That looks a lot like Nick," she said.

"I guess we know what happened to —"

11

Ron paused and slowly turned toward the stairs. Did he hear a low growling whisper? No one else appeared to be in the room with them when they entered the house. Just the legion of plants and a trio of heads mounted and displayed like trophy bucks.

"I don't like this at all."

Christina nodded. A worried frown crossed her lips.

"Neither do I. Something really unsettling is going on in this place."

She turned and walked past Ron. He followed her to the foot of the stairs. Christina froze. Ron also stopped in his tracks. A different sound greeted them this time. A low moan. It came from the top of the stairs.

Christina swung the flashlight beam upward. Nothing. Ron saw no source for the noise. She started forward. Ron reached out and grasped her right arm again. He tried to pull her back but Christina pushed back against his hand.

"What are you doing?" Ron said. "You don't go toward strange sounds in a place like this. You move away from them as fast as possible."

"Don't you want to find out what's going on here?"

"I'm more worried about joining the other heads hanging over the mantle if we stay here too much longer."

Christina yanked her arm out of his grasp and started up the stairs again.

"You can always go wait in the car if you're scared," she said without looking back at him. "I don't like this either, but we need some answers."

Ron scowled and trudged up the stairs behind her. He wasn't about to go back and sit in the car by himself. Sticking close to a girl like Christina who could use magic seemed like a smarter and safer choice at this point. Still, it didn't mean he needed to feel happy about that choice.

Coarse carpet covering each stair muffled the noise from their footsteps. Vines with matching small dark red leaves wrapped around the banister on one side of the staircase. They resembled ivy, but their color seemed all wrong. Ron didn't expect to see a red vine there. He reached out to touch a leaf.

"No! Don't do that!"

Christina's hand seized his wrist. She pulled Ron away from the vine. He glanced at his wrist and flashed a little smirk at her.

"It's just a plant. I don't think it's poisonous or anything."

"I don't think we should touch anything in here."

Ron pinched his lips together and nodded a second later. He couldn't argue with that logic. A creepy vibe ran through this whole place.

Shadows swallowed up places where the flashlight beam didn't fall. The stairs connected to a landing that narrowed into another hall after a few feet. More odd-looking vines crawled down each wall. Christina traced walls and vines with the flashlight. She stopped and focused the beam on a bedroom near the middle of the hall.

A dull dark red glow emerged from the doorway. It spread out into the hall like a dense fog for only a short distance before fading into shadows. Ron and Christina glanced at each other. Her grip around the flashlight tightened. He licked his lips and his throat tightened as he tried to swallow.

"I think our answer is down there."

Christina's gaze drifted back to the red glow again. She took a step forward and suddenly stopped. A low moan echoed through the hall. Ron's hand trembled a bit as he grasped her arm. He wanted to shout at his muscles and nerves and order them to stop quivering, but it wouldn't do any good. They wouldn't listen. Not in this place. Ron felt similar tremors attacking Christina as she swung the flashlight beam in the same direction where they heard the moan.

The beam illuminated a lower portion of the wall on the left side of the hall. Christina gasped and pressed her hand over her mouth. Ron's mouth simply hung open.

"God, that's so much worse than anything we saw downstairs," he finally said.

A body, partially cocooned in layered vines, was pinned against the wall. Lacerations crossed the face and neck. Blood had splattered out in multiple directions from each one. Eyelids were only partially open with the visible portion of the eyeballs rolled back. The mouth hung open; a frozen expression of absolute horror still lingered on the lips.

"This is bad." Christina's voice descended to a frightened whisper. "This is so bad."

Ron raised the lug wrench and jabbed the end into the cocooned body. A torn Pizza Wagon cap fell off its head and landed on the floor. The body itself remained motionless.

"Definitely dead."

A shiver shot through Christina. She pinched her eyes shut and turned away. When she opened them again, a second later, her lower lip started to tremble.

"We're not alone."

Ron turned, facing the same direction as Christina. A woman adorned with a flowing black gown now stood outside the doorway. Shadows, along with a black cloak and veil, hid much of her face. Only her eyes were visible. They possessed a dark red glow matching what they had seen emanating from the bedroom.

"Run."

Christina's words echoed Ron's own thoughts. The flashlight beam bounced up and down off the ground as they charged down the stairs. Ron stumbled on a middle stair. The lug wrench tumbled out of his hands and struck the banister.

He reached out to grasp the banister and steady himself. A vine sprang forward with the speed of a coiled snake. It wrapped itself around Ron's wrist and dragged him closer.

"Get it off! Get it off!"

Christina stopped near the bottom of the stairs and jerked her head around. The flashlight beam fell on Ron's arm. A second vine shot toward him. Ron's breaths grew shorter and more rapid. His eyes widened as the second vine closed in on his upper leg.

Then the vine halted as if it smacked right into an invisible brick wall. At the same time, the first vine recoiled and pulled away from Ron's wrist. Both vines backtracked and resumed their earlier spots wrapped around the banister.

Ron rubbed his jacket sleeve to confirm no plant material remained behind. He looked up and saw Christina standing on the stair directly in front of him with her left hand thrust out toward him. A pair of fingers pointed at the vines.

"I'm still in one piece," he said.

"Good." She motioned to the door. "Now let's hurry."

They cleared the final few stairs and reached the entryway. A low whisper followed. Immediately, the front door slammed shut as if an invisible hand drew it to the door jamb. Ron glanced back at the staircase. The woman in black stood atop the stairs. Both hands extended toward the bottom stair.

Christina yanked the doorknob. The door didn't budge an inch. Ron looked back a second time. Their adversary drew closer. Now she hovered over the middle of the stairs.

"We're trapped! God, this isn't happening."

"It isn't happening. Have a little faith."

Christina closed her eyes, uttered an odd word Ron didn't understand and clenched her right fist. The knob popped out from the front door like a cork launching from a champagne bottle and clanked against the floor. Christina opened her eyes again and she broke into a relieved smile.

11

"What did I tell you?"

She pushed the door open, and they both sprinted to her car. Ron heard an angry howl as they reached the porch steps. It shook every door and window.

He dared not look back. Not while getting into the car or backing out of the driveway. Only when the car peeled away, and the cul-de-sac grew smaller and faded in the rear-view mirror did the thumping deep inside his chest finally return to a normal rhythm.

Ron knew one thing. He owed Eric an apology.

12

One more stop. That's all they needed.

Trevor stared straight ahead. He looked past all five linemen with a hand planted on the ground. His ears didn't wander to raucous cheers from the bleachers. One thing alone commanded his attention. His eyes locked on the quarterback with the precision of a scope on a sniper's rifle.

The quarterback lined up in shotgun formation. Trevor watched his eyes dart back and forth, scanning the defense as he barked out the snap count. He shifted up to the edge. When the center snapped the ball, Trevor sprang forward with the tenacity of a sprinter bursting out of the blocks.

He blitzed around the edge as the quarterback checked down his receivers. Trevor barreled toward him like an enraged bull and met him in the backfield right as the quarterback raised his arm to throw. He plowed straight into his shoulder before the quarterback started his throwing motion and quickly knocked his opponent sideways onto the turf.

The football squirted out of the quarterback's hand and bounced onto the grass near Trevor's feet. No whistle. Trevor scooped it up in his hand before the quarterback scrambled over to blanket the ball. He dashed forward. Sweat trickled down his forehead. Nothing but green grass and white hash marks lay ahead of him. No one could catch Trevor before he crossed the goal line. The referee quickly raised his arms.

Touchdown.

Game over.

The crowd erupted in cheers. Trevor tossed the ball over to the back judge and pumped his fist in the air. He glanced at the scoreboard and soaked it all in. Less than a minute remained on the game clock and Deer Falls now held a nine-point lead. Centennial didn't have enough time left to mount a comeback now. His dream of an undefeated season remained alive.

Several teammates mobbed Trevor in the end zone. They hugged him and exchanged high fives. Trevor trotted over to the sideline and took off his helmet. Coach Barker immediately marched over to him and smacked him on the back.

"Nice play, Judd. You picked a perfect time to come up with your first defensive touchdown of the season."

Trevor pointed to the scoreboard.

"It's the first of many."

"I don't doubt it," Coach Barker replied. "One more reason I'm glad you're our sideline."

Zeroes flashed on the scoreboard as the final seconds ticked off the game clock. Deer Falls would be undefeated going into region play and the Bucks just knocked off the number one ranked team in their classification. This had the makings of a special season and Trevor had played a crucial role in it all so far. Adrenaline, mixed with a few scattered butterflies, surged through him while going through the customary post-game handshake line at midfield. Neither of his older brothers won a state title. He had a real shot at accomplishing something they couldn't ever do.

The celebration didn't stay confined to post-game speeches in the locker room. Trevor converged with several teammates at one of their houses for an impromptu party. Music popped at full blast from the speakers. Football players and cheerleaders clustered on couches and chairs. Laughter and conversations rippled throughout the living room and kitchen.

Trevor stayed on an island of his own construction. He leaned against a wall at the foot of the stairs. A beer bottle, still half-full, rested in one hand. His eyes were fixed on the bottle alone. The party surrounding him had turned into white noise his ears filtered out.

"Trev, man, come join the party. You deserve it."

He looked up to see a fellow linebacker standing in front of him. His teammate wore a satisfied smile Trevor wanted to paint on his own face. The smile seemed to extend through his freckled cheeks and right up to his curly red hair. Trevor didn't think he had any similar smiles left inside himself.

"I just need some time alone. Me and my beer."

"Dude, seriously, you have to come out here. Jasmine is back on the market. She's got her eye on you.

Trevor squinted at him and scowled.

"Leave me alone, Noah."

Noah scoffed and shook his head. He rested his hand on Trevor's shoulder.

"You might not get another chance. A girl with tits that perfect doesn't cross your path every day."

Trevor ripped away Noah's hand and pushed him backward. The other linebacker stumbled a bit and he dropped the can in his other hand. Beer splashed out and quickly created a fresh puddle at the bottom of the stairs.

"What the hell? Who crawled up your ass and died?"

"Let me spell it out for you. I want to be with Lisa and no one else. We were in love. Some asshole took her from me and stole a part of my life."

Tears threatened to seep out of Trevor's eyes. It didn't feel fair. Lisa should have been there to see his big game like all the others. He missed seeing her on the sideline. He missed her. Period. Trevor planned to ask Lisa to marry him after they graduated in the spring. They were supposed to go to the same college and start a new life together. None of that could happen now that she was dead. Chatting up another cheerleader just to get inside her pants didn't hold any appeal for Trevor right now.

"I'm sorry, dude. Lisa was a great girl. But you have to try to heal and move forward."

"You stupid shit!"

Trevor smashed the bottle against the wall. Beer and shards of glass splattered everywhere.

"I just barely went to her funeral and now you want me to forget about her? Who the hell does that?"

"Chill. That's not what I meant. Just calm the fuck down, okay?"

Trevor pointed the jagged end of the beer bottle at his teammate. Noah threw up his hands to shield himself and backed up a half-step.

"You can go fuck yourself with a stick. I'm outta here."

Trevor hurled the rest of the bottle against the floor. Another spray of glass shards scattered across the carpet. He stomped through the kitchen and out the back door. Trevor fumbled for his keys as he marched across the grass. They spilled out of his hand and struck the curb before he reached his truck.

He shouted and kicked the front tire nearest to the curb. Trevor stooped down and moved his hand across the cement, trying to figure out where he dropped those damn keys. Everything had become a bit blurry. The sidewalk. The road. His truck. All blended into one giant, hardened, shapeless mass.

Trevor finally wrapped his hand around the elusive keys and scooped them off the cement. He stumbled forward and planted his arm against the truck fender to keep from tumbling over. A dull throbbing overtook Trevor's head. He didn't really feel up to driving. But only one thought dominated his mind. Get out. Drive as far away from this party as he could get. It's all he could do to keep from beating up Noah until he turned into a bloody shell of himself.

Trevor climbed into the truck and peeled away from the house. He needed to go find some other place where he could think. Away from all the noise.

Why did this have to hurt so damn much? He just wanted to forget everything in moments like this one. Trevor never even got to say goodbye or hold Lisa in his arms one last time. Her killer robbed him of seeing her smile, hearing her laugh, and feeling her warm lips press against his own ever again.

They couldn't even allow an open casket. Her parents told him Lisa's body had been destroyed beyond recognition. Those words choked up Trevor as much to hear them as it did for Lisa's parents to say them. Justice. That's what he wanted. He didn't care what anyone said. Her death was no freak accident. Lisa had been murdered. Plain and simple. And he just knew Christina had to be behind it all. Once Trevor could prove it, he vowed to do to that damn witch what she had done to Lisa. That freak would get what she deserved.

Streetlights gave way to reflector poles as he hit the Deer Falls town limits. Trevor headed up the highway toward the ranches. Lisa always loved horses. He could sit there and park and think about the fun times they had riding together. Trevor crisscrossed the yellow line a couple of times as ranch land clustered along the horizon.

He slowed down as he reached a stained log fence marking the eastern boundary of the ranches. Trevor peered out of the windshield at the opposite side of the road. A woman clad in a billowing black gown stood in the gravel behind the white line. She stepped on the asphalt as his truck approached and then crossed to the yellow line.

"What the hell?"

Trevor slammed on the brakes. The truck jerked to a halt only a few feet from the woman. Beams from the headlights fell on her and illuminated her from head to toe. A hood attached to her cloak covered her head and a matching veil obscured much of her face. The woman in black wrenched her head upward and stared right at Trevor. Both eyes burned with a distinct chill.

Trevor's manners overtook his anger and grief. He rolled down the window.

"Are you all right? Do you need a ride somewhere?"

Her eyes softened. She said nothing but started walking toward the truck. Trevor pressed a small button and unlocked the passenger side door for her.

"Door's unlocked."

She opened the door and climbed into the cab. The woman in black gazed at Trevor again. He couldn't tell for sure, but her eyes reflected a concealed smile under that veil.

"Where are you going?"

"North."

Her words entered his ears in the form of a whisper as feathery as the hair peeking out from under her hood. A strange energy surrounded the woman. Trevor could feel it. She already seemed unlike any person he had seen or met before tonight. He shifted back into drive and continued down the highway.

They passed by one mile marker and another and another. Trevor tried to ask her a couple of questions. She didn't say much. Her relative silence didn't deter Trevor's efforts at conversation. The more he stole glances at the woman in black, the more intrigued he became with her.

"Stop here."

Trevor obeyed her request and pulled his truck off the highway and onto a small rest area. He saw lights from one ranch house several yards ahead and lights from another about a half-mile behind them. No residence occupied this particular spot. Trevor parked the truck but left the engine running.

"I just wanted to give you a proper thank you for giving me a ride."

Her hand slithered across his knee. Trevor turned and glanced at the mysterious woman. His eyes narrowed and his lips tightened. He slid back against the seat. Trevor's heart quivered like a hammer repeatedly struck it.

"Look, I don't even know you ..."

Trevor trailed off. Memories of sharing kisses with Lisa sprang into his mind. On so many occasions, they drove out here and parked near the ranches. Sometimes they made out in his truck. Other times, Lisa snuggled up against his shoulders and they talked while he held her in his arms. It didn't feel right to kiss and caress a stranger he barely met in the same way.

The woman in black leaned in closer to him and lifted the veil from over her mouth. An aroma of coriander flowers wafted past his nose. Her lips pressed against his lips. Trevor's eyes widened and his whole body stiffened. His arm shot out to push the woman away.

Suddenly, his eyes closed. His arm loosened and trailed down the side of her neck. Trevor drank in the kiss with the intensity of a thirsty man indulging in a glass of water. When he opened his eyes again and pulled back from her lips, the woman in black no longer sat before him. A familiar face had taken her place.

"Lisa? Is that you? What's going on?"

His fingers ran through her blond hair. It felt as real as it did in the last moments they spent together. Everything he loved about Lisa was there, right down to the promise ring on her finger. She tenderly traced her fingers across his cheek and over his lips. Lisa worked her way down to his hand, which she then took up in her own, and began kissing his fingertips.

"I've missed you so much," Lisa said between kisses. "I needed to be with you just one more time."

Trevor felt lightheaded. Maybe he downed one beer too many at the party. None of this could be real. She died. He went to the funeral. He placed flowers on the casket and watched it get lowered into the grave. How was this even possible? Yet, she sat before him and both looked and felt as real as anything else inside his truck.

"Babe, it's really me." Lisa looked at him through her lashes and gave a flirty smile. "Do I have to beg for your kisses? Because I will beg."

Trevor leaned forward without hesitation this time. His left arm encircled her back. Their lips parted at the same time and his tongue darted inside her mouth. Trevor savored the kisses for a moment before pulling back and trailing his lips across her jawbone. Lisa let out a satisfied moan.

This felt better than a dream. If it really was a dream, Trevor didn't want to wake up.

He brought his lips back to hers again and plunged his tongue in a little deeper the second time around. Lisa squeezed his right hand and guided it onto her breast. Trevor massaged the breast as he prepared to slide his hand under her blouse.

A sharp stabbing pain suddenly ripped through his mouth. Teeth sank deep into Trevor's tongue.

His eyes popped open.

Trevor wrenched back from Lisa. Only Lisa no longer sat before him. The woman in the black gown had returned. Her dark eyes shifted into a steely gaze and her veil had been drawn back from her mouth.

Blood now enveloped her lips.

His blood.

Trevor screamed and cupped his left hand to his mouth. Blood dribbled out between his fingers. He grabbed the keys out of the ignition and fumbled to open the door.

The woman in black spit out the portion of Trevor's tongue trapped inside her mouth. It landed on the floor mat.

"Come back over here, lover. We're not done yet."

Trevor shuddered and whimpered. The door finally popped open. He rolled out onto the highway. His left hand made a bloody imprint on the asphalt. Trevor staggered to his feet and cupped his hand to his mouth again.

A ranch house lay only a short distance away. 200 or 300 yards. Trevor could make it. Then he could get help. He just had to outrun this crazy bitch. Without the truck keys, she wouldn't get far. All Trevor had to do was concentrate. Pretend he was carrying a football and trying to return a fumble or an interception back for a touchdown.

He could do it.

He had to do it.

The woman in black opened the passenger side door and walked to the front end of the truck. She planted herself before the now darkened headlights and started rotating her hands in a circular motion. Both headlights popped on again, illuminating the highway and Trevor as he fled. Soon, a blue flame appeared between both hands. It flickered no brighter than a flame on a tiny candle at first. The flame soon grew larger and rounder until it reached the same size as a baseball.

She unleashed a scream and hurled it toward Trevor. He glanced back and saw a fireball headed straight for him. Trevor sprinted toward the fence, hoping to dodge it and force the fireball to hit the logs instead. He slipped on some loose gravel and crunched down on his knees. The ball of flames closed the gap as Trevor tried to scramble to his feet.

Blood kept oozing from his mouth.

It now covered his entire chin.

Trevor grabbed a fence post. The fireball popped like a bubble and splattered against his back. Flames spread out in all directions across his body.

12

Trevor screamed and continued trying to scramble over the fence. He reached the top but immediately toppled backward and landed hard in a patch of crabgrass. His skin turned black like charcoal as flames turned white. Not so much as a spark fled from him into the surrounding grass.

The flames stuck to Trevor's body like glue as they stripped away every last ounce of flesh. Not a single flame faded away until finishing the job they were designed to do. Only a charred skeleton remained to mark the spot near the fence where Trevor had fallen.

13

Casey did nothing to hide his disappointment. His lips hung out in a visible pout. It told Ron all he needed to know. Christina worked to persuade him that they didn't intentionally exclude him from their trek to Nick's house.

Ron knew he made a huge mistake letting word of it slip out in the first place.

"Sorry." She gave him a reassuring pat on the shoulder. "It didn't cross my mind. Everything happened so fast."

Casey looked down at the rubber track circling the football field. He inspected the white lines separating each running lane and refused to make eye contact with Christina or Ron. Getting him to simply shrug off what he perceived to be a deliberate snub would not come easy.

"I would have met you over at the house. One text and I'd be there."

"I know. We're tight. I don't know where I'd be without a friend like you here."

Casey's pout finally loosened a bit. His lips hinted at a smile as he looked at Christina again.

"Maybe we can go back in the daylight and check it out again."

Ron choked a bit on the water he squeezed into his mouth from his bottle. He spent the better part of a week trying to forget about what he saw in there. Casey had to be out of his mind. Ron dropped the water bottle on a patch of grass bordering the track and tilted his head.

13

"Go back there? Are you serious? What makes you think that's a good idea?"

"Why not? You got out of there the first time around without even a scratch."

"Doesn't mean we'll do it again."

Ron glanced over at Christina. His eyes pleaded for added resistance against Casey's suggestion. Snooping around Nick's house again redefined the whole concept of a bad idea. Ron still struggled to erase that image of the cocooned body they stumbled upon in the upstairs hall. Behind closed eyes, those mummified heads mounted above the living room fireplace reappeared no matter how much he tried to block them out.

"Casey, take our word for it," Christina said. "That whole place has a freaky vibe to it."

"What do you mean?"

They all turned to see Cassandra standing in front of them out on the track. Ron wondered where she had come from. He didn't remember seeing her hanging out with Casey and Christina in the group's usual spot in the bleachers. They all started gathering there over the last few days to watch his soccer practices.

"It's kind of a long story," Christina said.

"I have time to kill," Cassandra replied. "Tell me."

Christina flashed a strained smile at Ron. He got a distinct impression she didn't want to keep dredging up their shared experiences in that house either.

"They checked out an abandoned house without me — even though I was the one who told them about it in the first place."

Casey obviously had no problems volunteering information.

"What's so special about this house?"

"Another student who used to live there suddenly disappeared without a trace. His parents did too."

"Really?" Cassandra raised her eyebrows and surprise threaded through her voice. "What do you think happened to them? Does anyone know they're missing?"

"Something killed them and took possession of the house? I don't know. I can't tell you for sure since I didn't actually get to see anything."

As soon as he said those words, Casey made a point to look directly at Ron and Christina one more time. He really wanted to drive home his displeasure over getting left out of their earlier expedition to Nick's house. Cassandra glanced sideways at both teens and then back at Casey.

"Doesn't sound like a house that any of you should be visiting."

"You know what? You're absolutely right." Christina clapped her hands together. "No need to go back so that woman in black can take a second crack at us."

Cassandra turned her gaze back to Christina and quickly shot her a curious look.

"Woman in black?"

"It's apparently some sort of monster or ghost that tried to attack them," Casey suggested.

"A monster? That sounds ridiculous."

"How so?"

Casey seemed genuinely surprised and disappointed to hear Cassandra dismiss his theory. Ron didn't understand his reaction. He figured Casey would have grown used to being met with skepticism by now.

"Everyone knows those things are just a myth," Cassandra said. "They don't exist. It's a proven fact."

Ron envied Cassandra. He wished to be as skeptical as her again. But now he'd seen just enough since coming to Deer Falls to know some strange things were indeed going on around this town and those things just couldn't be explained away.

"I stand by what Christina said earlier," Ron replied. "Everything about that place freaked us both out. I mean everything."

"What specifically was freaky?"

"Dried out mummy heads on one wall. A pizza delivery boy cocooned on a different wall. Strange vines growing all over the place."

A little shudder raced through Ron as he listed it all off. Cassandra fiddled with a lock of her hair. Her eyes trailed the football field from one end to the other. She finally looked at the other three again with a hint of concern in her eyes.

"Did you get a good look at this woman in black?"

Ron grabbed his water bottle off the ground and glanced over his shoulder toward the locker room.

"Not really," he said. "The whole place was dark, and she had a veil covering most of her face."

Cassandra stared at him for a moment and then shook her head.

"I'll say it again. You all are better off staying away from that place."

"Why? We need to find out what's going on there."

Casey wasn't about to yield on his dogged quest to see the house.

"Why do you care?"

"If there's a monster on the loose, we need to find a way to stop it."

A bemused smile emerged on Cassandra's face as soon as he said those words. Ron didn't need to read her mind to get an idea of what she really thought. Her reaction had skeptic written all over it.

"There's another option that comes to mind." Cassandra's tone started to match the tone of an adult growing weary with a small child's stubbornness. "We can let someone else worry about those imaginary problems."

"I'm going there right now!" Casey insisted. "And I'll bring back proof I'm right."

Ron and Christina exchanged nervous glances as the foursome approached the gymnasium. Neither shared Casey's enthusiasm for checking out Nick's house again. They barely escaped in one piece on their visit. Ron didn't feel confident about their escape odds on a return trip.

Neither did Christina.

"I don't think it's such a good idea," she said. "I'm not one who usually shies away from investigating things, but whatever is in that house is bad news."

"Nothing you say is changing my mind." Casey raised his chin in the air and gave her a defiant look. "I'm going over there."

Cassandra shrugged and grasped Casey's hand.

"I guess if we can't talk you out of it, then I'll at least go and keep you company."

He glanced down at Cassandra's hand and smiled.

"We're not asking for your permission." Casey took on a triumphant tone toward Ron and Christina. "If you don't want to go back to the house, don't go."

Christina closed her eyes and shook her head. The hairs on Ron's neck stood up as he thought about what lay in store for those two at that house. He couldn't let it happen — even if Casey annoyed the hell out of him. What he saw on those walls gave him a good idea of potential fates ahead for them if they went into that place alone.

"You win," Ron said. "I'll take you there."

Christina gnawed on her lower lip. Ron knew she didn't want to go back. Neither did he. But maybe the two of them together would be enough to keep Casey and Cassandra out of trouble.

"Strength in numbers," Ron said, turning to her.

Christina nodded.

"Strength in numbers," she repeated in a defeated tone.

Ron struggled to shake off the bad feeling welling up inside of him while he changed out of his soccer uniform and put on a pair of jeans and a long-sleeved shirt. The same thoughts circulated through his head over and over as he drove from the school straight to Nick's house.

What would they find there this time around? What if the woman in black discovered the group lurking around in a room and went after them again? Christina got herself and Ron out of harm's way the last time. Still, her ability to use magic had to have some limits.

Ron pulled up to the house and the foursome piled out of his car. Everything looked peaceful from the outside. He noticed the same car occupied the same spot in the driveway as last time. More leaves cluttered the hood, windshield, roof, and trunk. Add a few more and it will start turning into compost. Ron chuckled briefly at the image it presented in his mind.

"What's so funny?" Christina asked.

"It's nothing," he said. "Just looked at all the leaves covering the car and wondered what it would look like as a compost heap."

She flashed a cute smirk at him.

"Yeah ... funny."

One thing had changed. The front doorknob had been put back into place since their last visit. Ron gazed up at the windows on the bungalow's second level. Did one or more sets of eyes watch them, even now, from the darkened room above? How could the woman in black not anticipate intruders showing up again?

Casey wandered over to the mailbox. It had grown overstuffed with mail to the point that a couple of random pieces spilled out and decorated the curb.

"Wow." He poked at the letters, bills and ads crammed into the open mailbox. "This is turning into a mini trash can."

Cassandra ignored the mailbox. She cut across the grass and marched up the porch steps. The other three scrambled after her. Ron caught up to her on the porch. As she reached for the copper knocker adorning the front door, he quickly grabbed Cassandra by the shoulder and pulled her back.

"Are you crazy?" he said. "We don't want to alert the woman in black to meet us at the front door."

Cassandra's blue eyes turned skyward. When she glanced at Ron again, she gave him a funny look.

"Who leaves their door unlocked?"

"How do you think we got inside the last time?"

She sighed and turned the knob. It didn't budge.

"Satisfied? Let's knock."

"No! That's a bad idea."

Ron reached out to stop her hand again. Cassandra pushed him away and raised the copper knocker. She gave the door a pair of hard raps.

"What have you done?"

Christina's eyes darted to the front window. She saw no movement behind the blinds yet. Still, any chance of their return going unnoticed had now vanished.

Ron gnawed on his lower lip, ran his hand through his light brown hair, and glanced back at the car.

"We've gotta bolt from here, guys. Only a matter of time before that woman shows up."

"I don't actually see or hear anything."

Ron realized Casey was right. He also didn't see anything stirring beyond the blinds. Random birds chirping in nearby trees supplied the only noises outside the house. The entire cul-de-sac seemed to be devoid of supernatural activity, or any actual human activity for that matter.

"See? No one answered. Nothing happened." Cassandra turned away from the door and started back down the steps. "You all have vivid imaginations. That's where it ends. Now let's go."

"We didn't exactly make this garbage up," Christina snapped. "It really happened."

"Maybe we can find another way inside?" Casey pointed to the side of the house. "The back door could be unlocked."

13

"Are you serious?" Ron said. "Let's just call it a day and go. I'm not about to try and force my way back into this house."

Casey ignored Ron's protests and climbed over the side of the porch. He dropped down on a short, narrow brick walkway winding past the garage into the backyard. Christina charged down the steps behind him and rounded the corner with the determination of a runner making one final kick to reach the finish line. Waves of frustration and worry rippling through her eyes were matched in Ron's own eyes. He and Cassandra hurried off the porch as well.

When Ron reached the backyard, he spotted Casey emerging from an open shed door. He had hoisted an extension ladder onto his shoulder. Casey plodded across the grass over to the brick walkway. He shifted his grip on the ladder's aluminum legs a couple of times to keep from dropping it.

"Where are you going with that ladder?" Ron asked.

"I tried the backdoor," Casey said. "It's locked too. But the shed was open. Then I saw the ladder and the solution came to me."

Christina gave him a wary glance.

"What solution?"

"I'm gonna see if I can get up on the roof from the front of the house. I can get a peek inside the upstairs window. Find out what's going on in there."

"Are you planning on breaking into that room?" Cassandra asked.

"Well, no. But we can't seem to get a look inside another way."

Ron wondered if broken bones were the next item on the list. That ladder didn't look all that stable when Casey planted it squarely in the grass and pushed it up against rain gutters lining the front of the house. Christina's eyes followed him as he started up the ladder.

"This is a bad idea," Christina rested her chin in her palm. "Those doors are locked for a reason. Casey, come back down."

"No worries." Casey's voice exuded an enthusiastic confidence. "If

Indiana Jones can dodge booby traps in an ancient temple, I can handle climbing on the roof of this house."

"Fun fact: you're not Indiana Jones," Ron replied.

Casey waved his hand dismissively at Ron and continued up the ladder. His head was almost parallel with the rain gutters when the muscles in his forearms suddenly tightened. The ladder started to sway a little bit. Casey's hands clasped onto the ladder like eagle's talons. He pinched his eyes shut and gritted his teeth.

"It's burning!"

"That's not funny," Christina said.

"Help! Help!"

Smoke started wafting upward from both of Casey's hands. The ladder started to rock more violently and threatened to topple over like an overgrown tree branch on a blustery day. Cassandra started forward and reached out to steady the ladder. A terse scream erupted from her at the same moment flesh and metal made contact. She stumbled backward while cradling her hand.

"Hang in there, Casey. I'll get you down."

Ron stripped off his fleece jacket and wrapped the sleeves around his hands. He latched onto the ladder and pulled it away from the roof.

"I can't move my hands."

Tears streamed from Casey's eyes. Christina covered her mouth to stifle a scream. Ron lowered the ladder to the ground with Casey still on the rungs. As soon as metal touched grass, he dashed forward and wrenched Casey's hands off the ladder rung.

Open blisters coated both palms where patches of skin had burned off. What remained behind from the top layer of his skin had turned into a crinkled mess. Casey's lower lip quivered, and he panted like a frightened dog.

"Oh God! I've never felt so much pain in my life."

Ron dropped the jacket on the grass. It bore fresh scorch marks where it pressed against the ladder. He tore two strips off the bottom of his long-sleeved shirt. Ron wrapped a strip around each hand and helped Casey to his feet.

"I think we better get him over to a hospital quick." Ron fished his car keys out of his pocket. "Those are at least second- or third-degree burns."

He turned to Cassandra. She continued to cradle her own hand and pressed the palm against her shirt.

"How badly did you get burned?"

She squinted at Ron and refused to pull back her hand to allow him a better look at the extent of her injury.

"I'll survive. Help Casey."

Ron helped Casey into the front seat. Christina stood fixed in the same spot on the lawn. She stared at the extension ladder with wide eyes. Then, finally, Christina crept forward and poked the lowest rung with her finger.

She crinkled her nose and stepped back.

"It's completely cool now. Definitely magic."

Ron's eyes shifted upward, and he gazed at the upstairs window. He wondered if the drawn blinds concealed that woman in black. Did she watch them below as they fled while quietly planning her next attack?

"Someone is trying to send us a message," Ron said. "And they're willing to kill us to get the point across."

14

Dean slumped down against a brick wall only a few feet from a garbage can. His stomach rumbled as his internal gas tank hit empty. It needed fuel now. His eyes followed a truck that pulled up in front of the nearest gas pump. Dean scanned the license plate and noted a Utah plate, not a Colorado one. A middle-aged man stepped out of the truck and lumbered toward the main doors of the small convenience store.

A visitor.

Dean counted his good fortune. People from Utah who he encountered before were compelled to be generous more readily than tourists who dropped in from other places. Once the middle-aged man cast his eyes toward the garbage can, Dean made his move.

He caught up to his target before that man reached the door.

"Sir, I hate to bother you like this." Dean promptly extended his hand. "I haven't eaten since yesterday and I don't have enough money to get a meal. Could you spare some change?"

"I'm in a hurry." The middle-aged man stared past Dean's shoulder into the store window. "Can you pester someone else?"

Dean kept his hand fixed in the same spot.

"I just need a little bit. You can even buy me food if you want."

The other man fished his wallet out of his jeans. He opened it up and combed through a couple of bills with his fingertips. They must have been large ones. Hesitation to part with the money was written in the frown adorning the man's face.

"How about I buy you a breakfast sandwich from the gas station? Would that work?"

Dean smiled and nodded.

"That's perfect. Bless you sir."

He followed the other man into the store. Dean waited near the door while his benefactor grabbed some food and a pop and then headed up to the register to pay for everything. While watching him at the register, he heard a voice crackle over a police radio.

"We have a 10-54 and 11-24 near the ranches. Possible 187."

"187?" Dean's ears perked up at hearing a familiar voice. "Oh God, not another one."

"Body burned beyond recognition."

"On my way."

Dean shrank back as Deputy Palmer barged past him and out the front door. Images long buried in his mind were now resurrected and clawed back to the surface. Two former classmates burnt beyond recognition. They found what remained of their bodies near a swing set inside the main street park. That's when Dean first awakened to the trouble that had befallen Deer Falls.

Adam discovered the gruesome scene by chance and his brother had become hysterical by the time he found Dean to tell him. They went back to the place together. What Dean saw still haunted him. Like so many other memories from that time, it hung back in dark corners and then jumped out at him when he came too close. Dean's life turned upside down starting from that day, though he didn't realize it at the time.

Part of him wanted to dismiss the description of the body he overheard. But those words made Dean's hands tremble and his palms feel clammy. This mirrored the work of that same awful being who terrorized this town 55 years ago. Dean had to see for himself. He needed confirmation, so he could track her down and, once again, banish her back to where she came from.

Dean pressed the handle and pushed the door open.

"Wait a minute? Don't you want your food?"

He turned to see the middle-aged man walking toward him and holding out a breakfast sandwich. Dean nodded and snatched it out of his hands. He tore off the top of the wrapper.

"Thank you so much."

Without another word, Dean bolted out the door. He devoured the egg and sausage biscuit as he rounded the corner. Dean's attempts to run, after tossing the wrapper, devolved into a half-run, half-limp gait. He surveyed the alley behind the gas station as he searched for some form of transportation that could get him out to the ranches.

A bicycle caught Dean's eyes. It had balding tires and the paint had flaked off in several places. He found it parked up against a garage in a neighboring yard. His eyes darted to the front door of the house and back to the gas station. Dean shuffled around the fence separating the two properties and snatched up the old bike. Not his first choice. But he couldn't afford to be picky if he wanted to get out there before they took the body away.

Dean hopped on the seat and started pedaling. He winced as his knees bounced up and down. His right knee throbbed and pulsated each time he completed one revolution with the pedal. Dean pushed himself forward. He threw every breath and every muscle into covering the three miles he needed to cover to reach the ranches. Traveling such a short distance wouldn't take long. He only needed to gut it out for a few minutes.

Houses and trailers soon yielded to open fields and trees. An aroma of parched hay drifted through the mountain air. Before long, Dean came upon a pickup truck parked off to the side of the highway. Several yards further up the road he spotted a highway patrol car, an ambulance and a sheriff's truck all clustered around the same spot.

Dean squeezed a hand brake on the bicycle and stopped a few feet behind the first truck. He dismounted from the bicycle and plodded along the asphalt. Dean wanted to get a good look at the body without drawing unwanted attention to himself at the crime scene. Deputy Palmer crouched over a patch of grass, near the log fence, with a highway patrolman.

Dean stopped by the hood of the truck, a short distance behind them, and squinted at the same spot. The highway patrolman stepped back a couple of steps and revealed the dead body in question. Nothing more than melted flesh and hair turned to charred bone was left. Dean snapped his eyes shut and pressed his hand against his mouth to suppress an urge to gag.

He had seen this before.

Another sickening image clawed into his mind. Dean wanted to jam it back down inside the mental chest where he once locked it away and tossed out the key. Doing that wasn't possible now. Remnants of melted and blackened faces belonging to those two classmates paraded before his eyes again. A circle of ashes from their bodies lay heaped under the swings. No burn scars beyond their immediate vicinity were present. No one knew the explanation for their horrific deaths at the time. Dean, Adam, and Valerie all soon uncovered what led Bucky and Marge to meet such a gruesome fate.

A fresh image burst through the door once blocking it from entering. Blinding streaks of light and red mist flashed through the halls of the high school. Screams everywhere. Students sprinting in every possible direction. Frantic pounding and yanking on large metal doors. Every attempt to push those doors open proved futile. No escape possible.

That monstrous witch did it. She sealed everyone inside and then cornered them with the skill of a cat preparing to pounce on a mouse.

Dean smacked the palm of his hand against his temple and gritted his teeth. Now an image of Adam popped into his head. He shouted at the witch, ordering her to leave the others alone. The witch spun to face him. Fury burned within those reddish black eyes poking out from beneath the hood of her cloak. She thrust out her arm toward their little group as they took cover.

At once, Dean's eyelids peeled open again. The chest had been opened again. He knew what lay ahead. The witch would go back to the site of her defeat. She would feel compelled to finish the destruction she started. Someone needed to step in and find a way to stop her before time ran out.

He had to get to the high school. Now.

Dean hopped on the bicycle and pedaled as hard as his knee let him pedal. Once again, he refused to listen to his twitchy nerves and inflamed ligaments. Dean could not spare even the smallest moment to indulge in pain. Not while that chest remained open. Not while that awful thing roamed free in Deer Falls for a second time.

Trees and houses formed a blur on the periphery of his eyes as the highway took him back into town. Dean wondered how much time passed before the teen opened the chest after stealing it from him. Death and destruction had not spread as far as last time yet, so he still had a chance. But not much of one. Every day she remained free opened a window wider for her to build up her power.

As the street climbed toward the foothills surrounding the eastern edge of Deer Falls, the high school popped into view. Dean zigzagged to the other side of the street. His front tire hopped over the curb. The back tire couldn't quite clear it. Dean popped off the seat with his fingers still wrapped around the handlebars. He stumbled sideways and his elbow struck the curb. Dean winced and pinched his eyes shut.

When the nerves in his elbow stopped throbbing, he opened his eyes again. Dean rose to his feet and fished the bicycle off the sidewalk. He pushed it forward a few feet and rested the weathered bike against a tree across the street from the high school. Dean had a clear view of the front of the school from here. No students were going in and out of the main doors. No buses were parked in the bus lane. Cars dotted an adjacent parking lot.

Classes would still be in session for a while. Dean counted his good fortune. If he could sneak inside, he'd hide somewhere and wait for the witch to show herself. She had to be here. Dean worried for a moment if he would recognize her. She had the ability to change her true appearance at will and make herself resemble a different person. Could he trust his eyes to not deceive him? He had to stay sharp.

Dean glanced up and down the street. He limped across the road toward the bus lane. Dean knew of a side entrance beyond the end of the lane where he could enter unnoticed. From there, he'd scout the halls and search for evidence of the witch's whereabouts.

Flashes of blue and red suddenly grabbed his eyes. A few notes from a siren penetrated his ears. Dean bit down on his lower lip and closed his eyes. He froze right in the middle of the bus lane.

"Where do you think you're going?"

Dean turned and saw a sheriff's truck pulling up into the bus lane only a short distance behind him. Deputy Palmer hung his head out the open window.

"Now, Dean, you know you can't go inside that school. That's called trespassing. You don't want me to put you in jail, do you?"

Dean turned away from Deputy Palmer again. His eyes wanted to lead his body up to the sidewalk, across the grass and through the side doors. There's no chance he'd ever make it that far before the deputy got to him. His legs remained stationary in the bus lane.

"Someone has to stop her." Dean said, without looking at the deputy or his truck.

"Who?"

"That monster. The witch."

"Not this again."

"I don't know who she's pretending to be. A student? A teacher? All I know is if we don't stop her, she will take over this town and destroy anyone who gets in her way."

"Dean, I don't have time for this nonsense."

"Nonsense?" He wheeled around to finally face the deputy. Dean's eyes flashed with rage. His voice climbed higher. "This is not nonsense! This is very real and very frightening."

"I'm not going to repeat myself."

"Don't pretend like you don't know what happened around here 55 years ago!"

The truck door immediately opened. Deputy Palmer stepped down onto the asphalt and pulled a pair of handcuffs off his belt.

"Do you want me to arrest you?"

"I've lost so much because of that vile woman. What she has stolen from me, I can never get back."

Dean's voice quavered as he said those words. Tears streamed down both cheeks. Memories of his last confrontation with her dug into his heart with sharp talons and shredded it like cheap paper. Deputy Palmer lowered the handcuffs and placed them back in their original spot on his belt.

"I know something isn't right," he said, while walking toward Dean. "I will get to the bottom of whatever is going on around here. But I need you to stay out of it. For your own safety and everyone else's safety too."

Dean sniffled and brushed away tears with his hand.

"I can't bear to go through this again. I can't."

Deputy Palmer pressed his hand on Dean's shoulder.

"I can't pretend to know what's going through your mind, Dean. All I know is I may have a serial killer on my hands. Two students found dead within a few days of each other. Other students reported missing."

It sounded worse than what Dean imagined. Things were escalating around here as quickly as last time.

"I need you to stay away. Go home Dean."

Dean's eyes dropped down to his feet and he nodded. He wouldn't go into the high school while Deputy Palmer remained here. Once the deputy left, however, that story would change. Dean vowed to come back as soon as eyes weren't on him and stake out the building. Someone needed to stop that witch from doing everything she intended to do.

That someone was him.

15

A dozen thoughts crowded into Ron's head as he approached the door to the principal's office. None were good. Every time he got called in here, it never ended well for him. Ron reached his hand out but stopped short of touching the doorknob. He didn't really want to be compelled to make a second effort to remove himself from Principal Reynolds' shit list. All of those missed soccer practices would have cost him a spot in the first XI on a more talented team.

Ron inched the door open with his fingers.

"Come in here, Mr. Olson. Have a seat."

He glanced at the desk and noticed a deputy sheriff standing next to the principal's chair. A different deputy than the one who showed up at his house. He wore a deep frown and rested his hands on his hips, one only a short distance from his holster.

Ron furrowed his brow when he noticed where the hand rested. Did the deputy expect someone to come in here and pull a weapon on him? He dropped his backpack next to a chair in front of the principal's desk and took a seat as directed.

"What's going on?"

"Deputy Palmer needs to ask you a few questions."

"A few questions? About what?"

Deputy Palmer cleared his throat.

"I'm hoping you can shed light on a couple of recent deaths around here."

"Deaths?"

"We discovered the body of one your classmates out near the ranches earlier this morning. Or what was left of it. Dental records identified the victim as Trevor Judd."

Ron's eyes widened and he swallowed uncomfortably. He hated Trevor's guts. But certainly not bad enough to go out and murder him. Obviously, someone else in this town didn't feel the same way.

"You have something you want to tell me, son?"

Deputy Palmer walked around to the front of the desk and leaned against it. His eyes locked on Ron with the same fierceness as an eagle circling its prey.

"So, I guess this means we're not taking state this year?"

Ron tried not to smirk, but he couldn't help allowing one to briefly cross his lips. Trevor never showed a single redeemable quality in any encounters Ron had with him. He didn't feel as broken up over the news as he supposed he was expected to feel.

"Do you think this is funny, Mr. Olson?" Principal Reynolds rose from her chair as sharply as her voice climbed in pitch. "Is the brutal murder of a fellow student a laughing matter to you?

Deputy Palmer turned to her and raised his hand. Principal Reynolds took it as a warning. She pinched her lips shut, but her glowering eyes conveyed all the other things she wanted to express in a stream of words principals weren't supposed to say to students.

"Don't try to be a smart ass," Deputy Palmer said, facing Ron again. "You're in a whole lot of trouble here."

"I'm in trouble?" A frown overtook Ron's face. "For what?"

"It seems like you and Trevor share a history of altercations with one another. You had a fight on the first day of school. And you almost came to blows a couple of more times after that first incident."

"I guess so. But it doesn't mean I killed him."

"Doesn't it?"

"I'm not that kind of person."

"Why were you at odds with one another so often?"

"He didn't like me because I'm a soccer player."

"That obviously bugged you, didn't it?"

Ron licked his lips and scrunched his fingers up on the end of the armrest. He had an idea where this path led. Deputy Palmer couldn't figure out the true culprit behind Trevor's death, so he wanted to pin it on him. Ron would become his scapegoat. His heart started thumping against his ribs. It finally dawned on Ron what this could entail.

Prison time.

A lifetime behind bars.

NO!

Ron wanted to scream out his innocence loud enough so everyone from one end of the school to the other heard it. He wanted to paint it in bright red letters where everyone saw it. Nobody would turn him into a scapegoat.

Ron stared, unblinking, at the deputy.

"Witnesses last saw Trevor on the night of our most recent football game." Deputy Palmer leaned forward, making every effort to tower over Ron in his chair. "Care to tell me where you were that night?"

Ron pinched his eyelids shut for a moment. They soon popped open again and unveiled light brown eyes filled with frustration.

"Look, I really didn't have anything to do with this. Do you want to know what I do after school? Ask my soccer coach. Ask my mom."

"You didn't answer my question, son."

"I didn't go to the game. I don't like football."

"So where were you after the game?"

"At home. Studying."

"Did anyone see you there studying?"

Ron drew a sharp breath and gnawed on his lower lip. It took all his energy to put a lid on his temper. His first instinct was to tell Deputy Palmer off for this unnecessary interrogation. But Ron also understood losing his cool here wouldn't end well.

"My mom and my little brother were both home that night. They can vouch for me."

Deputy Palmer squinted at Ron and frowned. It seemed obvious he didn't believe him. Still, the deputy grasped at straws. He didn't have a shred of evidence tying Ron to Trevor's murder because he didn't commit any murders in the first place. Ron knew one thing. He had enough of answering questions.

"Can I please go?" Ron started to rise from his chair. "I have to get to the rest of my classes and soccer practice."

Deputy Palmer hesitated to give him an answer. Ron watched uncomfortably while the deputy pulled out a small notebook and scanned over notes that he jotted down at the crime scene. He finally glanced up at him and nodded.

"We'll be in touch. I'm sure I'll have some more questions I'll need you to answer."

Ron snatched up his backpack and promptly barged out the door.

None of this made sense. Why were they singling him out? He barely even knew Trevor. Ron replayed the deputy's questions in his head while he walked back to his English class.

Something more than false accusations gnawed at Ron. It felt like more than a coincidence that someone killed Lisa and Trevor within a few days of one another. Their deaths both occurred after Nick's house had been abandoned from all outside appearances. But it hadn't been abandoned. Ron knew better.

Those surreal images from inside the house barged through the door in his mind and invaded his thoughts once again. Ron's efforts to not remember bore no fruit. What he saw reappeared with crystal clarity, as if someone transported everything from that awful place within the walls of the school and placed it in the hall before him.

Ron shuddered. All of these things were connected somehow. Deputy Palmer didn't say anything about Nick or the pizza delivery boy. Ron assumed he knew nothing about the house. He wanted to go back and reveal to the deputy everything he and Christina saw.

Giving into that urge wouldn't end well.

At best, Deputy Palmer wouldn't believe anything he told him. Hell, Ron wouldn't believe it himself if he hadn't experienced those things. At worst, his revelations would supply the deputy with more ammunition to pursue him as a suspect. Christina would be in trouble as well. Ron figured they craved a fresh excuse to harass her.

A smattering of students glanced up from their textbooks when Ron opened the classroom door. He barely noticed their whispers as he took a seat. Ron did catch a glimpse of Cassandra's eyes trailing him as he walked to his desk.

"What's going on?" she whispered, hiding the corner of her mouth behind her hand. "You seem upset."

"I never expected to be interrogated over a murder."

"Murder?"

"Someone killed Trevor. They found his body."

Cassandra suddenly turned her head and faced forward. Ron closed his eyes and sighed. A realization washed over his face that an unwelcome third party monitored his whispered conversation with heightened agitation.

"Do you mind if I have the floor now, Mr. Olson? These verbs won't conjugate themselves."

Ron opened his eyes and faced the front of the classroom. His English teacher stood before the marker board. She held a blue marker and pointed it at him like a knight brandishing a sword at a challenger. Ron sank down in his seat and kept his mouth zipped shut until the bell rang.

"So, someone thinks you're a murderer?"

Cassandra's question came a split second after the bell to dismiss their class peeled through the classroom. Ron shrugged as he snatched up his textbook and shoved it into his backpack.

"I got that feeling from the questions they peppered me with. Fighting with Trevor makes me their top suspect, I guess."

"He seemed like someone who has plenty of enemies."

Ron zipped up the backpack and hoisted it onto his shoulders.

"Are you kidding?" he said. "Trevor was this stupid town's meal ticket to a football championship. Everyone in this school celebrated him and put up with all his shit for that reason alone."

"People are the same everywhere."

"What do you mean by that?"

Cassandra pushed open the door and looked back at Ron. Her icy blue eyes seemed to be staring right through his body and centering on some distant point behind him.

"A soldier in the town where I came from elicited similar feelings. Everyone painted him as heroic. He did no wrong in their minds. Nothing could be further from the truth."

"What did he do?"

"He took a liking to a certain girl. Turned out, she didn't feel the same way. It didn't stop him. That soldier overpowered her one evening and raped her."

"God, that's horrible!"

"Terrible beyond words. I knew her. I understood her pain. She reported to the authorities what he did to her. They did nothing to punish the soldier."

Cassandra's expression turned grim as she recounted the story. Her eyes, for a small moment, seemed ready to burst under the strain of holding back a deluge of tears. Ron had an uncanny feeling Cassandra played a more prominent role in the story she shared than she cared to admit.

"Didn't they get a rape kit from her or anything? I can't believe they would ignore such a serious charge."

"The powerless have no recourse against the powerful. He resided in a protected class. She meant nothing to them. End of story."

Cassandra turned down a different hall than where Ron needed to go. He found himself following her down the hall anyway.

"What happened to her after that? What did she do?"

His questions stopped Cassandra in her tracks. She turned away and stared at the floor for a moment as if lost in thought.

"I better hurry to my next class," she finally said, glancing back at him. "Don't want to be late."

Cassandra's tale only served to heighten Ron's worries as they parted ways before his next class. He couldn't help wondering if his defense of his own innocence would also fall on deaf ears. No question Ron came to Deer Falls as an outsider. Shifting the blame to him rather than digging deep and finding the real culprit would certainly be easier for the cops around here.

Her story and his own concerns hung with him through soccer practice. After Ron overshot a teammate on a cross three times in a row, a whistle pierced both his thoughts and his ears.

"Come on, Olson. Get it together," His coach barked. "You two don't connect now, you won't do it in the game."

Ron wanted to remind Coach Rimmert how he led their team in goals in each of their last two matches. Then again, this wasn't the best time to dredge up that fact. He answered with a sharp nod and lined up outside the attacking third to start the passing drill again.

Getting chewed out did help Ron train his focus on soccer alone for the rest of the practice. Nothing else entered his mind right up until the team took a knee around Coach Rimmert to hear pregame instructions for tomorrow. Ron glanced over to the sideline and saw Christina walking over to the bench. He only heard bits and pieces of what the coach had to say after that point. Christina drew his attention. Did she endure her own interrogation in the principal's office? Trevor threatened her with violence the last time Ron had seen him alive. He had a feeling such an incident didn't go unnoticed.

"So, did you get to have a chat with our friendly neighborhood cops too?" Ron cracked a sarcastic smile as he walked over to her. "Or did I just get singled out for the hell of it?"

Christina responded with her own half-hearted smile. The corners of her lips barely turned upward before snapping like a rubber band back into a frown. Her eyes failed to conceal her annoyance.

"If I didn't know any better, I could have sworn the deputy sheriff was trying to force a confession out of me."

"I got a similar feeling when he talked to me."

"Don't get me wrong. I didn't like Trevor one bit. I thought he was an abrasive mean-spirited jerk. But I also wouldn't go out and murder him over it."

"Same here."

Christina brushed back a lock of hair from her cheek.

"At least Casey got spared going through the same third degree."

Ron instinctively glanced in the direction of the medical clinic on the other side of town.

"So how is Casey doing? Is he feeling any better?"

"His hands are still all bandaged up. They look rough. But he seems to be in really good spirits. He told me Cassandra came by to check on him too."

"I'm sure Casey loved seeing her."

"Yeah, he seemed to enjoy bringing it up."

Ron laughed. He pictured Casey's eyes staying glued to Cassandra and following her no matter where she went in the room. Not that he'd blame him for it. Cassandra was hot with a capital H. On the other hand, Ron found himself increasingly drawn to Christina. She looked cute and had a likeable personality from day one. As they bonded over soccer, and other things, his attraction to her only intensified.

A little smile crept over Christina's face as if she sensed Ron thinking about her. He licked his lips and snatched up his water bottle.

"So … um … what did the deputy say to you?"

"Just asked me where I was the night Trevor disappeared. He also grilled me on whether or not I clandestinely spent time out near the ranches practicing witchcraft."

"Are you serious?"

"Welcome to my life. This is the sort of garbage I deal with from people in this town. I'm used to it by now."

"You shouldn't have to be used to it."

Christina touched the back of Ron's arm and let her fingers trail down to his elbow before pulling away.

"I know I'm not the person they're afraid I am. That's what matters to me."

Ron gulped down some water and they walked from the football field down to the gym doors. How her interrogation played out troubled him more than his own. It wasn't just the idea that the authorities in Deer Falls were trying to pin this crime on them. What felt worse was the fact Christina experienced this level of fear and suspicion from people she lived around her whole life. It planted seeds of rage in his heart. Ron wanted to seize at least one of these idiots and channel his inner boxer working a speed bag.

Christina waited for Ron while he showered and changed in the locker room. Time had arrived for more soccer in the park. He tossed her a soccer ball as they walked out of the gym doors. They did some impromptu snake dribbling on their way to the parking lot.

Ron halted suddenly at the sidewalk. A disheveled gray-haired man clad in a heavy green jacket prowled along the cars. And he lingered too close to Ron's car for comfort.

"Hey! Get away from my ride!"

The man in the green jacket jerked his head up and shrank back from the bumper.

"I'm sorry. I'm searching for someone. I need to find them now."

"Who?"

"They escaped. I imprisoned them and they escaped!"

"Who?"

"A vile dangerous creature."

Ron folded his arms and drummed his fingers on his forearm.

"If I have to repeat my question one more time, I'm gonna lose it."

"A witch."

Ron glanced at Christina. Their eyes met and their lips curled into matching frowns.

"Let's go." She glanced sideways at the old man. "I see him in a vacant lot near the park all the time. He's crazy. Crazy Dean is what everyone calls him."

Dean threw up his arms in protest.

"I'm not crazy! Someone needs to listen to me."

"We don't have time for this." Ron turned back to him and stabbed his index finger at Dean. "Why don't you go find the other members of your anti-witch club and leave Christina alone?"

Ron grasped Christina's arm and took a half-step ahead of her, instinctively trying to shield her from the bum's presence. Dean crinkled both eyes and scrunched his nose.

"Her?" He pointed at Christina and shook his head. "This isn't who I'm looking for."

"Who are you looking for?"

"I'm not good with descriptions. I'm not sure if they even look the same after spending all that time trapped inside that chest."

"Trapped in a chest? What are you talking about?"

"Just answer me this. How many people have mysteriously died in the last few days?

Christina's eyes widened and she leaned forward. Ron swallowed hard. Maybe Dean had something useful to say after all.

16

Dean paced back and forth in front of Ron and Christina. "This is how it started last time." He closed his eyes and rubbed his hand across his cheek. "Random violent deaths. Unexplained disappearances. Before long, the witch unleashed her full power."

"What do you mean by full power?"

Ron wasn't sure he really wanted to know the answer to his own question. But they needed to understand what they were dealing with here.

A tremor gripped Dean's body for a second as if he saw a visual representation of his words behind his eyelids. Dean opened his eyes again and fixed his gaze on both Ron and Christina.

"Something more terrifying than you can possibly imagine." His lips trembled as those words escaped. "I failed in safeguarding the witch's prison. I can't fail in tracking her down."

Christina gasped.

"Do you suppose this is connected to all the things we uncovered in that house?" she whispered to Ron.

Dean lurched forward and grasped her shoulders.

"What house?"

"The Graber house." Christina pried his hands away from her shoulders. "Over in Willow Flats."

Dean stepped back. His face tightened and his eyes drifted past them. Both hands trembled even worse now.

"I have to go. I have to go now before it's too late."

"Whoa. That's not a good idea." Ron held up his hand. "That place is bad news."

"It doesn't matter. I have a job to do."

"We barely got out of there in one piece the first time around," he said, pointing to himself and Christina. "Between heads on the wall and strange vines everywhere and the woman in black —"

"Woman in black? Wearing a flowing gown and cloak?"

Christina's mouth dropped open. She trailed her fingers across her bottom lip.

"You've seen her too?"

"A long time ago. And I hoped not to see her again."

Dean turned and started to march away from both teens. Christina glanced at Ron and then pointed at Dean's back.

"Stop him! We can't let him go there alone."

"What do you want me to do? Tackle him?"

"If that's what it takes."

Ron rushed forward. Dean dug into his pocket and spun around. He brandished a small pocketknife with a slightly bent blade attached to a discolored handle. Ron threw his hands up and backed away.

"It took some scrounging to find this." Dean waved the knife at the two teens. "But I need to protect myself. Ever since that kid knocked me out cold and stole the chest. I can't be too careful."

Christina clapped her hands together as she caught up to Ron.

"She's gonna kill you," she said, pleading with Dean. "You gotta listen to us."

Dean fished a folded paper from the left breast pocket of his coat. The edges had grown crinkled and yellowed with age.

"I know how to stop the witch," he said. "I have it all written down here. It worked last time."

"You're just one person."

"You can throw an army at her. Without the right words, it won't do any good. I have those words."

Ron beckoned to him to draw closer and pointed to the parked cars. "Let's go together," he said. "We can drive there — all three of us."

Dean shook his head.

"No. I have to face her alone. I won't risk the lives of anyone else this time around."

He refused to turn around again. Dean walked backward, facing Ron and Christina, with the pocketknife blade extended forward. Once he reached the end of the parking lot, Dean stuffed the folded paper back in his coat pocket and hurried across the street. He snatched up an old bicycle parked by an aspen tree. Christina and Ron remained frozen in the parking lot, watching helplessly as Dean hopped on the bike and pedaled out of their sight.

"Shouldn't we jump in the car and drive after him?" Christina asked. Tangible concern threaded through her voice.

"He's made his choice," Ron said. "I really don't think we can do anything to stop him from seeing it through."

* * *

Dean's knee still throbbed when he pulled into the driveway outside the abandoned house. He pedaled slower than he liked, going only as fast as the knee allowed. He hopped off the bicycle and let it clatter against the cement. The whole yard surrounding the house felt lifeless. It wasn't simply an effect of an extra abundance of leaves blanketing grass and cement alike.

Silence dominated everything. No birds chirped from the trees or the sky. No cats meowed or dogs barked behind a closed fence. Dean scanned the cul-de-sac end to end. He neither saw nor heard signs of activity from the other houses.

Dean drew a jagged breath and limped across the grass. He pulled himself up the porch steps, grunting each time he lifted his leg. Resting his knee would feel so good right now, but he had no time to spare.

The witch obviously did not expect to see him. He had not been attacked amid this new rash of unexplained deaths and disappearances. Perhaps she did not know he was still alive. Maybe she still feared him from the last time they clashed.

Dean clung to both thoughts like a life preserver. He embraced fear as a potential weapon to use against her.

Still, his own heart pounded inside his chest as he twisted the doorknob. No one had bothered to lock the door. The front door popped open and he pushed it backward with his fingertips. Sunlight spilled into the entryway. Thick dark green curtains had been placed behind the drawn blinds covering the windows. Every speck of sunlight had been denied entrance until Dean opened the door. He stepped inside the doorway and walked into the living room.

Slam!

Dean wrenched his head around in time to witness the heavy oak door smack against the door jamb. It echoed through the seemingly empty house. Darkness enveloped Dean as sunlight dissipated like morning dew on grass.

Then he saw one flicker of light. Another flicker joined it. More flickers dotted the living room.

Candles sprang to life all over the place as though an invisible hand lit each one. New tremors crept into his hands. Dean clenched each hand into a fist and drew a long, deep breath. This all mirrored what he encountered last time with Valerie and Adam at his side.

"Let them go!"

Adam's voice bounced off the walls of Dean's mind. Once again, an awful scene he tried so hard to bury so many times unfolded. Adam emerged from behind an overturned table in the cafeteria. Chairs and tables lay scattered like fallen dominoes across the floor. Dean reached out and seized his brother's shirt sleeve. Adam looked down at his hand, brushed it off, and kept walking forward.

"No! We have to do this now."

"We're not ready," Dean protested. "If she realizes what we're trying to do here, she'll strike us down before we can speak more than two words of that incantation."

"It will only work if we get her in our line of sight." Adam glanced over his shoulder. His eyes held as much fear as the screams of students reverberating through the school's main hall. "I have to draw her attention and bring her to us before it's too late."

"Adam, please don't do this."

"I leave it in your hands. Start reciting the incantation when I give the signal."

Adam planted himself in the main hall next to the cafeteria. A glowing red mist billowed out of a classroom at one end of the hall behind him. It spread out into the hallway like storm clouds dashing across the sky.

"We're the ones you're after!" Adam's voice boomed loud enough to break through countless screams and metallic clanking of doors. "We found your chest! Show yourself."

A woman clad in a flowing black gown and matching cloak emerged from the gymnasium. Smoke billowed out into the hall ahead of her and obscured a generous portion of the witch's face. Her eyes flashed red and she marched toward Adam. He crossed himself and took off racing toward the mist.

"That's the signal." Valerie pulled out a folded piece of paper from her jacket. "It's now or never!"

Dean stared at the paper. At once, it grew crinkled in his hand. Edges cracked and turned yellow. He looked up and no longer crouched down behind a table inside the school cafeteria. Dean saw flickering candles dotting the living room once again. His fingers clenched the folded paper. Each breath came in short and shallow bursts.

Dean walked over and snatched a candle off a nearby end table. If any sunlight remained outside the house, he could not discern it. The witch had taken extreme measures to block out all windows. Not that it mattered anyway. Dean gained nothing from seeing the full extent of the horrors she unleashed inside this place. His sole purpose consisted of finding the chest, sealing her inside and burying it where it could not be found ever again.

A red glow emerged from around the corner at the top of the stairs. Dean groaned at the thought of conquering more stairs. He gritted his teeth and gingerly placed one foot in front of the other as he climbed each stair. Faint candlelight barely illuminated more than the stair immediately in front of him. Shadows at edge of the light assumed the shape of coiled snakes, ready to strike at a moment's notice. Dean dared not reach out his hand to aid his balance. He feared what form those shadows would take once he plunged a limb into their territory.

Shadows gave way to red mist once he reached the top of the stairs. It billowed out from a bedroom door and hovered above the hall floor in both directions. Dean knew he had found her lair. But the witch had not shown herself. Only a matter of time before it came to pass. She caused the front door to slam behind him. She lit every candle at once. No other force could claim responsibility.

"Show your face. Where are you?"

Dean meant to produce his words with authority as he entered the room. They instead took the form of an uncertain whisper.

A low whispering howl greeted him and scattered through the room. The door slammed behind him. Another tremor surged straight through Dean's body.

He dropped the candle onto the floor.

"Stay calm. Stay calm."

Dean paired those instructions to himself with a deep breath. Red mist snuffed out the flame. It emitted enough of a glow for him to still see the hardened wax base on the carpet. Dean bent down and wrapped his fingers around the candle again.

The flame burst to life once more.

"You dare to disturb me, old man?"

Dean needed no introduction to the voice behind him. It haunted him day and night for the last 55 years.

"What do you hope to accomplish here?"

"I intend to send you back to where you belong."

Dean turned and faced the chest on the dresser. It remained open. That's how the witch wanted it. An opened lid symbolized her freedom.

The witch positioned herself between Dean and the chest. She wore her usual black gown and cloak mixed with dark red hues. A thick veil obscured much of her face from Dean.

"You cannot stand against me alone. Leave now and I may decide to spare you."

Her words hissed inside his ears — acting as both a threat and a taunt to Dean.

"Drop the act." He scowled and looked at the floor, then up at her again. "I know who you are. I defeated you once already. And I can do it again."

A look of recognition washed over her red and black eyes. She waved her hands in a sweeping motion. Red mist fled from around her and Dean. The witch passed her hand over her face like a shade being drawn in front of a window.

A splash of blue appeared in each eye and spread out like a spider web until it consumed the whole iris. The veil disappeared as her hand passed over it. Dean's heart pounded even harder as she threw back the hood on her cloak to reveal her shoulder-length deep brown curls.

"Cassandra."

Her name on his lips sounded less like a greeting and more like an epithet. Cassandra circled him. Her icy blue eyes narrowed. She smirked as she sized up Dean.

"So, it really is you. In a way."

Dean glanced at the chest and then at the folded paper in his hand. He had her in his line of sight. But he couldn't figure out how to open it up and read the incantation without drawing her attention. He could not risk letting her destroy the paper before he got all the words out.

"Your body is all broken down with age." Cassandra's voice took on a triumphant tone. "Time has not been kind to you. You're hardly the adversary I faced last time."

"I won't fail."

"You seem so certain of yourself."

"I can't fail."

Cassandra cast her eyes toward the chest and smiled again.

"That's just it." She circled him a second time. "You already failed. You spent your whole life trying to keep me in that chest. And you could not do it."

Tears coursed down Dean's cheeks. Cassandra's taunts were true down to the last word. He failed. His promise to Valerie died unfulfilled. Keeping that promise felt so certain when he held her in his arms, trying to ease the pain raging throughout her body.

Another unwelcome image emerged from the depths of his mind. Both Dean and Valerie began reciting the incantation as Cassandra pursued Adam down the hall. A horrific scream from his brother followed. It rattled Dean enough that he stumbled over his words.

He lunged forward, only to have a hand restrain his arm and pull him back behind the table.

"You can't do anything for him now." Valerie's eyes darted between

Dean and Cassandra. Those eyes pleaded with Dean to not risk his life in an act of sacrificial revenge. "We have to finish this!"

Dean and Valerie resumed the incantation from the beginning. Cassandra spun around. She unleashed a shrieking howl that pierced the air and raised both arms. The table concealing them flew straight up into the ceiling. Cassandra thrust her arms downward again. This motion sent the table crashing back to the ground. Dean rolled out of the table's path just in time. Valerie wasn't quick enough. Broken remnants of wood and metal rained down on her.

The last word of the incantation passed through Dean's lips as Cassandra raised her arm to strike him dead. Her howl returned, fiercer this time, accompanied by a rushing wind. Dean pinched his eyes shut until the awful noise died away. He scrambled to his feet and pursued the vanishing red mist back into the empty classroom holding the chest.

Dean slammed the lid down with an emphatic thud. He tucked the chest inside his arm and marched out of the room.

His triumph felt hollow and short-lived. A burnt husk of what used to be Adam lay in a heap near the lockers. It only grew worse when he returned to the cafeteria. Cassandra's final act of fury pinned Valerie under a twisted and broken heap of a table. Dean set the chest on the floor and crouched down. He ripped debris off her as fast as his hands could pull it away.

When he got to the last piece, Dean gasped.

A table leg had snapped into three pieces when it smashed against the ceiling. One jagged chunk of wood struck Valerie in the lower back. It plunged through her abdomen like a spear. She lay in a growing puddle of her own blood. Both legs were frozen against the floor.

"God, no!" Dean lifted his girlfriend into his arms. He brushed back her hair. "Valerie!"

Tears flowed freely for both teens. Valerie bit on her lower lip for a moment as if trying to summon her remaining strength.

"I'll always love you."

"Stay with me."

"It's starting to hurt less ... please ... Dean ... promise me."

"Anything." He tenderly stroked a lock of her hair. "I'll do anything you want."

"Don't let that chest ... see the light of ... day ... again."

The light fled from her eyes after those final words. Dean cradled Valerie's lifeless body in his arms.

"I'll protect all of them," he whispered. "You have my word."

Dean sobbed and looked over at the chest again.

Everything around the chest dissolved. It no longer sat on the school cafeteria floor. The chest resumed its former place on the dresser. He found himself back inside the bedroom, standing before Cassandra. She glanced at the chest and again at him. That same devious smirk decorated her face.

"You took everything from me!" Dean's face turned crimson, and his eyes burned with anger. "You stole my life!"

He wanted to rain blows on Cassandra and beat her into oblivion. It would do no good. Even if she allowed him to touch her, Cassandra would simply repair any damage through her dark magic. The thought of causing Dean untold pain filled her with delight.

"You mean to tell me you spent your entire life guarding my chest?" Cassandra clapped her hands together and closed her eyes. "Just as foolish as those pitiful monks who thought they could bury it in a wilderness and move on with their lives."

"Shut up."

Her eyelids snapped open again.

"You should have left me alone. Now your brother, your parents, your precious girlfriend are all gone. Was it worth the cost, Dean?"

Tears flooded Dean's eyes and raced down his cheeks anew. He hurled the candle at Cassandra's torso. Hot wax splashed on her gown, inviting the diminutive flame to spread across the fabric. It conquered this new territory at a rapid pace.

Dean unfolded the paper in his hand. Cassandra gazed down at the spreading flames and cooled them with a touch of her fingers. Her head snapped back up at him. That blue hue in her eyes flashed back to red and black.

"Invoco hod caelum et terra ..."

Dean squinted at the paper. Some words had faded with time. Smudges had taken out letters here and there. His memory betrayed him as he tried to fill in the gaps.

"Ignum ... arca ... ad fine ..."

Cassandra shrieked at him and stretched out her hand. Dean lowered the paper and stared at the chest. It remained unchanged.

Same red glow. Same hovering mist.

"Old fool." Cassandra glanced behind her at the chest and then back at him. "You can't even see those words to read them properly. That's just got to eat you up."

Cassandra drew the paper out of his hand. It floated over to her. She tapped it with her index finger, and it evaporated into a wisp of smoke.

"Let me show you how a true incantation is done."

Cassandra fixed her eyes on the floor before Dean.

"Et crescere os, lignea area et consumat habitatores natus est stultus."

Her words hissed forth through her clenched teeth like a fierce wind.

Carpet dissolved under their feet at the same time, leaving behind a bare wooden floor. Wood cracked violently below his feet. Dean could not move either leg. A stabbing sensation gripped both ankles. It reached through both sides of his shoes and dug into skin and bone.

Dean cried out and jerked his head downward. Floorboards had formed into jagged wooden teeth. The floor attacked his legs with the tenacity of a hungry animal devouring a meal.

Dean tried to wrench his lower body out of this giant wooden mouth. He struggled to free his limbs from between the chomping teeth. Blood and chunks of flesh blasted toward the ceiling with the same intensity of water spraying from an outdoor fountain. His screams cluttered the bedroom and bounced off the walls. Cassandra's fierce eyes and determined scowl did not soften until only a thick puddle of blood, flesh and bone shards remained.

17

Christina handed Ron the smartphone. When he clicked on a new text message, his smile quickly morphed into a frown.

"Bad news?"

Ron looked up at her and nodded.

"My mom can't make it to the game." He handed the phone back to Christina. "Eric's here. You're here. She can't be bothered."

"Do you think she'd really miss it on purpose?"

"See for yourself."

Christina clicked on the text in question and gave it a quick glance. His mother's message seemed innocuous enough. Ron knew better. Same old excuses.

So sorry sweetie. Urgent video chat with my publisher. I'll make it up to you soon.

"Always some excuse." He turned away and started across the soccer field. "I should be used to it now, I guess."

Ron tried to downplay his mom's latest absence as the match progressed, but her missing out on one of his best performances of the season to date stung him even more. Deer Falls raced out to a 3-0 lead over Arapaho Valley in the first 30 minutes.

Ron had a hand in each goal.

He put his team on the board in the seventh minute after taking a cross and threading it inside the near post from just outside the top of the 18-yard box. Then, in the 19th minute, Ron stripped the ball from an outside midfielder and sprinted up the right flank on a counterattack. He drew their goalkeeper out for a one versus one challenge, danced around his left side, and then blasted the ball into the back of the net.

Arapaho Valley started marking him more vigorously each time Deer Falls possessed the ball after that point. Ron turned the tables on them, flicking the ball out to a teammate near the penalty spot on another attack. They teed it up and hooked the ball over the keeper's right shoulder for goal number three in the 28th minute.

It didn't take long for Ron to see how his dominant play impacted on the other team. Wide open, glaring eyes greeted him. Reddened faces with tensed muscles followed his movement on the pitch. Seeing it all only caused Ron's satisfied smile to stick around longer. He relished being a source of pure frustration for an over-matched opponent.

Thunderous cheers rippled through the stands after each goal. On the third one, Ron marched toward the touchline and tossed up a salute to the home fans. Christina and Eric laughed, and both answered him with a salute.

Christina leaned over to Eric's ear, when he turned away again, and cupped her hand against her mouth.

"He's going to goad the other team into drawing a bunch of yellow cards if he keeps this up."

Eric nodded.

"That's how my brother rolls."

She glanced back at the field. Christina raised her eyebrows and leaned forward. A woman clad in a flowing back gown and hooded cloak stopped a pair of players warming up behind the visiting team bench. She stooped down and whispered in one player's ear, then the other. Her outfit resembled the same one Christina had seen on the mysterious woman inside the abandoned house.

17

This was no coincidence.

Christina's heart jumped into her throat. Somehow, the woman in black tracked down her and Ron.

After both players heard the whispers, their eyebrows lowered and pulled together. A determined scowl washed over each teen's face. They sprinted to the midfield line.

"Sub! Sub!" The opposing coach called out.

The referee turned and beckoned at both players to come onto the pitch. Christina shifted her eyes from the two opposing players back to the touchline. The woman in black wheeled around and started walking toward the south goal. Christina turned and tapped Eric on the arm.

"Keep an eye on those two players that just checked in for the other team." She raised Ron's smartphone for Eric to see. "Text your brother's phone if something strange happens."

He glanced at the phone and then shot her a puzzled look.

"What do you mean? What's going on?"

Christina stood up.

"That's what I intend to find out."

She threaded through a row of seated fans toward the stairs. Keeping her eyes trained on the woman in black wasn't the easiest task. Some longer-legged fans obstructed the path between bleacher seats. Christina stumbled over feet at two different points and offered a hasty apology each time.

Once she finally reached the stairs, Christina raced down to the grass and darted behind the bleachers. She emerged on the other side only to realize the woman in black had vanished. Christina fiddled with a lock of her dark brown hair while she surveyed the whole field and the bleachers.

No trace of the mysterious woman.

Christina sprinted toward the chain link fence separating the field from the parking lot. She stopped at the gate. Cars peppered spaces throughout the lot. Nothing appeared out of the ordinary. Christina glanced down at Ron's smartphone and swiped the screen. No new text message alerts.

"Looking for someone?"

Goosebumps sprang up on Christina's arms. Her legs refused to move, as if they were suddenly glued to the asphalt beneath her feet. The voice entered her ears as a feathery whisper but felt as cold and sharp as an icicle.

"Who are you?" Christina did not turn her head to see who stood behind her. She kept her unblinking eyes fixed on a parked car ahead. "What do you intend to do to us?"

"Why do you insist on troubling me?"

"Why did you murder all those people? Why attack us?"

That feathery voice took on a harder edge.

"Your meddling is not welcome. I will not be imprisoned again."

"Imprisoned? Where? Who are you?"

"I am one not to be challenged. That is all you need to know."

Christina closed her eyes. Shallow breaths escaped her lungs. All she wanted to do was push her feet forward and run away — springing out of the blocks like a sprinter. Christina dared not look over her shoulder into her antagonist's face. It only promised to make the menacing tone in that voice feel worse.

Her legs remained rooted to the ground like twin tree trunks.

"Look at me!"

A hand squeezed Christina's cheeks and jaw. Her eyes popped open again. The woman in black stood before her. Both veil and hood obscured her face just enough to keep Christina from discerning identifying features beyond a pair of reddish black eyes.

"I know you and your friends sent that old man after me to take away my freedom." Pure rage darkened those eyes like billowing storm clouds. "Now you all will pay the price."

The woman in black raised her other arm and drew it back by her hood. It remained suspended in that spot, waiting to strike like a snake preparing to unleash venom into unsuspecting prey. Christina twisted and jerked her head as she fought to wrench her face free from her adversary's grasp.

At once, a small strain of rock music ripped through the air. The woman in black looked down at Christina's pocket. Christina did not let the distraction go to waste. She gave a hard shove with both hands and ripped herself free from her grasp. The woman in black stumbled backward. Her fingernails left a pair of drawn-out scratches across Christina's cheek.

The woman in black stretched out her arm and unleashed a plume of red dust from her fingertips. Christina threw up both hands in a crisscrossed pattern. The dust halted in mid-air and dropped straight down on the asphalt.

"No!"

A shriek escaped the woman's lips. The strain of rock music returned. Christina pulled Ron's smartphone out of her pocket and swiped the screen. Two new message alerts appeared.

911. Ron's in danger.

Please hurry.

Christina's eyes grew as wide as saucers. She glanced at the woman in black. Her veil barely concealed a fresh smile.

"Say farewell to your friend. He's about to lose much more than a simple game."

Without another word, a reddish black fog formed around the woman. It covered her from head to toe. When the fog dissipated, no trace of her remained.

A chorus of shouts and screams from the bleachers reached her ears. Christina took off on a dead run back toward the soccer field.

She hoped she wasn't too late.

* * *

Ron barely gave Arapaho Valley's two newest subs a second look when they first trotted out to midfield. He felt confident his side could hang onto a three-goal lead going into halftime. Even if the other team did pull one or two back, he'd just unleash plenty of other shots on goal against their porous backline.

Arapaho Valley lined up for the kickoff after the third goal. Both subs shifted up top near the midfield line and scooted over to the left side where Ron stationed himself. Each sub locked eyes with him and scowled.

A smirk washed over Ron's face anew.

Really? They sent in two fresh players off the bench just to mark me? He thought. *Their coach must be feeling desperate.*

Ron read a cross to the outside midfielder and bolted into the passing lane. He latched onto the ball and pivoted to start a counterattack up the left flank. Both subs charged at him. Ron faked left toward the touchline and dribbled the ball right to get around the first sub.

He laughed. This felt too easy.

Out of the corner of his eye, Ron saw the second sub slide in toward him. Their lead foot collided with his lead foot. It poked the ball away. The sliding foot undercut both of his legs and sent Ron tumbling forward. He landed on his shins and rolled onto his backside.

Ron slammed his fist into the grass.

The second sub booted the ball to a teammate and stared back at Ron still lying on the ground. His facial muscles were drawn taut, and his jaw was clenched.

"Stay down."

Ron pulled himself up into a sitting position. He shook his head.

The other boy marched over to the same spot and stood over him.

"I told you to stay down."

Ron rose to his feet. He returned the unbroken stare he received in equal measure. Then, Ron grabbed a fistful of three on the other boy's no. 13 jersey.

"You'll have to make me, you little dick."

A whistle pierced the air. Then, a moment later, the referee appeared and wedged himself between the two boys to diffuse their confrontation.

"Knock it off or you're both getting yellow cards." The referee pushed Ron back. He finally let go of the other boy's jersey. "Do I make myself clear?"

Ron nodded and turned away. He bit down on his lower lip and looked down at the ground. Arguments and complaints he wanted to make to the referee flooded his mind. It wasn't worth the risk of getting on his bad side. Last thing Ron needed was to draw two yellows, or even a straight red card, and end up getting tossed out and suspended for the next game for his efforts.

The referee blew his whistle to resume play. Deer Falls scored another takeaway after the restart. The holding midfielder latched onto the ball and threaded it between a pair of defenders toward Ron. As soon as his foot touched the ball, Ron felt a pop before he turned to start his attack. The first sub drove his shoulder into Ron's chest as he poked at the ball. His blow knocked Ron off balance and sent him crashing to the ground where he landed with a thud on his hip.

A whistle blew again. Ron grimaced and looked up. The first sub stood over him, mouth open, flashing clenched teeth. He heard his angry breaths as acutely as the wave of boos from the crowd.

"You dirty asshole!"

One of Ron's teammates marched up to the first sub and gave that boy a hard shove in the middle of his no. 7 jersey. The first sub backpedaled and fell into the grass. The referee blew his whistle again. Players from both teams jumped in to restrain their teammates. He walked over to each player one at a time and showed both a yellow card. The referee then whipped out a small notebook and pen and jotted down the offending players' names and jersey numbers and the game time.

A teammate extended his hand and pulled Ron to his feet. Both no. 13 and no. 7 had rejoined one another, though multiple players and the referee now stood between them and Ron. They paced nonstop until they sensed Ron looking in their direction. Both players suddenly fixed their eyes on him and squared their bodies toward him. Rage decorating their faces had grown even more intense. Ron shot them a puzzled look. Something seemed odd about their body language. It didn't seem consistent with the run-of-the-mill frustration he expected from players on a losing team.

Another whistle and restart followed. This time around, Ron's focus drifted away from the ball. He kept seeing no. 13 and no. 7 doggedly marking him. They trailed him like twin shadows as he darted from the left side over to the right side of the pitch.

One midfielder blasted a long ball a few yards ahead of Ron, hoping he'd spring free and get to it first. All the defenders were trailing, setting up for a perfect one versus one with the keeper. Ron zigzagged as he sprinted up the right flank, trying to shake the two subs. He reeled in the ball, pivoted, and raced toward the 18-yard box.

Both subs closed in on Ron from opposite directions. No. 7 slid in with spikes up on his cleats and knocked Ron off his feet. At the same time, no. 13 charged into his right side and leveled Ron. He flipped up in the air and crunched down on his left shoulder.

Ron pinched his eyelids shut and grabbed his upper arm. He lay on the grass, drawing in short and heavy breaths. Throbbing in his shoulder matched his pounding heartbeat. These weren't simple fouls.

These two Arapaho Valley players were deliberately trying to injure him and knock him out of the game. Neither one made any pretense about going for the ball at this point.

The referee's whistle sounded again. Ron opened his eyes and saw two players towering over him. No. 13 and no. 7. Their eye color had changed. Both players looked almost inhuman, as if they had turned into wild animals clothed in human skin.

"This is only the beginning," no. 7 said.

No. 13 chimed in with a low growl.

"We're gonna make you beg for your death."

The referee appeared behind the two Arapaho Valley players and blew his whistle again. He pulled a red card from his pocket and grabbed no. 7 by the shoulder.

"That's it! Both of you are out of here."

No. 7 wheeled around and snarled. His right hand shot forward. Fingers wrapped around the referee's windpipe. He raised him off the ground. Gurgling sounds escaped from the referee's mouth. He kicked his feet and clawed at no. 7's arm, trying to dislodge his hand from around his throat.

Ron's eyes widened. He scrambled to his feet, grimacing and clutching his shoulder as he put weight on his arm. No. 13 unleashed a loud shriek. He tackled Ron from behind and sent him tumbling to the ground again. A pair of hands grabbed the back of Ron's head and slammed his skull into the ground.

He rolled over and threw his forearm up in the air in a clothesline motion. The forearm smacked no. 13 directly in the mouth. A tooth popped out and fell on the grass. No. 13 glanced down at it and back at Ron. He cocked his left fist and started raining blows down on Ron's face. One punched landed. Then another. Ron threw up his uninjured arm again to try to ward off the blows. It did little to prevent the sting of knuckles against his cheekbones and eyes.

Two of Ron's teammates seized no. 13 from behind and yanked him backward. Ron sat up. They pinned the arms of Ron's attacker to his sides for a moment. Then no. 7 charged toward both teammates.

"Look out!" Ron shouted.

His warning reached their ears too late. No. 7 leveled one of Ron's teammates with a brutal tackle. Once one arm came free, no. 13 grabbed the other teammate's head with both arms and smashed his face down into his knee. Both boys crumpled to the ground in a heap and lay on the grass moaning.

Both teams spilled out from the sidelines. Coaches and players converged on no. 7 and no. 13 to subdue and restrain the two boys. The rest of the officiating crew fled from the field. Fans jumped out of their seats. Panicked shouts and screams rippled through the bleachers.

No. 13 charged toward Ron again as no. 7 faced down the crowd trying to intervene. Ron scrambled away from his attacker toward the touchline. In one fluid leap, no. 13 pounced onto Ron's back and brought him to the ground again.

"You should have stayed away from the abandoned house." His words and tone sounded programmed. "Now you will face her wrath and suffer her vengeance."

Abandoned house?

Those words cut into Ron like knives and turned his belly to ice. The woman in black found him.

His thoughts at once turned to the bleachers. Where was Eric? Where was Christina? He had to free himself and warn them of the danger. They were all targets.

No. 13 flipped Ron over to his backside and clamped onto his chin. "Now we end this."

At once, Ron's attacker lifted into the air above him. Ron slipped out of his grasp. No. 13 screamed and thrashed as if an invisible hand now held him in place. Ron heard a familiar voice.

"Go to sleep."

No. 13's eyes snapped shut. All his muscles relaxed, and his arms dropped to his sides. His body lowered to the ground until he flopped on his side when his feet touched grass. Ron soon saw Christina, her anxious eyes examining him.

"I got here as soon as I could. Are you okay?"

"I'll live — I think."

Christina clasped his hands and helped Ron to his feet. He grimaced again, pulled away his right hand, and clutched his shoulder near the collarbone.

"I think they did something to my shoulder."

"We better get you to the clinic."

No. 7 lay on his side sleeping in the grass just like the other attacker. Christina subdued both players.

Ron got to see the full scope of the damage for the first time. The referee lay in a motionless heap just inside the 18-yard box. His eyes were open and empty. A band of skin crossing his throat had turned purple. Both teammates who tried to pull no. 13 away from Ron still lay on the ground. Blood covered one teammate's nose and mouth. The other held his hand against his rib cage. Both players groaned and sobbed while paramedics tended to them.

Two other players and Coach Rimmert also lay sprawled on the grass. A jagged end of bone poked through Coach Rimmert's skin where his wrist had been snapped. Each player had a bruised and bloodied face.

Ron wrapped his uninjured arm around Christina and drew her into a tight embrace. He shut his eyes and let his head rest against hers.

"I'm so glad you were here to save me."

18

Much of the throbbing in Ron's shoulder subsided once the pain medicine the doctor gave him kicked into action. Blinding pain now gave way to staring at a wall in the clinic examination room. Ron bounced his left heel against the exam table while he sat waiting for the doctor to return with his diagnosis.

He pulled out his phone from his pocket and swiped the screen again. No word from his mother. She never called or texted him back. Did she not see the text he sent her, telling her he had to go to the clinic? Ron sometimes wondered if she cared enough to bother to even check her text messages.

A door opened. Ron looked up from his phone to see a doctor walk in, holding an open folder. He glanced up at Ron and smiled.

"I got back your x-rays, and the news is better than expected." The doctor looked down again and pressed his finger on the chart inside the folder. "We discovered a grade one acromioclavicular joint sprain in your left shoulder."

Ron frowned.

"That doesn't sound like good news."

"Trust me, it could be much worse. You only suffered a partial ligament tear. No surgery is required. It should heal within the next two to three weeks."

"Two to three weeks?"

"Of course, you'll need to wear a protective sling. You also need to apply ice to reduce swelling on the shoulder. I'm going to prescribe 800 mg of ibuprofen to help ease the pain, along with some exercises to strengthen the shoulder and aid in recovery."

Ron's mouth dropped open. He shook his head.

"I can't sit out for two or three weeks. We're right in the heart of our season."

"You took a pretty good beating out there." The doctor closed the folder and his eyes settled on Ron again. "Orbital bone contusions. A gashed lip. You're fortunate this is the worst thing that happened to you today, son."

Ron didn't feel fortunate.

Dealing with an arm stuck in a sling for a couple of weeks represented one more setback in his soccer pursuits. None of this would have happened if he had not been forced to move Deer Falls. It only made him burn hotter over his mother's failure to respond. She may not have borne responsibility for the attack, but she certainly deserved a ton of blame for putting him in this position in the first place.

The doctor fitted Ron's arm with a sling and then handed him a prescription for his pain medication. Ron entered the waiting room displaying the same frown that emerged when he heard the diagnosis.

Christina rose from a nearby chair. She clasped his free hand.

"What's the word?"

"Shoulder sprain. I gotta wear this sling for at least two or three weeks until the ligament heals."

"That sucks."

"Tell me about it. Guess I won't be playing soccer, or driving, or doing anything worthwhile for a while."

"It could have been a lot worse."

Ron glanced at his sling and back at Christina.

"I suppose. But it doesn't feel that way."

Christina pulled her hand away and trailed it down his upper arm. "Trust me. It had the potential to get really bad. Those two players who attacked you didn't do it of their own free will."

Ron stared blankly at the door. The faces and words of both players popped into his head again. Their rage and brute force were equal doses of unnatural.

"They said some things to me no one in their position could have known."

"Like what?"

"Mentioned the abandoned house. Told me I'd suffer her vengeance."

Christina pushed open the clinic door and they walked outside.

"The woman in black is behind all of this."

"What woman in black?" a voice behind them said.

Ron and Christina both turned. Deputy Palmer approached them, walking from his truck toward the clinic door.

"What woman in black?" he repeated.

Deputy Palmer gazed down at Ron's sling and then moved onto the bruises surrounding his eyes. He acted as though he were taking mental notes on his appearance.

"I don't know who she is," Christina said. "I saw her on the sidelines before everything happened. She said something to both players who attacked Ron. Whatever she said whipped them into a frenzy."

"Did she now?" Deputy Palmer gave her a quizzical look and then turned back to Ron. "And did you see this mysterious woman too?"

"I wasn't looking over at their sideline but, yeah, I have no doubt she was there."

"What makes you so certain?"

"We've seen her before. I don't think she really likes us that much."

Deputy Palmer nodded. A thin smile formed on his tight lips.

"Hmm. How is it that you two seem to be involved in all these incidents?"

Christina frowned.

"What are you suggesting?"

Deputy Palmer pulled out a notebook from his pocket and flipped it open.

"Where do I start? Two teens involved in fights or arguments with one or both of you at school are dead. At the same time, multiple students have disappeared and no trace of them has been found."

He looked up from his notebook and jabbed his index finger at Ron.

"Now you're involved in a soccer brawl that resulted in one confirmed fatality and multiple serious injuries. What am I supposed to think?"

"We are not behind this," Ron replied. "Ask that vagrant — what's his name? Dean? — Ask him about the woman in black. He's also seen her."

"That's assuming she didn't kill him first," Christina said. "We never saw Dean again after he took off for that abandoned house."

Her face did nothing to mask the concern building inside her as Christina spoke those words. Ron knew she still agonized over not being able to stop Dean from going to that house alone.

"Crazy Dean?" Deputy Palmer barely suppressed the laughter fighting to escape his lips. "He's your character witness? Good God. You two are really digging yourselves a deep hole here."

"You don't believe us? Go check it out for yourself." Ron motioned in the direction where he thought the abandoned house was in proximity to the clinic. "We're not making this shit up."

"Tell you what I'm gonna do: I'm gonna go question those two Arapaho Valley boys in my custody." Deputy Palmer turned away, walked to his truck door, and opened it. "I'm gonna dig into the soccer brawl and find out why they attacked so many people."

The deputy climbed inside his truck and slammed the door behind him. He peered back out of his open window at Ron and Christina.

"And, finally, I'm gonna figure out how you and the girl factor into all of it, son."

Ron bit his lower lip and stood there like a statue as Deputy Palmer backed up his truck and pulled out of the parking lot. So many things raced through his mind he really wanted to say to that idiot cop. Casey pegged Deer Falls exactly right. People in this town were willfully blind when it came to any supernatural phenomena.

He kicked a parking block in front of him.

"I guess we're on our own in dealing with this."

Christina answered with a short nod. She gazed solemnly down the road where Deputy Palmer had driven away from them.

"I always figured we were on our own from the start."

* * *

Ron didn't have to wait long to encounter his mother. As soon as Christina dropped him off at his house and he opened the front door, Emily emerged from her office. Her eyes trailed him from head to toe and her mouth popped open.

"What happened to you?" Emily stood in front of Ron with her hands on her hips. "Did you get in another fight at school?"

Ron glanced at his shoulder and back at his mother. His hardened face revealed his feelings like an open book.

"If you bothered to show up for the soccer game, you would have had a front row seat to take it all in with your own eyes."

"What's that supposed to mean?"

"It means, Mom, I got attacked by two players from the other team."

"Did you do something to provoke them?"

Ron flashed an angry smile and shook his head.

"I'm always the one at fault in your eyes. My arm's in a sling. And my face is all bruised. Damn. I definitely brought it all on myself."

18

Emily reached out and touched his uninjured shoulder.

"Don't play the martyr. That's not what I'm saying at all. I'm just trying to understand what's behind all this conflict."

Ron brushed her hand off his shoulder. He refused to look his mother in the eyes. If anyone deserved blame for this situation, she did. Moving to Deer Falls was her idea and her idea alone. No one else wanted to be here. Ron knew he wanted to be back in Commerce City. He suspected Eric shared those same thoughts, even if he didn't openly admit it.

"Can I just go to my room now?"

"No. I want to talk. We used to talk, Ron."

"Things change. Sometimes you don't get a say in the matter."

Emily's eyes started to tear up. She sniffed, trying to fight back those same tears.

"I'm trying to make the best of this situation. I really am. I'm sorry I can't give you everything you think I'm supposed to give you."

Ron tugged at his sling and continued to avoid eye contact with her.

"All I know is my life would be a lot better back in Commerce City. Back with my friends. Back with Dad."

Emily squinted at him and frowned.

"No, it wouldn't. You don't understand. I brought us all here for a fresh start."

Ron finally locked eyes with her. His glare could have melted a block of ice.

"Fresh start? This is about you, Mom!" he said. "Me? I come to a school where I don't fit in. I play on a bad soccer team in a small town no one cares about."

"We all had to make sacrifices."

"And you know the best part? I nearly got killed in a random soccer game because I rubbed some supernatural baddie the wrong way. Tell me how this is a better life for me? Tell me!"

Emily shook her head.

"Supernatural baddie? What are you even saying? Why can't you tell me what's really going on?"

Ron stomped past her toward the stairs. He stopped at the foot of the stairs and wheeled around.

"Dad would understand. He'd back me up."

"No, he wouldn't."

Emily cast her eyes down to the ground. Those words left her lips barely more audible than a whisper inside a chapel.

"Of course, you'd say that."

She looked up at Ron again.

"Your dad didn't want you. Or Eric. Or me. He abandoned all of us."

"You mean you kicked him out?"

"He cheated on me! That's why we got divorced, Ron. He left me for another woman. I couldn't stay in that house after that."

Emily's revelation hit Ron's ears like a clap of thunder. He sunk down onto the bottom stair. Ron buried his face in his free hand. Memories flooded into his head. Soccer games. Ski trips. Camping. Trading endless goofy jokes. What his mom said didn't fit with the father he thought he knew.

"Dad wouldn't do that. How could he do that?"

"He did it. Without an ounce of remorse."

Ron felt betrayed. By his father. And by his mother for keeping this hidden from him.

Emily sensed his thoughts.

"I know I should have told you sooner. I should have told both you and Eric sooner. I wanted to protect you. I didn't want you two to hate your dad."

Ron stared at his mother's face again. Her teary eyes pleaded for understanding. He couldn't find it within himself. Not right now. Everything about his dad turned out to be a lie and his mother hid that lie from him.

He stood up and barged right past her. Ron yanked open the front door.

"I need to get out of here. Clear my head."

"No. You need to stay here. We need to talk this out."

"Nah. I'm good." Ron turned back and offered a curt wave. "I've had my fill of talking for one night."

Emily wiped away her tears and scowled at her son.

"If you walk out that door right now, you better not walk back through it unless you're ready to apologize."

Ron refused to say another word. He answered his mother by letting the door slam behind him.

19

Ron didn't bother to look back, even for a second, after storming out of the house. His momentum carried him down the driveway and to the sidewalk. He gazed down at his sling, grunted, and kicked a loose pebble. It bounced off the cement and took two skips on the road before landing on the yellow line. His lower lip hung out more than normal as Ron tried to suppress tears threatening to spring to the surface.

Betrayed by both of his parents. They ruined his life. His father didn't love him. His mother didn't trust him.

Where could he go from here?

Ron forced one foot in front of the other, driven by a fear of standing still too long. If he stopped to think, it would only open a door for him to collapse on the sidewalk in a quavering heap of sobs. He didn't want to unleash such raw emotion where random strangers were allowed to gawk at him. Only a short step from there to someone creating an obtrusive photo or video, followed by a stupid meme mocking the whole episode once it all went viral.

His path took him toward the same park where he and Christina spent so many hours playing soccer and talking. Ron whipped out his smartphone as he neared the park entrance. Maybe he could get her to join him. Christina was the only good thing about Deer Falls.

I need to talk. Meet me at the park?

19

A pair of smiley emojis popped up below his brief text only a few seconds later.

On my way.

Ron stared unblinking at his smartphone.

His thoughts drifted to his dad. It occurred to him that he didn't remember the last time he heard his voice. Ron hadn't seen him since the move to Deer Falls. Was it true? Did his father just abandon his family?

Ron slumped against a border wall by the park entrance and scrolled through saved text messages on his phone. He clicked on his dad's phone number. The last text dated almost two weeks ago — one Ron sent. His dad never responded to him.

Responses to all his previous texts seemed more abrupt than Ron remembered.

Hang in there. You'll always be my #1 striker.

I'll work something out.

My hands are tied. Sorry, Ron.

In a meeting. Text you later.

Maybe down the road?

Ron dropped the phone into the grass and rested his elbows on his knees. He buried his chin in his hand. Tears rolled down Ron's cheeks. It didn't feel real. His dad truly didn't want to be in his life. Did his parents even engage in a custody battle like he once thought?

Life had turned into a waking nightmare.

"Ron? What's wrong?"

A soft voice called out his name. Ron sensed a note of hesitation, revealing a fear of interrupting him. He looked up and gazed at Christina. Her hazel eyes revealed concern hidden behind her face. Ron brushed away the tears and sniffed.

"I'm starting to understand what hell feels like."

Christina dropped down on the grass and leaned against the wall beside him.

"I'm sorry about your shoulder. Sitting out for a few weeks has to feel like an eternity."

"It goes deeper than that."

"What is it?"

"Tonight, I found out the truth about my dad."

"What truth?"

"I know why my parents really got divorced."

"What did he do?"

"He cheated on her. He cheated on my mom."

Christina trailed her hand into Ron's and clasped his palm tight.

"I'm so sorry. I had no idea."

Ron looked down at his hand and back at her. He flashed an appreciative smile.

"I always looked up to my dad, you know? We were tight when I was little. I can't believe he'd do something like this to Mom ... and to me."

"Have you seen him or talked to him recently?"

Ron slipped his hand out of hers and snatched up his phone from the grass. He tapped on the screen, unlocked the phone, and brought up his dad's old texts in full view again.

"I want to call so bad. Just unleash every thought swarming my head. Tell him what I'm feeling and why I'm feeling it."

"You should do it. He needs to know he hurt you."

Christina's advice made sense. It would feel therapeutic to let loose and let his dad have a piece of his mind after all this time. He dialed the number.

One ring. Two rings. Three rings.

No answer.

Then the voicemail popped up. It instructed Ron to leave a message at the beep. He hurled his phone down into the grass this time. The recorded voice on the other end belonged to a woman he did not recognize.

"He didn't pick up." Ron anticipated the question forming on Christina's lips and beat her to it. "My dad just doesn't care. It's obvious to me now."

Christina rescued the phone from its landing spot. The screen protector bore a new scratch where it bounced off a random rock hidden among the grass blades. She handed the phone back to Ron.

"I care. I promise that I truly care."

Ron allowed a small smile to creep out from the corners of his mouth again. He turned and wrapped his uninjured arm around her in an embrace. Christina leaned in and soaked it up. Her feathery brown hair rested against his cheek.

She smelled like cherry blossoms. Ron loved it.

Suddenly, he clenched his teeth and grunted. A twinge of pain shot through his shoulder. Almost like an invisible hand plucked his ligament like a guitar string.

"Sorry. I must have bumped your shoulder."

Christina pulled back a bit but remained inside his other arm.

"Only three more weeks to go."

Her eyes brightened.

"I've got an idea. I know a remedy for fast tracking your recovery."

"Lay it on me." Ron looked down at his sling and back at her. "I'm willing to try anything if it means ditching this stupid sling faster."

She smiled, extended her hand, and quickly helped Ron to his feet.

"Follow me."

***

Christina's house had to be fun to live in during the summer months. It had so many front-facing windows. Anyone inside could expect to be bathed in sunlight or moonlight around the clock if they so wished.

Ron was down with that idea. He embraced soaking in warm rays of sunlight with the same zeal as a cat settling in for an afternoon nap.

They weren't alone.

Lights switched on inside the living room as they walked up the porch steps.

"Looks like my dad's home." Christina fished her keys out of her pocket and opened the door. "I didn't think he'd be back from his conference until tomorrow."

Ron did his best to stay in the shadows right behind Christina. He didn't want to field questions about his bruised face if he could help it. Her father ended up showing a highly inquisitive side when Ron met him the last time he came over here. Those hopes were dashed once her father popped his head out from the hallway.

"Hi sweetheart."

He flashed a warm smile at Christina, walked over and gave her a quick hug. Then her father pulled back, glanced at Ron, and gave a low whistle.

"What happened to you? I hope the other guy looks worse."

Ron returned a weak smile. He did not see the bruises covering his face, but he felt their presence. Those suckers went right down to the bone on both cheeks.

"I got attacked at my soccer game today."

"Where was the referee in all of this?"

"It's a really long story."

"Well, I hope the ref gets disciplined for letting the match get out of hand so badly."

Ron frowned and shuddered. A snapshot of the referee's strangled corpse sprawled on the field barged into his mind.

"I've got a hunch his refereeing days are over."

Christina scrunched up her face and winced. Ron wasn't sure if the visual of the referee or his comment caused it. He shot her an apologetic look.

"So, who won the game?" Her father asked.

Christina shrugged.

"I don't know if it counts to be honest. The game got called at halftime after they arrested both players who attacked Ron."

"On the bright side, I scored two goals and assisted another."

Ron's lips curved into a slight smile. He welcomed the chance to think about something other than a dead referee.

Christina's father laughed.

"Hey. That's always good news. We need someone who can score like that to help Colorado. The lack of offense puts too much pressure on Tim Howard between the pipes."

"Don't I know it." Ron's voice grew a bit more animated. "I don't know why they can't get some quality strikers in there. We have an awesome defense. The Rapids are wasting a world-class keeper."

Christina glanced at the clock on the wall. She tugged on Ron's uninjured arm.

"I hate to interrupt, but we better go see what we can do about these bruises and the sprain." She turned to her father. "Dad, can you grab some gauze, candles, and a water basin for me and bring them to the study? I need to go track down my emerald pendant, Calendula flower salve and Geranium oil."

Her father's face went blank.

"Are you sure it's a good idea to do what I think you're about to do?"

"Relax, Dad. He knows."

"He does?"

"I told him all about my magic."

Christina's father gazed at Ron for a moment and sized him up as if he were peering deep into his soul. His lips finally broke out into a smile.

"If you trust him with your secret, that's good enough for me."

Christina directed Ron to lie on a couch in the study. She took a lamp off an end table and pulled the table around to the front of the couch. She then left the room to fetch the necessary materials. Her father entered a few moments later and set gauze, some candles and a basin filled with water on the table. Christina soon reemerged in the room, bearing a couple of small bottles, and wearing the pendant around her neck.

"I'll leave you to it." Christina's father said. "Let me know if you need any help."

"Thanks, Dad." She kissed his cheek. "You're the best."

Once they were alone in the room, Christina opened the curtains and turned off the lights. Moonlight flooded through the window and splashed across Ron. Christina surrounded the basin with candles of equal sizes. They loomed over clear water like miniature statues built from wax.

"Don't you need matches or a lighter?" Ron asked.

"Not really."

Christina moved her hand over the candle nearest to her and snapped her fingers. A small yellow flame burst out of the wick. She repeated the same action with each candle until a perfect circle of flame glowed on the table.

Ron's mouth gaped open. Color drained from his face for a moment before he caught himself and sealed his lips shut again. Christina seemed more adept at using magic the more he got to know her.

"Pretty cool, huh?"

Her words almost seemed like a plea for approval from him.

"Yeah. I can definitely say I haven't seen anything like it before."

Christina immersed the gauze in the basin. She opened both bottles. She poured some Geranium oil from the first bottle into two gauze strips. Each strip Christina placed upon his facial bruises. Then she rubbed the Calendula flower salve from the second bottle into another

19

damp strip of gauze. This piece she slid under Ron's soccer jersey and across his shoulder.

Ron winced a bit as she applied the gauze.

"Sorry if it hurts," Christina said.

She closed her eyes and exhaled deeply.

"Repeat the words I say. This will only work right if we do this together."

Ron nodded and closed his eyes as well. Christina began reciting an incantation.

Beautiful bright healing moonlight.

Heal me with all your might.

A tingling sensation rippled through Ron's skin as he echoed those same words. It sprouted in his toes and continued up through every limb, then his torso and his face before culminating in the crown of his head.

Bright light, shining light.

Heal my hurts and make all right.

Tingling turned to warmth. It soon rushed from all corners of Ron's body and formed patches concentrated in his face and shoulder.

As I say,

So shall it be.

Ron's eyes popped open. He looked down at his shoulder. It glowed where moonlight fell upon the gauze. Ron felt the same glow in his cheeks and eyes. He turned his head and gazed at Christina. Her arms were raised above her head. Each hand stretched toward the window drawing in moonlight. The emerald inside Christina's pendant acquired a silvery hue and started to glow.

That warmth beneath his skin intensified. Ron felt bones and ligaments mending. Each afflicted cell evaporated like dew before a rising sun. A fresh vibrant cell took its place.

When he no longer felt even a twinge of pain, all glowing lights vanished from Ron's body as suddenly as if someone had flipped an unseen switch controlling each one. Ron scanned the room. Only normal moonlight and candlelight remained. His eyes wandered back over to Christina. She opened her eyes again. They sparkled as they soaked in the moonlight.

She let her arms drop and smiled.

"How do you feel now?"

Ron reached up and pulled away the gauze from his face. He pressed his fingers against his cheeks. The cheekbones and orbital bones no longer ached from contusions. Ron sat up. He reached under his jersey and pulled out the other gauze strip. Then Ron probed the shoulder with his fingers.

He didn't recoil from pain this time.

"This is so amazing." Ron jumped to his feet and ripped the sling off his arm. He cast it on the couch. "I've never felt better. This is like a miracle."

"That makes me so happy. I wasn't sure how this would turn out."

"You mean you've never done this before?"

"A healing incantation? No. I've always been too nervous to try it out. But I wanted to do something to ease the pain."

Ron rounded the end table and embraced her. Christina yielded to his embrace and slid her arms around him.

"You are so good to me. How can I ever thank you?"

Christina bit down on her lower lip as she smiled.

"I've got an idea."

She leaned in toward Ron and tilted her head. Ron mirrored her motion. Christina's olive skin, hazel eyes and dark brown locks seemed even more enticing than before. His hand brushed her cheek. Their eyes closed and lips parted at the same moment. He pressed his lips against hers and their embrace tightened.

A surge of adrenaline zipped from head to toe through Ron. This sensation felt so new. Christina was not the first girl he ever kissed, but this kiss shattered the memory of all others that came before it. So much passion. So much warmth. It felt as if his heart would explode and rain down like confetti.

When their lips retreated from one another, Christina's eyes met Ron's and seemed to drink in his entire soul. She trailed her finger along his jawline.

"I've wanted to do that for a long time."

Ron let his hand trail from her neck down through a wavy lock of hair. A broad smile spread over his mouth and soon conquered his whole face.

"I feel the same way. I'm so lucky to have found someone as special as you here."

Christina's gaze drifted from Ron's eyes back to his lips. Her lips parted slightly. Ron leaned in once again. His lips brushed against her cheek, hinting at another kiss, before connecting with her mouth a second time.

They plunged into this new kiss deeper than the first.

20

Christina and Ron jumped almost in sync when they heard her father's voice outside the study. Ron pulled back and peered over her shoulder. They were the only ones inside the study, and he saw no one else in the doorway — yet.

"How's everything going down there?" Her father repeated.

His voice sounded much closer this time.

"Feeling fine, sir." Ron took Christina's hand into his own and gave it a light squeeze. She returned his squeeze with one of her own. "Your daughter is a miracle worker."

Her father appeared in the doorway. His eyes trailed from the discarded sling on the couch to Ron's shoulder and face and he gave a nod of approval.

"No need to be so formal around me, Ron. I told you last time you can call me David."

"Sorry. It slipped my mind, I guess."

David walked up to Ron and patted him on his healed shoulder. Christina's hand slipped out of Ron's own.

"This is what magic is really about." David turned to his daughter and wrapped Christina up in a warm hug. "I'm so proud of you, sweetheart. You're doing good things and realizing your true potential."

Christina closed her eyes as her cheek brushed against his.

"I'll always make you proud of me, Dad."

David smiled. Christina returned the smile, as she pulled away again, but also stared at her father with unblinking eyes. He glanced at her, then at Ron, before finally catching on to the words she left unspoken.

"Ha. I don't want to be that nosy parent everyone hates. I'll get out of your hair."

Once David left the study, a question arose in Ron's mind. He thought about Casey's burned hands. Christina had an ability to heal, but she had not used it on him. Why? Christina peered into his eyes and fiddled with the pendant around her neck. Her eyes drifted down to his lips and back up to his eyes again. She sensed Ron's internal question before it formed in his mouth.

"What's wrong?"

"I guess I'm puzzled about Casey. Why didn't you help him with his burned hands?"

Christina's cheeks turned crimson. Her shoulders slumped and she looked past Ron toward the moonlit window.

"Don't you think I wanted to help him? Casey is my friend."

"Don't get me wrong. I'm truly grateful for what you did for me. I just guess I don't understand."

"I couldn't do anything with Cassandra there. I was afraid of how she would react to me if she knew about my magic. And I put Casey in jeopardy because of my fear."

Her voice choked a bit as she said those last words. Ron chewed on his lower lip and shook his head. He felt like a total fool for bringing it up. This obviously weighed on Christina's mind more than he realized.

"I didn't mean to make you feel bad." Ron's voice took on a more apologetic and sympathetic tone. "It must be a huge burden to be forced to hide your true self from so many people."

He reached out and tenderly stroked a lock of Christina's hair. She clasped his hand and pressed it against her cheek.

"It wasn't always this way," Christina said, closing her eyes. "I wasn't always afraid to be open about it."

"What happened?"

"Let me show you."

She let go of his hand and walked over to the basin filled with water. Ron joined her at the table. Christina reached out and touched the water's surface with her fingertips.

"Illuminate."

At once, the water rippled as if a stone had skipped across the surface. Those ripples soon smoothed out and the water became as clear as a mirror. Only it did not offer reflections of Ron and Christina. To Ron's surprise, it presented an entirely different scene. He saw a backyard on a late summer day. Surrounding trees filled with leaves at peak green.

Near the middle of the backyard, Ron saw a play set. Swings. A slide. Monkey bars acting as a bridge. Sunlight gleamed off metal posts. A large aspen tree cast leafy shadows over one end of the monkey bars. An older boy climbed a ladder at one end and crawled across the top of the monkey bars to a spot just under the tree. A little girl slid down the slide and started running toward the tree.

Ron recognized her at once. Christina. She was no more than eight or nine years old.

"That's my older brother James." Her eyes remained fixed in an unbroken gaze on the water. "He always loved to pull crazy stunts when we were little. Totally fearless."

Too fearless for his own good. Ron shuddered as her brother stood up and tried to grab onto a tree branch above his head. James pretended it was a vine and he was Tarzan, even making a jungle call. Ron wanted to shout out to him and plead with him to get down from the monkey bars. What he witnessed didn't feel like a memory. The entire scene played out in real time like a present event.

"Everything changed for me and for my family forever on this day."

The metal proved too slippery under James' feet. His shoes lost their grip. The tree branch snapped off in his hand. James tumbled backward off the monkey bars. Christina and her brother both screamed. He groped at the air wildly as he fell backward. Ron winced and pinched his eyelids shut as James did the same.

"Keep watching."

Ron obeyed Christina and snapped his eyes open. James had not collided violently with the lawn. His body slammed to a halt only a few feet above the tips of the grass blades. James opened his eyes and turned his head toward the slide. Ron also turned and what he saw made his mouth drop open.

Both of Christina's arms were stretched out toward her brother. She clenched her teeth. Beads of sweat dotted her forehead. Color drained from James' face. His lips trembled. Christina lowered him until he lay flat on his back in the grass.

"In that exact moment, I learned I could use magic." A tangible strain gripped Christina's voice as she relived those raw emotions from that day. "My brother obviously felt terrified. So did I. I didn't want to believe any of this was real."

Ron fixed his attention on the water again. James scrambled to his feet. Christina looked down at her own hands and then gazed at her brother. She started to approach him to see if he was hurt. Christina only took a couple of steps forward before he backed away from her. James turned and bolted toward the fence. She called out for him to stop, but her plea went ignored.

"I felt so alone and scared in that moment. But I soon found out I wasn't alone."

Ron watched as the younger version of Christina turned toward the backdoor of her house. The screen door flew open. Her father raced out across the grass. Christina stood paralyzed in the same spot, like a deer frozen in bright beams of a car barreling down a country road. David swept his daughter up in his arms.

She buried her head in his shoulder.

"Don't be afraid." David gave the younger Christina a reassuring pat on the back. "You have a wonderful gift, just like your mom."

"Just like your mom?"

Ron repeated David's last words as he glanced up from the water basin. Christina broke eye contact with the water, looked at him, and nodded.

"My Mom possessed the same abilities. I never realized it because she died suddenly when I was barely old enough to remember her."

"I'm so sorry you lost her at such a young age."

Christina gazed at him through half-closed eyes and flashed an appreciative smile.

"I feel connected with her through my magic," she said, turning back to the water basin. "Dad experienced similar feelings when he saw me save my brother. He loved my mom more than anything else in this world. He told me it felt like a small part of her had remained behind in me."

"So what happened after that?"

Christina's smile melted away. She mashed her lips together and swallowed hard.

"I made a terrible mistake. I lashed out at someone with magic."

She touched the water and it rippled again. A new scene popped up before Ron's eyes.

This time, he saw groups of children gathered on a playground. One group divided into two teams and played a basketball game. Another group played freeze tag. A few kids gathered in an adjacent grassy field to play soccer.

Christina emerged from a pair of doors belonging to a school building bordering the south end of the playground. She raced across the blacktop, hoping to join up with a team before a new game got going. A blonde-haired girl with a long ponytail zeroed in on her as

Christina weaved around a hopscotch grid.

"Why don't you just hop on your broom? You'll get there faster."

Her jeering words stopped Christina in her tracks. She turned and marched straight over to the blonde-haired girl.

"Ooh, did I upset you?" The other girl cracked a smile and took on an even more sarcastic tone. "Are you gonna cast a spell on us now?"

Two other girls playing hopscotch with her laughed at the taunts. Christina's lower lip trembled, and her eyes narrowed.

"Just leave me alone."

The other two girls saw how those taunts got under her skin. They couldn't resist following their friend's lead.

"Watch out Mykayla!" One of her friends, a red-haired girl with freckles, took a turn poking the bear this time. "She's gonna turn you into a toad or make you eat a poison apple."

Christina's knuckles turned white as she balled her hands into fists.

"Shut up."

Mykayla laughed and circled her.

"You're so lucky we don't still burn witches like you at the stake."

More laughs greeted her words.

Christina unleashed a violent scream and suddenly thrust her arms out at Mykayla. The other girl flew backward and slammed into a tether ball pole a few feet away. Christina glowered at her and marched toward the pole. She stabbed her index finger toward Mykayla and started moving it in a circular motion. The rope connecting the ball to the top of the pole wrapped around the other girl at an alarming speed. Mykayla screamed and cried as she pushed against the rope. Her friends pleaded for Christina to release her.

Still, the rope drew tighter and tighter.

Ron stepped back from the basin as he watched this all unfold. His hand instinctively cupped his mouth. Christina seemed possessed by an unquenchable rage. What did she do to this other little girl? He dared not envision the outcome in his own mind. The images that popped up would not be good.

Then, all at once, something snapped inside Christina. Her countenance softened. She dropped her arms to her sides. The rope around Mykayla slackened and, once it loosened enough, she fell on her knees and sobbed into the asphalt. A smattering of light purplish bruises remained where the rope pressed into her flesh.

"I nearly killed her in that moment." Christina's voice pierced an uncomfortable silence inside the study. "In a fit of rage, I did the one thing you're not supposed to do with magic. I caused major harm to someone else."

Her words had a trembling lilt to them. Ron could tell this incident haunted her to the core. He searched for the right words to reassure her.

"You were a little girl being bullied. Almost anyone in that situation would've snapped."

"I wasn't justified, Ron. Magic is supposed to help people."

"And you've done that. You stopped your brother's fall. You pulled that player off me and healed my injuries."

Christina bowed her head and waved her hand over the water basin. The living mirror vanished, and the water returned to its normal state.

"I still worry. Every day, I worry about losing control and hurting someone. Everyone knows what I did to Mykayla. They fear me. They ridicule me."

Ron put his arm around her and drew Christina closer to him.

"I don't fear you. In fact, I think I love you."

She gazed at him through her eyelashes and a grateful smile emerged again. Christina clung to his shoulders and allowed herself to soak in another hug. After a few seconds, she tilted her head and sought out his lips again. This latest kiss felt even better than the others to Ron. Their connection with one another seemed to deepen with each second that passed.

Their kiss led into another embrace. Christina nestled her head against Ron's neck. A scent of cherry blossoms filled his nose and mouth.

"I love you too," she whispered.

They stood silent in each other's arms while basking in the moonlight. Ron caressed her hair. Christina simply closed her eyes and cherished the warmth of his toned chest and arms.

Then, at once, Christina's eyes snapped open again and she raised her head.

"I have one other good thing I can do with my magic."

"What's that?"

"I can figure out how to send that woman in black back to where she came from."

"How are we going to do that?"

"I hope you don't mind homework. We're going to have to do some digging to find out who she is and how to stop her."

Christina turned toward the window and stared through the glass as if probing for their common adversary. Ron glanced at the clock on the wall behind them. Time was not on their side. They had to work fast to find a solution.

The woman in black tracked them to the high school. No doubt remained in Ron's mind what potential outcome lay ahead for both he and Christina. Once this mysterious woman figured out they were both still alive, she would return to finish the job she started on the soccer field.

21

Eric gave an indifferent shrug when he heard his mother's request. Emily knew he didn't figure she had much to worry about. Ron made a habit of being a drama king. Perhaps the whole situation would resolve itself soon enough. But her fears refused to let Emily believe a happy outcome lay ahead.

"Sure. I'll text him." Eric extracted his smartphone from a back pocket in his jeans. "But I just think he's pouting. I'll bet that's why he's not answering. He's probably holed up in the tree house or something."

"Don't you think I checked outside already honey? This isn't like him. This isn't like him at all."

Emily wrapped her arms around herself. Her eyes kept darting back to the clock on the microwave oven. Dinner had come and gone, and Ron had not returned. No call. No text. No clue to his whereabouts.

"Don't worry, Mom. I'm still here. We'll track him down. Figure out where he went."

Eric planted himself on a stool at the kitchen counter. He fired off a text just like she requested, leaving the screen visible to Emily.

Where you at? You coming home?

He waited a couple of minutes. No response. Not even a simple emoji. Eric tried again.

Mom's freaking out. Talk to me.

"Do you have any idea where he may have gone?" Emily fiddled with her car keys lying on the counter top. "Is there a place where he likes to hang out?"

"There's a girl he seems to like. Christina. He might be with her."

"Do you know where she lives?"

Eric shrugged.

"Not a clue."

Emily licked her lips and drummed her fingers against the counter top. She wished she had the power to take back the argument they had earlier in the evening. Ron's silence only heightened the dread and guilt weaving through her mind like a spider web. Her boy stormed out of their house all bruised and beaten and she ordered him not to come back.

"Please come home," she whispered, staring helplessly at her text messages.

Eric jumped off the stool and marched toward the kitchen door. Emily jerked her head up from the phone.

"Where are you going?"

"The tree house." Eric grabbed a small flashlight from a nearby drawer. "I've got a telescope up there. Maybe I can see if he's somewhere nearby."

* * *

Ron noticed message alerts from his brother. He didn't bother to open his texts. No doubt, Eric wanted him to reconcile with their mother. She could sit and stew over everything she said and did for a while as far as he was concerned. Ron had bigger fish to fry. He muted his phone and focused on the task at hand with Christina.

Uncovering what they needed to know about this witch would take much more than doing a simple Google search on a smartphone. Ron and Christina ran a few key words through the search engine without much success. The town library offered their only other option. Christina hoped to find some helpful clues in the archives of the old weekly Deer Falls newspaper.

They took Christina's car to the library. It lay only a few blocks away from her house. When they reached the front entrance, all except a few lights were turned out. Ron yanked on the door handle. It didn't budge. Everything had been locked up for the night.

"Don't suppose we could pick the lock?" Ron pressed his face up against the glass, trying to see if anyone was still inside. "You got a hairpin or a paper clip?"

Christina shook her head.

"That won't be necessary."

She closed her eyes and spoke an unfamiliar word. Ron didn't know what the word was, but it didn't sound like English. Christina reached out and touched the lock with her finger. It suddenly turned as if she inserted an invisible key. She opened her eyes again and pulled the door open.

"Nothing to it," Christina said.

Ron looked at the lock, then back at her, and grinned.

"Who needs lock picking skills when you have magic?"

They crept inside the library's main room. A pair of overhead fluorescent bulbs illuminated the area behind the circulation desk with an icky white glow. No other lights were on throughout the room. Glass panels checkered the outer walls, allowing moonlight to flood across shelves, tables, chairs, and computer stations. It cast long shadows down aisles between shelves.

Christina grabbed a leather office chair and sat at a computer behind the circulation desk. Ron pulled up a second chair and sat next to her. She clicked on the library's home page.

"What are we looking for exactly?"

Ron glanced back at the door as he asked that question. His eyes then trailed up to the ceiling and he surveyed every corner to see if security cameras were anywhere. They were ultra-quiet sneaking in here, but Ron still wondered if someone somewhere noticed them breaking into the library anyway.

"I want to know exactly what happened to Crazy Dean in the past."

Christina clicked on a link labeled Colorado Newspaper Archive. It pulled up a page with links to back issues of every newspaper in the state, going back more than 100 years. Another link took her to the Deer Falls Bulletin, the weekly community paper, and she brought up a search bar on the page.

Ron gazed over her shoulder at the computer screen. Christina typed in keywords witch and Dean. The search pulled up an issue from the paper from 55 years ago. A large black-and-white photo of a high school drew Ron's attention. Windows were shattered across the front of the building. Smoke rose from behind blackened brick.

"Arson Suspected in School Fire."

Christina leaned forward as she read the headline. Her lips tightened and she glanced sideways at Ron.

"It says here dozens of people were killed or injured when a fire broke out in the gymnasium during a basketball game."

"How did the fire start?"

"Doesn't say. One survivor, Dean Lambert, was taken into police custody under suspicion of starting the fire."

Ron lowered his eyebrows and half-squinted at the computer screen.

"Dean? As in Crazy Dean?"

Christina nodded.

"It says Lambert carried a small chest with him at the time of his arrest. According to the article, he claimed it held a disembodied witch he imprisoned."

Ron thought back to their encounter with the old bum. He mentioned trapping the witch in a chest at one point in time. Where was that chest now? It obviously held the key to getting rid of her.

"We gotta find that chest," Ron said. "I'd bet my life it's in that abandoned house."

"Yeah, but we need to find out more about this witch first," Christina replied. "Who is she? Where did she come from? Why is she doing these things?"

Christina scrolled further down the article and clicked the next page. More black-and-white photos of the school interior popped up. Chalk outlines dotted the scorched floor a short distance from melted and twisted bleachers. The scoreboard and one basketball hoop remained intact. These were the only undamaged items in the whole gym.

A sketch underneath the photos quickly drew Ron's eyes. It showed a slender teenage girl with dark hair wearing jeans and a blouse. The girl possessed striking, yet empty eyes. Those eyes seemed to leap off the page and stare directly at him. Ron looked away and shuddered. He had to remind himself it was only a sketch.

Christina's eyes also wandered down to the sketch of the girl accompanying the article.

"Artist's rendering of alleged second arson suspect," she said, reading the caption underneath the sketch.

"Doesn't she look familiar to you?" Ron asked.

"Very familiar." Christina rested her chin in her hand and closed her eyes, while trying to visualize where she had seen that face before. "Something about all of this isn't sitting right."

Her eyes popped open again and Christina pulled up another tab on the computer. She typed the keywords witch, chest and trapped into the search engine. The first page in the search results led Christina to a website devoted to medieval folklore. She scrolled through links to various myths until coming across one titled *Pandora Reborn.*

Christina clicked on the text and opened a new window. Ron scooted his chair closer to hers to get a better look. He had no interest in diving into the article itself, but the illustration caught his eye.

It showed a woman in a flowing gown suspended in the air above an open chest. Her body appeared fully formed from her head to her torso. Her legs gradually dissolved into a thick mist rising out of the chest.

Ron's gaze fixed on the woman's face. She possessed the exact same features as the girl in the police sketch from the old newspaper article. His breathing quickened.

"That's definitely the same woman. It has to be."

Christina nodded in agreement.

"Who is she? Why is she here in Deer Falls? What's her purpose? It doesn't add up."

She started reading the article aloud. The legend it recounted seemed so surreal to Ron. A young English maiden turned to witchcraft to avenge a personal wrong. She laid waste to an entire village until finally restrained by an order of monks. Using a powerful incantation, the monks stripped the woman of her body and sealed her dark soul inside a small chest.

This chest was meant to be her prison until the end of time. It continued to be guarded by other monks from that same order for centuries until it disappeared.

At the bottom of the page below the end of the text, a second illustration appeared. This simple box encased a string of words unfamiliar to Ron. He scanned the phrase over and over.

Invoco hodie caelum et terram signum potentiae intus arca ad finem.

Definitely not English. Ron did not recognize the language and he had no idea how to pronounce more than a couple of words.

"What do those words mean?"

"According to the legend, that's the same incantation used to imprison the young maiden in the beginning."

The idea that a simple combination of words possessed so much power would have seemed insane to Ron only a short time ago. After seeing Christina's magic firsthand, his eyes were opened to how much impact even a small action had. Part of him wished to return to that simpler time when outsmarting an opposing player on the soccer field stood out as his most pressing concern.

"Somehow the chest ended up here," Christina said, after studying the final words of the legend. "Someone opened it in Dean's youth and, now, it's open again."

"I can see why he became so unhinged." Ron kept staring at the incantation. "This witch murders a bunch of people in her time. Gets loose once and does the same. Gets loose a second time and, well, here we are."

"Something is unusual about these sketches though. You can see her face in both. But I've never seen her without a veil and hooded cloak covering her up."

"What are you saying?"

"Maybe she didn't try to hide her identity as much the first time around."

"So how does that help us?"

Christina glanced down a short hall leading toward a couple of storage rooms.

"The night she burned the high school may not have been her first time there. Maybe there's some other evidence of the witch's presence."

She sprang from her chair and started down the hall.

"Print off copies of that incantation. We're going to need it."

Christina entered a storage room at the back end of the hall. Ron followed her into the room while the printer spit out freshly printed pages. Christina knelt on the tile floor, combing through a pair of boxes she pulled from a nearby shelf. A small stack of old Deer Falls High yearbooks were piled between boxes. She added another one to the stack as Ron entered the room.

21

"Do you really think there will be a picture of her in a random yearbook?" Ron asked.

"It's worth checking out."

Near the bottom of the box, Christina finally found the object of her search. A yearbook dated 55 years earlier. She pulled it out and balanced it on top of the makeshift yearbook stack. Ron knelt next to Christina as she flipped open the cover. They scanned through a dozen pages filled from top to bottom with photos. She trailed her finger across each photo.

At once, Christina's finger froze on a photo from a pep rally. Her eyes widened and her hand shrank back from the yearbook.

"That's not possible. It can't be her."

Ron rested his hand on the opposite page. He squinted at the faces in the crowd. On the front row, he saw the same thing Christina had seen. His mouth dropped open.

He knew that face.

"Cassandra? She's the witch?"

A tremor raced through the length of his spine. He looked at Christina. She wore the same frightened I-saw-a-monster look Ron imagined adorned his own face. He could not deny what he saw. Everything about the girl in the yearbook photo matched Cassandra's features, right down to her eyes.

Christina's lips trembled and she shook her head again and again. She wrapped her arms around herself.

"How did we not see this? We're in more danger than I thought."

"God, where do you think she is now?"

"Casey!" Christina jumped to her feet. "She's been over to see Casey at his house. We gotta save him."

Ron didn't need to be told twice. He snatched up the printed copies of the incantation as they raced out of the storage room and then out of the library. Time wasn't on their side or on Casey's side.

* * *

Emily heard a loud knock at the front door from inside her office. She stared, unblinking, at her laptop screen.

No new words joined the others on the half-empty page in the past hour. Emily tried to force herself to write to divert her mind from agonizing over her son not coming home. But she could not feel or visualize any words. Her gaze kept drifting to framed photos on the wall. Two were family portraits. She stood with her husband and her two boys against a wooden fence bordering a park near their old home.

That happy scene felt like another lifetime.

A second knock came at the door. This one proved much louder than the first. Emily rose from her chair and poked her head outside the office.

"Eric? Is that you? The door's unlocked."

No response. Eric was nowhere in sight.

She looked at the locked door and then down at her phone. Could it be Ron? He hadn't called or sent a text since storming out. Maybe he was ready to talk again? A glimmer of hope arose within her that this was the case.

Emily drew in a slow breath to calm herself. She glanced through the window next to the door. Ron hadn't returned like she hoped. An unfamiliar girl, around the same age as him, stood under the porch light. Emily frowned and looked down at her phone. Who on Earth stops by this late at night?

The girl raised her chin as Emily turned the deadbolt and cracked open the door. She owned the most striking blue eyes and thickest dark curls Emily had seen on another person.

"Sorry to bug you so late." Her visitor flashed a quick smile and took a step toward the door. "Just stopped by to see if Ron's home."

"Ron?"

"Do I have the wrong house? I'm sorry."

Emily shook her head.

"No. He lives here. I don't think we've met. Are you one of his friends?"

The girl nodded.

"You could say that. I'm Cassandra."

Emily opened the front door a little wider and extended her hand. Cassandra shook it.

"It's nice to meet you, Cassandra. I'm afraid you came at a bad time. Ron's not here right now."

"Really? Did something happen to him?"

"He got in a fight with other players at a soccer game today. Got banged up quite a bit."

"Sounds terrible. Is he okay?"

"I hope so."

Cassandra held the corners of her mouth rigid. It appeared to Emily as if she were suppressing a smile. The girl took another step closer to the door. Emily looked down at Cassandra's feet and back at her eyes. She started to push the door back to its original position.

"I can tell him you stopped by."

"Do you mind if I just wait for him here? I really need to talk to him. It's urgent."

"Cassandra, honey, it's late. Why don't you just call him or text him?"

Cassandra stiffened and raised her chin. She closed her eyes for a moment. Then, her lips loosened, and slipped into a smile.

"You're right. I should call."

"It's nice to have met you, Cassandra. Good night."

Emily pulled the door shut and turned the deadbolt again. She trudged toward the stairs and made a left turn toward the kitchen. Something about Cassandra made her feel more than a bit uneasy. A small glass of wine would calm her nerves. Emily glanced back at the front door out of habit and froze inside the kitchen doorway. She slowly backtracked toward the stairs and turned to face the door again.

Cassandra stood inside the house now. Her icy blue eyes peered at Emily. Each one flickered with a seething hatred. Emily whipped out her smartphone from her pants pocket.

"What do you think you're doing?" she said. "How did you get inside? I didn't invite you in here. Do you want me to call the police?"

"I thought about what you said to me outside. There are better ways to get in touch with Ron than making a phone call."

"I don't know what you want with my son, but I'm putting a stop to it right now."

Emily started to dial 911. She only punched in the first two numbers before the phone suddenly popped out of her hand. Emily looked up and saw Cassandra's arm extended toward her. Her hand drew away Emily's phone like a magnet latching onto a screw.

Emily's face turned pale like she saw a ghost. Her eyes widened and she backed up a couple of steps from her unwanted visitor.

"What the hell?"

Cassandra spread her arms wide. She pointed her fingers downward. At once, both front door locks turned and bolted shut again. Emily took off on a dead run toward her office. The office door slammed shut before she reached it. Emily grasped the doorknob and it refused to budge. Also locked — just like the front door.

Cassandra raised her right arm and uttered a strange word. Both of Emily's arms snapped to her sides and her feet lifted off the floor. She kicked the air. No amount of leg movement could stop her upward trajectory.

"You aren't going anywhere," Cassandra hissed in a low voice.

22

Ron raced through one intersection after another toward Casey's house. He didn't slow for stop signs and simply zoned out occasional screeching brakes and angry honks greeting him as they passed other cars. They had no time to spare.

Cassandra could be there even now.

Christina texted Casey. No response. She dialed his number. One ring. Two rings. Three rings. No answer.

His voicemail popped up.

"Dammit Casey! Pick up the phone."

Worry swam through Christina's eyes. Ron shared her concern. What did Cassandra have planned for him? Were they too late?

Ron slammed on the brakes as soon as they pulled into the driveway. He and Christina both lurched forward and pressed against their seat belts. Ron flung open the door and was already halfway outside the car before he fully unlocked his seat belt. Both he and Christina sprinted to the front door.

She pounded on it with her fist.

"C'mon Casey. Please be okay. Please be okay."

The porch light clicked on. A dog barked inside the house. A few seconds later, the doorknob turned, and the front door popped open. Casey stared at both Ron and Christina and scratched his head.

"What's up? You both look like you've been chased around town by a ghost."

"Is she here?" Christina glanced over Casey's shoulder, trying to see past him into his front room. "Have you seen her?"

"Who?"

"Cassandra."

"Not for a little while. I enjoyed her last visit though."

A little grin appeared on Casey's face as though he held back some juicy details. Ron started to wonder what her visit entailed.

"We gotta find her, Casey." Christina grabbed his shoulder and looked into his eyes. "She's the woman in black from the abandoned house. We're all in serious danger!"

Casey laughed and brushed her hand off his shoulder.

"Nah. Cassandra's cool. Actually, hot. But there's no way. She was there with us. She got burned on the ladder like me, remember?"

"Dude, she fooled us," Ron said. "We found evidence. She's been around for centuries."

"Centuries? She doesn't look that old to me."

"Cassandra knows we're on to her. She used magic to influence a couple of soccer players to try to kill me earlier today. She's the one behind all the deaths and disappearances."

"How come I've never noticed her using magic?"

"Because she's hiding it from you," Christina said. "Witches can conceal their magic."

Casey flung the door open.

"Come on in. Let's go bag us a witch."

Christina let out a relieved sigh and walked inside. Ron gave Casey a curious glance. Something about his body language seemed off. Casey kept avoiding eye contact with both him and Christina. His eyes also kept darting to a back room inside his house. At once, Casey slipped behind them and slammed the front door shut.

He locked the deadbolt.

22

"What are you doing?" Christina wheeled around and faced him. "We gotta get out of here and track her down right now. Cassandra won't stop until we're all dead."

Casey stiffened and shook his head.

"You have Cassandra pegged all wrong. Your jealousy blinds you to who she really is."

"My jealousy?"

"You know she's twice the woman you are. Cassandra appreciates me. I can't let you hurt her."

Casey snatched a gold-colored candlestick holder off a nearby table. He brandished it in front of him like a small sword. Christina and Ron both started backing away from the candlestick.

"Whoa. Easy there." Ron held up his hands. His eyes darted around the room looking for something he could throw at Casey. "This isn't a game of Clue. Put the candlestick down."

Casey swung the candlestick at Ron. He snarled at him with the fierceness of a cornered dog. Both of Casey's eyes changed colors, mirroring the changes in the two soccer players who had attacked Ron earlier.

"He's under Cassandra's spell," Christina said.

"Can you snap him out of it?"

"I'll do my best."

Christina closed her eyes and clasped her hands together. Casey snarled and swung the candlestick at her. Ron stepped in his path and deflected the blow away from Christina. The candlestick crunched down on his forearm. Ron grimaced and plowed directly into Casey with his healed shoulder. He stumbled backward and fell on the floor, still growing the whole time.

At once, Christina's eyes opened again. She cupped her right hand and waved it in Casey's direction.

"Hear me, spirits. Free this man's mind from the hex entangling it like a web."

Casey's snarl instantly erased from his face. His eye color returned to normal. Confusion washed over his face as his eyes darted between Ron and Christina.

"What's going on? What are you doing here?"

"You're kidding, right?" Ron scoffed. He turned to Christina. "Did you also give him amnesia?"

She shrugged.

"I don't know what the side effects of that spell are."

Casey shot a puzzled look at Christina.

"What spell?"

"Bruh, you attacked us and snarled at us like a wild animal." Ron approached Casey and helped him to his feet. "Cassandra wound you up good."

"Cassandra? Where is she?"

"You haven't seen her?"

"Not since last night. At least, I don't think so."

Ron and Christina exchanged concerned looks.

"What do you mean?" she said.

"My mind is blank. The last thing I remember is laying on my bed while Cassandra straddled me."

A satisfied grin crept over Casey's face as he said those words. Christina's cheeks turned a shade of red and she cast her eyes to the ground. Ron pinched his lips together and just nodded. Finding out Casey had sex with Cassandra offered up a twist he didn't see coming. One glimpse of Casey's half-closed eyes and persistent smile told Ron an image of her slender naked body carved out a permanent home inside his head.

"I can see how she put you under a spell now." Christina did not mask the disappointment in her voice. She continued to avert her eyes from him. "You invited her to take control of you."

22

“It’s kind of hard to turn down sex,” Casey replied. “She came here to check on me a couple of times after my hands got burned. Our talking turned to kissing and when she showed me her boobs —”

“We don’t need a play-by-play recap of what happened.” Christina said, glaring at him. “I just need to know if you’re ready to stand with us against her.”

“Why? What did she do?”

“Cassandra is the woman in black. She’s the one responsible for all the recent deaths and disappearances.”

Casey’s face fell like someone had delivered the most painful insult imaginable.

“How’s that possible?”

“She’s a witch,” Christina replied. “Until recently, she had been sealed away inside a chest and prevented from working her magic. We need to put her back in that chest where she belongs.”

Casey rubbed his bandaged hands down the length of his face as he absorbed this revelation from her. Ron sympathized with his reaction. He and Christina were plenty shaken by the news when they uncovered it at the library. It had to feel much worse for Casey. He finds a girl who took an interest in him beyond friendship, and she turns out to be a centuries-old malevolent being who put him under a spell. A definite punch in the gut and kick to the balls. Ron counted himself fortunate he instead chose to pursue a relationship with Christina.

“How do we stop her?”

Casey sniffed back a tear or two as the tone in his voice grew more somber.

“We dug up an incantation.” Ron fished the pages he printed off at the library from his jacket pocket. “It’s supposed to bind her inside the chest.”

He handed copies to both Casey and Christina. Casey stared hard at the incantation and looked at Ron again.

"Hope one of you knows how to say these words. It'd really help if these ancient incantations came with a pronunciation guide."

Ron answered with a nervous chuckle. Casey's observation made sense. He had no idea what the words even meant. How could they do the incantation right if they had no clue how to say anything?

"Just sound them out," Christina suggested. "We need to all be able to do this."

"I don't know the first thing about using magic," Casey replied.

"We all have to be ready. If one person fails to recite the full incantation properly, then someone else needs to step in and finish the job."

Casey grinned.

"But you won't fail! You're like Sabrina the Teenage Witch and Kim Possible rolled into one."

"Kim Possible?" Ron snickered. "You actually watch a girl's cartoon?"

The grin instantly dropped from Casey's face. He looked down sheepishly at the floor.

"Um … well … maybe. It's not exactly a girl's cartoon."

"Whatever you say, bruh."

Christina crossed her arms and tapped her foot against the floorboards.

"Are you two done? We gotta jump on this now. The longer Cassandra is free, the more damage she can do."

Damage.

That word struck Ron with the force of a ball bouncing against a brick wall. If Cassandra went to Casey's house, did that mean she would target his house or Christina's house next? Did she know where they lived? Ron had never taken her to his place. But they weren't dealing with an unknown monster here. Cassandra went to school with them. She befriended them and knew them well enough to enable her to track down each one of them anywhere in town.

22

Ron plucked his smartphone out of his jacket pocket. A new text message icon appeared on the screen. He clicked on the message.

Eric sent it.

HELP! Mom has vanished! Where are you?!

Ron's jaw clenched up. He squeezed the smartphone until his knuckles turned white.

"What's wrong?"

Christina draped her arm around his shoulder. Ron showed her the text from Eric. She gasped.

"Oh no. Ron. I'm so sorry."

Ron bolted toward the front door. Tears streamed down his face and his cheeks became red. All the images he saw in the abandoned house flooded into his mind.

The severed heads.

A cocooned body.

Cassandra already proved how capable she was of doing horrific things. He feared the worst for his mom.

"We gotta get over there right now. If that witch did something to my mom, I'm gonna kill her."

Ron flung open the door. Casey and Christina quickly joined him in a sprint to the car. It was simple math really. If his mom had become Cassandra's latest victim, that witch would be subtracted from existence.

He would find a way to make her pay.

It only took him a few minutes to reach his house. Each minute felt like an hour to Ron. One scenario after another unfolded inside his head. What happened to his mom? What about Eric? Was his brother safe? He visualized his house engorged in flames with the lifeless bodies of his brother and mother in the rubble or overgrown with deadly vines like Nick's house.

Would she be waiting there for them to arrive?

Were they walking into a trap?

Christina dialed up her father while Ron's thoughts raced and pressed the speakerphone button. A relieved sigh escaped her lips when he answered. Christina interrupted David before he got too far into chiding her for being out past curfew.

"I know I shouldn't be out this late. I'm sorry. But Dad, you got to listen to me. This is important."

"What's going on?"

"Remember how you told me that Mom once taught you how to block out witches from entering your home?

"I do. Is something wrong?"

"Very wrong. Do those things she told you about. I'll let you know when it's safe."

"Honey, are you okay?"

"I hope so. I have to face down an evil witch."

"I don't think that's such a good —"

"Dad, I have to do it. She'll kill us and destroy the whole town if I don't stop her."

Silence permeated the car. Her dad said nothing. Only troubled breaths escaped his lips.

"Dad? Dad?"

"Be safe, sweetheart. I love you."

"I love you too, Dad."

Christina ended the call and pulled into the driveway. She barely parked the car before the doors all flew open. The three teens sprinted toward the front door. Someone flung it wide open earlier. Shards of glass lay scattered on the porch. A window above the glass possessed a jagged gaping hole. Lights were still turned on inside the house.

"Mom! Eric! Where are you?"

Ron's eyes darted about the living room. No sign of his brother or his mom. No sign of a struggle or anything else out of place other than a broken window and a large rock lying on the carpet.

"Ron!" Christina's voice came from his mom's office. "You better hurry."

Ron raced into the office and saw Casey and Christina standing in front of Emily's laptop. A black veil was draped over the screen. It matched one belonging to Cassandra. The same veil she used to disguise herself as the woman in black.

"Cassandra was here."

Those three words from Christina sliced through Ron like a knife. His lips trembled and he dropped to his knees. Ron could not control the sobs. Cassandra took his mother from him. He didn't want his last memory to be storming out on her after an argument. If only he had the power to turn back the clock. Ron would tell his mom he was sorry. He would tell her how much he loved her.

Cassandra stole his life.

Forget about sealing her inside a chest. She had to be destroyed, never to return.

Christina dropped to her knees beside Ron and embraced him. He buried his face into her shoulder. She tenderly ran her fingers through his hair.

"I should've been here. I could have saved my mom."

"She would have killed you too."

"I hate her so much now."

"So do I. She's pure evil."

Ron looked up from Christina's shoulder. He noticed Casey walk over to the laptop and pick up the veil. He turned it over in his hand and put it back down. Then Casey moved on to checking out a nearby bookshelf and table. Both stood upright. In fact, no signs of a struggle were present anywhere. Just like there were no signs of Emily's body.

"I don't think your mom's dead." Casey said, turning back to Ron and Christina. "No sign of a body. No sign of an attack. Just a veil."

"I don't think mom's dead either."

All three teens snapped their heads toward the door. Eric stood in the office doorway. Ron slipped out of Christina's arms and jumped to his feet.

He wrapped his little brother in a bear hug.

"I'm glad you're safe."

"Hey! Let go of me. You're squeezing me harder than a python."

Ron scowled and pushed him backward.

"So, what do you think happened to your Mom?" Christina asked.

She mimicked Casey in picking up the veil and examining it closer. The discarded fabric almost felt like a taunt from Cassandra. Perhaps she intended to lure them into a trap.

"From the backyard tree house, I watched a high school girl enter the front yard," Eric said. "I climbed down to see who she was. When I made it around to the front door, she had vanished."

"Did she break the window?"

"No. That was me. All the doors were suddenly locked. I didn't have a key to get back in, so I threw a rock through the window. When I got inside, mom was gone and so was the girl."

Eric turned and faced Ron. A trace of hope swam through his brother's eyes.

"I think she kidnapped her."

Christina closed her eyes as she pondered Eric's story. For the first time since leaving Casey's house, a glimmer of hope welled up inside Ron. Given the gruesome deaths inflicted by Cassandra elsewhere, no sign of a dead body meant one thing.

This had become a rescue mission.

"We've got to go back to the abandoned house," Christina said, opening her eyes again.

Casey shuddered and his eyes darted down to his bandaged hands.

"That's suicide."

22

"This is my mom." Ron punched a fist into his other hand. "If she can still be saved, we need to get her back from Cassandra and then send that monster back to hell."

The thought of going back inside that house made Ron's skin crawl. Still, no turning back. Cassandra would pay for whatever she had done to his mom. He wanted to make sure she didn't stick around to see another sunrise.

23

Everything seemed too quiet and dark.

It struck Ron how lifeless the whole cul-de-sac had become when he opened his car door. Where were the chirping crickets? How come he didn't hear any cats yowling or dogs barking? Ron had grown used to those sorts of noises peppering his own neighborhood at night. None of those things were present here. Not even the smallest pin drop sound. No lights — not even porch lights — illuminated the other houses.

"Do you think she's watching us right now?" Casey's eyes were glued to the front of the house as he climbed out of the backseat. "This completely feels like a trap."

"I don't think she's ready to play her hand yet," Christina said. "She's done a pretty good job up to this point of keeping all of us in the dark."

Leaves now covered the car in the driveway as thick as snow after a winter storm. A weathered bike lay a short distance away from the car. More fallen leaves mingled with shaggy patches of front yard grass. Now stripped of every remaining leaf, the large willow tree stood guard over the house — towering like a wooden giant with spindly arms and fingers. It looked imposing under a moonlit sky. The house exuded a stronger unwelcoming vibe than before. It also lay shrouded in near darkness, except for an ethereal red glow emanating from the upstairs window.

23

A gust of wind kicked up and tugged at Ron's shirt and jeans as he cut across the front yard. He zipped up his jacket and thrust his hands into his pockets. Once Ron reached the porch, a bolt of lightning streaked across the sky along mountains crowding the horizon. A loud clap of thunder followed on its tail.

Christina and Casey soon joined him on the porch. She tried the doorknob. This time around, Cassandra had left it unlocked. Christina turned the knob and flung the door open.

"This seriously feels like a trap." Casey pressed his face up against the window in a futile effort to see through darkened blinds and thick green curtains. "Can't we recite the incantation somewhere else and just pick up the chest when we're done?"

Christina shook her head.

"It doesn't work that way. She has to be in our line of sight for it to take effect."

At once, leaves crunched behind them. Ron flinched and shrank back from the doorway. He turned to face Christina. Her entire mouth trembled, and it wasn't from the cool night air. Casey stood rigid in the middle of the porch and his breathing quickened. All three teens slowly made a 180-degree turn.

Cassandra stood at the bottom of the porch steps. Beads of sweat dotted her forehead and both cheeks were flushed. Cassandra's jacket and jeans bore horizontal tears. Both looked like giant claws ripped through each article of clothing.

Edges of surrounding fabric were stained red.

"Wow, I'm so glad I found you guys." Cassandra's breaths came forth in quick bursts mirroring Casey. "This is so scary."

Ron stared at her and refused to blink. A deep scowl formed on his face even as a shudder raced from head to toe. He wasn't in the mood for whatever mind games Cassandra wanted to play.

"What did you do to my mom, you evil bitch?"

Cassandra blinked at him rapidly and her mouth dropped open.

"What are you talking about? This strange woman in a black gown just attacked me. I barely escaped from her in one piece!"

"Drop the act," Christina replied. "All of us know who you really are."

Cassandra stamped her foot in the grass.

"Listen to me! I looked everywhere for you. We all have to get out of here. Go somewhere safe to hide. We're all in danger."

Casey fished his copy of the incantation from his jeans pocket. She instantly whipped her head in his direction.

"You believe me, don't you? All of this is freaking me out. Come over here and hold me."

Cassandra licked her lips and her eyes darted about nervously. She extended her arms to Casey, inviting him into her embrace. He swallowed hard and clenched his jaw. Memories of the night he spent with Cassandra lingered fresh in Casey's mind. Her influence was not an influence easily shaken.

He started to slide the incantation back inside his pocket.

"I really want to go to her side," Casey whispered. "Help me."

Christina slid over next to him and clasped Casey's arm to keep him from succumbing to her invitation. She stared at Cassandra with steely eyes and a determined expression.

"We know you're trying to drive us from this house. We know you want us to stay away from your chest. Your tricks won't work on us this time."

Cassandra's icy blue eyes narrowed to a slit. A subtle half-smirk washed over her face. She let her arms drop to her sides.

"Fine. We'll do it your way."

A reddish black hue washed over each eye. Her lips parted, revealing clenched teeth. Sweat vanished from her brow and her cheeks turned pale white. Cassandra's torn clothes rippled, swirled, and blended until coalescing into a flowing gown that mirrored her new eye color.

Ron, Christina, and Casey were all rooted to the porch. Their eyes and mouths fell wide open in equal proportion.

Cassandra thrust out her right hand toward the porch. At once, the front door slammed shut behind them. A loud crack followed. Ron glanced up.

"Look out!"

He dove over the porch railing. Christina and Casey followed a split second behind him. A large wood beam crashed down on the porch. Splinters and paint chips flew in multiple directions.

Cassandra laughed.

"This is where it gets fun."

Christina pushed herself up with her arms onto her knees. Dead blades of grass and leaves clung to the front of her jacket. She raised her hand and started swirling her index finger in a circular motion. Leaves shot straight up into the air from one end of the front yard to the other.

"Oh, that's right. You dabble in magic." Cassandra rolled her eyes and laughed again. "Your simple tricks won't save you against my real powers."

"I'm so much stronger than you think," Christina replied.

All the leaves matched the swirling motion of her finger. Christina brought her hand in front of her until the finger pointed directly at Cassandra. At once, leaves zoomed through the air in all directions toward the witch. They enveloped her head like a swarm of angry bees until all she saw were leaves. Cassandra shrieked as she tried to swat the leaves away.

"Get inside! Hurry!" Christina's words grew strained as she focused her energies on keeping all the leaves blanketing their target. "I can't keep this up very long."

Both Ron and Casey scrambled to their feet. Ron charged up the porch steps first. He twisted the doorknob. It wouldn't budge.

"Dammit! She locked it."

Casey glanced down at the broken wooden beam. He hoisted it up off the porch.

"There's more than one way to get inside."

Ron nodded and grabbed hold of the beam too. They turned and swung it like a battering ram into the window. Glass shattered around the end of the wood. A large hole remained when they pulled the beam back out and tossed it back on the porch. Ron thrust his elbow into the surrounding glass and knocked another chunk loose. Casey followed his lead and knocked a second chunk loose with his forearm. They rained blows on broken glass until the hole grew large enough for everyone to climb through into the living room.

"Let's go!" Ron shouted.

He reached inside the broken window and ripped the blinds out of the fixture holding them. The blinds tumbled to the carpet in a heap. Ron then pushed aside the heavy curtain just enough, so they had room to climb through fast.

Christina backpedaled toward the porch, never dropping her hand or finger. Leaves now engulfed Cassandra from head to toe. As soon as she swatted a few down, others flew in to fill the gap. Christina only turned away once she reached the bottom porch step. She raced up the steps and climbed through the window behind Ron and Casey.

As soon as Christina's last leg passed the windowsill, the leaves burst into a curtain of blue flame. They disintegrated and Cassandra walked through the flames. Her reddish black eyes held a glimmer of flame inside them. Cassandra cupped her hands together and another blue fireball began to take shape inside.

"I think we better get away from the window."

Ron started backing up as soon as he spoke. His leg muscles tightened, anticipating a forthcoming sprint out of the living room. Christina scanned the room, looking for some way to combat the fireball. Her eyes lit up as soon as she saw a mirror hanging on the opposite wall.

"We can't outrun it. But I think we can stop it."

"How?" Ron asked.

Christina pointed to the wall.

"Grab the mirror."

Ron snatched the mirror from the wall. Cassandra faced the living room and thrust her hands toward the house. The fireball zipped through the air on a collision course with the window. Christina rushed forward and smashed a sofa cushion up against the hole they made in the glass. She took the mirror from Ron and held it up in front of her.

"Get directly behind me." Christina glanced at both Ron and Casey. "We don't need to give that fireball any extra targets."

A burning whoosh echoed through the room as the fireball punched a hole through the cushion and the edge of the curtain. Twin plumes of smoke from singed fabric drifted toward the ceiling. The fireball followed the same trajectory. Inches from the plaster, it took a sharp curve and flew in a straight line toward the chandelier.

"It's gonna drop right on top of us."

Casey hunkered down and threw his arms over his head like a makeshift helmet.

"Reflect this fireball no more but absorb its flames!"

Once she shouted those words, Christina hoisted the mirror above her head as the fireball closed in on their position. It rippled with the same intensity as the surface of a pond on a windy day. The fireball slammed to a halt right above the mirror. Wisps of flame swirled downward like a star falling into a black hole until the last traces of the fireball finally vanished.

Ron gazed into the mirror as Christina brought it down in front of her and rested the bottom edge on the floor. Instead of seeing his reflection, a large blue fireball occupied the space on the other side. She had imprisoned the flames within the mirror.

Ron planted a kiss on her cheek.

"That's freaking awesome. Is there anything that you can't do?"

Christina smiled. Her smile quickly evaporated though when a loud cracking sound filled the room.

"Down!"

She dropped to the floor and covered her head and neck. Ron and Casey did the same. What remained of the living room window exploded in a shower of glass. Shards of glass scattered in all directions. The curtain caught some of it. The rest rained down on the three teens, pelting them like hail.

Ron uncovered his head and looked up when the final glass shards had fallen. Cassandra floated in through the window and touched down onto the floor in front of them. The corners of her mouth turned up into a slight smile, but her eyes flashed with rage.

"You just won't die, will you?"

"You can't always get your way," Ron said.

He glared at Cassandra. Ron wondered what torments she inflicted on his mother. Was she even still alive at this point? He grabbed a large glass shard and rose to his feet.

"A piece of glass? Really?" Cassandra scoffed. "What exactly do you think you're going to do?"

"This is for my mom!"

Ron hurled the most jagged end of the glass shard at her. Cassandra thrust up her hand. The shard froze in midair. She turned the hand around so her palm faced her body. Her motion caused the shard to change direction and it sped back toward Ron. He flung his arm upward to block his face and throat. The glass shard struck his forearm and buried itself deep into muscle tissue. Ron clenched his teeth and dropped to his knees.

Only the upper portion of the shard still protruded from his jacket sleeve.

"You need to do better than that, Ron." Cassandra stood over him. "I'm a powerful witch. A little piece of glass isn't going to stop me."

"See if you can stop this."

Christina scrambled to her feet and stomped on the mirror. A large crack spread from one end of the frame to the other. She kicked it toward Cassandra, and it collided with her foot. Ron rolled out of the way. That same fireball Christina trapped earlier ascended from the broken mirror. It enveloped the hem of Cassandra's gown. Blue flames climbed the fabric on all sides. She looked down at the flames and let out a furious shriek.

"Atque extinguere flammas crescente."

Upon saying those words, Cassandra traced her finger across her belly. A dark mist formed near her navel, circled her torso, and spread down the gown on all sides. It snuffed out the flames on contact.

"I'm no longer amused." Her voice descended to a guttural hiss. Ron never heard anything else so unsettling in his life. "You all will learn what true pain means."

Casey retrieved the incantation again and unfolded the paper.

"Invoco hodie."

Cassandra faced him and thrust her hand in his direction. She lifted her fingers up. His feet lifted off the ground at the same time. Casey tightened his grip on the paper as he floated toward the ceiling.

"Caelum et terram."

She cast her fingers downward, pointing them at the ground. Casey crashed hard onto the floor. He groaned and rolled over on his side. Cassandra drew back her hand like she pulled an invisible string toward herself. The paper at once flew out of Casey's fingers and landed in her own.

"You all went to significant trouble to trap me in that chest again. I can't let it happen."

The paper vanished from between Cassandra's fingers in a puff of smoke. Ron scrambled to his feet. He and Christina both helped Casey stand up. They backed away from Cassandra as she walked over to the mantle. Cassandra waved her hand and suddenly one of the mummified heads popped free from the wall. It floated over to her.

"This is the fate of all who dare to threaten me."

Cassandra spun around and held out the head. Empty eye sockets and dried out skin, combined with full teeth and hair, made it a truly frightening sight.

"Why are you doing this Cassandra?" Christina asked. "What has anyone done to you to deserve death?"

Cassandra crushed the head with her hand. She let broken remnants drop to the floor.

"Your pathetic town has earned nothing less. The powerful here oppress the weak. Nothing has changed from what I experienced as a young maiden."

"What do you mean? What happened to you?"

"A loathsome knight destroyed everything precious to me. So, I repaid him with what he deserved. My reward? Imprisonment inside a chest by monks who feared me."

Her words struck a chord with Ron. He remembered Cassandra's story about the girl raped by a soldier. Now Ron understood the deeper meaning behind that story. Cassandra was that girl. At one time he would have felt sympathetic to her plight. No such feelings stirred within him now. Nothing she experienced justified her turning into an absolute monster.

"You're right. The knight deserved to be punished," Ron said. "But we don't deserve this. We've tried to be friends with you from your first day at school."

Cassandra closed her fingers tight as if squeezing an invisible orange.

Ron started gagging. He tugged at his throat as his breaths grew more labored.

"Friends don't try to force friends back inside a chest."

Suddenly, both remaining heads above the mantle popped free from the wall. Cassandra jerked her head around just in time to see each one flying straight at her. Both heads smacked her in the face and knocked the witch backward. Her grip around Ron's windpipe loosened. He gasped loudly and rubbed his throat.

Christina grabbed his shoulder.

"Are you okay? Can you breathe?"

Ron winced and nodded.

"This is the second time you've saved my life. I owe you a lot more than one."

Christina planted a quick kiss on his lips.

"Let's hurry. I think her chest is hidden somewhere upstairs."

They bolted out of the living room toward the stairs. Christina snapped her fingers when they reached the bottom stair. A candle lit up near the entry way. She snatched it off a nearby table. It punched a hole in thickening darkness that gathered in absence of direct moonlight.

"Watch out for the vines, Casey." Christina shined candlelight at the wall, revealing a vine skulking at arm level. "Ron and I found out about them the hard way last time."

"Yes, Casey, do be careful. Those vines really do have a mind of their own."

No one needed to look behind them. They knew Cassandra was hot on their heels again. Casey suddenly let out a scream.

"It's got my foot!"

Christina shined the candlelight on Casey's legs. A large vine wrapped itself around both limbs and bound them together. Before she had a chance to reach out and force it to let go, the vine retreated toward the wall and dragged Casey along for the ride. Two more large vines latched onto his arms and pulled him up against the wall. Baby vines burst from the wall and wrapped around his body until sealing him in a cocoon with only his face left exposed.

Ron charged up the stairs, hoping to reach the top before any vines touched him. More vines shot out from the wall on one side and the banister on the other. They knocked him off his feet and swarmed over him on top of the stairs until he became wrapped in a cocoon matching the one immobilizing Casey.

“No!” Christina shouted.

She swung around to face Cassandra.

A few seconds too late.

That awful witch was ready for her.

Ron watched helplessly as Cassandra circled her hands in the air and pushed them forward. Her motion threw Christina backward. She reached out instinctively to grab the banister and soon found a vine wrapped around her left arm. It pulled her in. Two more vines weaved around both of her legs, trapping her against the wood.

Christina pressed the candle in her free hand against the vine on her arm. Molten wax dripped on the vine and caused it to shrink back. Cassandra quickly snatched the candle away. She slammed Christina’s arm against the railing and held her wrist in place until another vine secured her right arm. Baby vines sprouted from the wood and formed a cocoon around Christina matching the ones around Ron and Casey.

Cassandra smiled and snapped her fingers on both hands. A trail of candles lit up along the wall, illuminating the stairs.

“I’ll give you credit. You three put up a much better fight than I expected from any of you. Now it’s at an end.”

Christina bit down on her lower lip and pushed against the web of vines restraining her. Each vine wrapped tighter around her body, forcing a sharp cry out of her.

“I wouldn’t do that if I were you.” Cassandra waggled her finger at

Christina. “Fighting the vines will only make your pain grow worse while they drain away your energy and soul.”

“When we get free, we’re going to destroy you,” Ron said. “That’s a promise.”

Cassandra turned and marched up to the spot on the stairs where he lay cocooned. She trailed her fingers through part of Ron’s unruly mop of light brown hair and flashed a wicked grin.

“No. What you will do is share in your mother’s fate.”

24

Eric didn't care what Ron told him to do. Staying at Max's house until Ron and his friends took care of everything did not feel like a practical option. He always had a much closer relationship with his mom than Ron did, especially since their father exited the picture. If anyone deserved to spearhead a rescue, Eric was the one.

That's why Eric pedaled at a furious pace down Main Street in Deer Falls as the midnight hour approached. His bike's headlight flickered and bounced whenever the front tire crested the smallest bump. An occasional passing car offered the only sign of life or activity in the town. Interspersed between a few streetlights, a row of darkened buildings lined both sides of Main Street.

The sheriff's office offered the only exception. Some lights were still on inside. Eric skidded to a stop along the sidewalk in front and pushed down his bike's kickstand with his foot.

"I told you it'd still be open."

Eric glanced back over his shoulder. Max pulled up behind him on another bike. He hopped off and rested his hands on his hips.

"I still think this is a bad idea." Max paused and coughed as he worked to catch his breath again. "We just barely escaped from that place the last time."

Eric's eyes burned hot with annoyance. Max's whining didn't bug him most of the time. This wasn't one of those times.

"My mom's in danger! I gotta do something. I have to rescue her."

"I know. I'm sorry. I just don't see what we can do to help her."

"I guess we'll find out. We're going back to that house. And this time we'll bring some help with us."

Eric marched up the steps and pushed open the main door. Max kept glancing back at their bicycles and then down the street as he followed a couple of steps behind. They walked up to the front desk.

"Can I help you boys with something?"

A deputy poked his head out of an office near the back. His stern eyes and slight frown told Eric he already pegged them as a pair of troublemakers before hearing a single word.

"My mom has been kidnapped," Eric said. "She disappeared earlier tonight after some mysterious girl showed up at our front door."

The deputy beckoned both boys to draw closer.

"Come back here and have a seat."

Eric and Max both entered the office. They sat down in two chairs in front of a desk. The nameplate on the desk belonged to Deputy Shawn Palmer. Open file folders and papers were spread across the desk. Other papers plastered with photos and detailed writing were pinned to a rolling bulletin board near the desk. Eric did a double take. One photo looked familiar — a head shot of the pizza delivery boy that the old man monster attacked and killed at the abandoned house.

Deputy Palmer took a seat behind the desk and faced the two boys.

"Do you know approximately what time your mother vanished?"

"Around eight o'clock, I think." Eric squinted and scratched his head. "It was already dark when the girl I told you about showed up."

"Any sign of forced entry?"

"It all seemed weird. I saw her coming while up in the tree house in our yard. I climbed down to see who it was. When I got to the front door, she had vanished. And all the doors and windows were locked."

"The doors and windows were locked?"

"Yeah. I had to break a window with a rock to get back inside. Mom wasn't anywhere."

Deputy Palmer glanced at Max.

"Did you see the same things?"

"I wasn't there, sir."

Max looked at his feet, the floor, and anything else that kept him from making eye contact with the deputy.

"My brother Ron can vouch for my story," Eric replied. "He already took off in search of our mom."

Deputy Palmer's brows knitted together when he heard the name of Eric's brother.

"Ron? Is your brother Ron Olson?"

"Yeah … you know him?"

The deputy closed his eyes and sighed.

"Yes, son, I know who he is. Where's your brother right now?"

Eric cast a worried glance outside the office door.

"He went to an abandoned house with a couple of friends. We think she was taken there by a witch."

"A witch?" Deputy Palmer slammed his fist on the desk. Both boys jumped in their seats. "God, I really don't have time to deal with this nonsense."

"I'm telling the truth!" Eric protested. "You've got to help us. It's your job!"

"Kidnapping is a serious crime," the deputy replied. "I want to track down the culprit, son. But I can only help you out if you stop with the tall tales."

Eric looked at the floor and frowned. What did he have to do to make cops in this town believe him?

"Can you tell me what the girl looks like?"

"I couldn't get a good look at her, sir. It was so dark. I know she had dark curly hair."

Deputy Palmer leaned forward.

"I don't really have much to go on here."

"Please." Eric glanced outside the office door a second time. "I'm really worried about my mom. I don't want to lose her."

Deputy Palmer stared at the open files spread out on his desk. He scowled and buried his chin into his hand. Eric noticed for the first time two files on his desk featured photos of Ron and Christina. Was the deputy investigating his brother? Did he think he was behind all these things the witch had done?

Eric started to wonder if turning to the cops for help was the right idea.

"You win. I'll go check this out." Deputy Palmer dropped his hand and looked at the two boys again. "Tell me where this house is."

"I don't know the exact address."

Fresh hesitation crept into Eric's voice.

"Can you show me where the house is?"

"I think so. Maybe."

"Look, son, I can only help your mom if you help me first."

"Yeah. I can find it."

Eric's internal compass wasn't as strong as he thought when they left the sheriff's office. Deputy Palmer turned down three different streets. All were the wrong ones. None led to Willow Flats. By the third wrong turn, a scowl became as deeply etched on his lips as a crack in an aging sidewalk.

"This is turning into a mammoth waste of my time, son," Deputy Palmer said. "I'm not in the habit of arresting kids, but I'm ready to make an exception."

Max pulled out his smartphone and pulled up the video from their aborted prank on the pizza delivery boy. As soon as Eric caught a glimpse of the video, he shot Max a dirty look. When the camera passed over the number on the front of the house, Max paused the video and handed it to the deputy.

"Here's what the house looks like in the day, sir."

Deputy Palmer pulled off to the side of the road and took the phone from Max. He studied the frozen frame of the house and then resumed playback from the video.

"Care to tell me what you boys were up to here?"

Max and Eric both gulped. Neither boy anticipated him playing the rest of the video. When he saw the attack on the pizza delivery boy, the deputy nearly jumped out of his seat.

"Holy shit! What happened to that kid?"

"We don't know!" Eric waved his hands frantically. "We jumped on our bikes and then started pedaling for our lives."

Deputy Palmer paused the video again and set the phone down.

"I think I know where the house is now. I recognize that part of Willow Flats."

He pulled back onto the road and turned on his lights and siren. It took only a few minutes to reach the cul-de-sac. Eric saw Ron's car parked in front of the house when they pulled up in the deputy's truck.

No sign of Ron, Christina, or Casey.

"What happened to the Pizza Wagon car?" Max said.

Eric shrugged and turned to the spot in the driveway where they last saw it parked. Not seeing that car around spooked Eric even more. The deputy wasn't kidding when he said they hadn't found any evidence of the pizza delivery boy's murder. It occurred to him people didn't simply die in this house. All traces of their existence seemed to be erased as well.

Deputy Palmer grabbed a flashlight and opened the driver's side door. Eric cracked open the other door.

"Wait a minute, son. Where exactly do you think you're going?"

"I just thought —"

"Stay here in the truck."

Eric reluctantly pulled the door shut again. The deputy slammed his door. He drew his pistol from the holster on his belt and clicked on his flashlight. Eric mumbled some choice words he wanted to say to Deputy Palmer, but only once he figured the deputy had moved safely out of earshot.

Eric quickly turned and smacked Max's arm.

"Hey, thanks for throwing me under the bus!"

"What are you talking about?" Max recoiled and backed away. "I didn't do anything."

Eric pointed to the phone.

"The video? Funny how you suddenly didn't accidentally erase it after all."

"Sorry. When they told us that they found no evidence of anything, I panicked."

Eric abruptly turned away. He rested his hand on the passenger door handle.

"You seriously still want to go in there?" Max asked, turning to him. "That's whacked."

"I'm worried about my mom." Eric's eyes trailed Deputy Palmer as the deputy finished examining the front porch and shined his flashlight into the living room. "I can't just sit here in this truck waiting and wondering."

"The deputy will find her."

"I don't trust him."

"Why not?"

Mental snapshots of those files on Ron and Christina appeared in Eric's head again. He questioned Deputy Palmer's motives. Eric got a distinct impression the deputy seemed less concerned about finding his mom and more focused on pinning all the strange happenings on Ron and Christina.

"I've got a feeling he thinks my brother is to blame for all of this."

"What are we supposed to do about it?"

"Follow me."

Eric kept his eyes glued on Deputy Palmer. Once the deputy climbed through a gaping hole that used to be living room windows, he made his move. Eric cracked open the other door and slid out of the cab of the truck, dropping gently to the asphalt. Max drew a long breath and joined him outside.

Seeing the damage to the house up close blew Eric's mind. Something bad took place before they got here. What happened to Ron? Did he find their mom? Was he hurt or dead? Not knowing solid answers to those questions ate at him.

Eric pulled out his smartphone and texted Ron.

No answer.

"We've gotta find a different way inside," Eric whispered. "Maybe there's a back door."

They walked around the garage and soon found the back door. Unlocked. Eric gently turned the knob and poked the door open. It led into a small kitchen. Drawn blinds on each window created a stifling darkness. Eric flipped on a light switch. A fluorescent bulb flickered on overhead and just as quickly shorted out.

Max stared up at the now darkened fixture.

"Did the power just go out?"

Eric pulled open the top drawer under the kitchen counter and started combing through the contents. He wrapped his hands around a small flashlight and turned it on. The beam seemed so small and weak compared to darkness that devoured the rest of the room like a giant mouth. Still, it offered enough light to at least show Eric and Max where they were going.

Eric rummaged through a utensil drawer next and found a set of six steak knives. He pulled out three knives and handed them to Max and kept the others.

"In case we need to defend ourselves," Eric said.

Both boys concealed the knives inside their jackets. They tiptoed out of the kitchen and crossed a short hallway into a small den. Eric trailed the flashlight beam along the wall. Some odd-looking plants dotted the room. Nothing else appeared out of the ordinary.

"Where are you, mom?" Eric muttered.

Max froze.

"Did you hear that?"

"What? Where?"

"Behind us."

Eric heard it now. Footsteps. They drew closer. One step. Then another. He pulled the flashlight beam away from the wall and grasped a knife handle inside his jacket. Eric's breaths grew faster and heavier. He slowly pivoted his body around until he faced the doorway leading into the den.

A second flashlight beam greeted him from the other side of the doorway.

"What part of 'stay in the truck' don't you boys understand?"

Deputy Palmer lowered his pistol and his flashlight. Eric and Max both exhaled loud enough for everyone to hear it.

"It's safer for everyone if you two go back outside. Let's go."

He waved his flashlight toward a second door leading from the den out to the living room. Eric and Max walked past the TV and sofa in the direction where the beam pointed and opened the door. A chilly blast of mountain air greeted their faces. Broken glass lay scattered across the floor.

At once, Eric heard three voices. All came from near the stairs. One sounded like Ron.

"Hey, I think I hear my brother in the other room," he said, looking over his shoulder.

Eric's muscles stiffened and his feet clamped to the floor. A darkened figure entered the den behind Deputy Palmer and Max. The flashlight beam matched the tremors in Eric's hand as he centered it on this new person in the room.

They were clad in a hooded cloak and hunched over, leaning on a walking stick. Part of the hooded figure's face wasn't clearly visible. Eric wished the whole face had stayed hidden. What he saw painted a horrifying picture. Their flesh hung from their bones like melted wax that suddenly cooled in an instant.

Deputy Palmer simultaneously raised his pistol and his flashlight.

"Put your hands where I can see them. Raise them nice and slow."

The hooded figure's eyes trailed up to the deputy. Eric had no idea if he was looking at a man or woman. Whoever stood before them didn't even seem human. One thing he did know. This was the same being who tore apart the pizza delivery boy before his eyes.

"I said hands up. NOW!"

The hooded figure bared a set of dark jagged teeth at Deputy Palmer. They delivered an ear-piercing shriek. Eric and Max both answered it with their own screams and bolted through the doorway into the living room. The mystery visitor in the den raised their walking stick in the air and charged toward the two boys.

Deputy Palmer stood his ground. He fired the pistol. A bullet struck the hooded figure in the shoulder. They snarled and didn't slow a step. Deputy Palmer unloaded the clip into his intended target as he backed toward the wall. One bullet after another struck them in the chest and both arms. It did nothing to slow their advance.

Deputy Palmer's eyes slid over to the walking stick. It possessed an end sharpened like a spear and appeared to be crafted from bone. His pistol clicked. No more bullets remained in the chamber. The hooded figure thrust their walking stick forward.

It pierced Deputy Palmer in the navel.

He grimaced and clutched at the walking stick as the sharpened end plowed through his bowels and ripped through his back. The stick finally stopped deep inside the wall behind the deputy.

It pinned Deputy Palmer against sheet rock like a human kebab.

Deputy Palmer gagged up blood and it dribbled down his chin. He wrapped his hands around the walking stick as the hooded figure threw back their hood. Their facial features smoothed out and hair lengthened until a young dark-haired woman stood before him. Eric recognized her as the same girl who kidnapped his mom.

Ron called her Cassandra.

She traced her finger across his cheek and smiled. Tremors wracked the deputy's body as he coughed up a fresh batch of blood.

He reached for his police radio.

"10-78 … Code 3 … Officer needs assistance." Deputy Palmer struggled to form words while gasping for breath. "Deputy Leeds … please hurry."

His attacker drew back a couple of steps. Cassandra crossed her hands before her chest and gradually pulled them away from her body. At once, every bullet Deputy Palmer fired into Cassandra emerged from her skin. Holes in her flesh closed again and not so much as a scar remained behind. Each bullet spun in the air and pointed back at the deputy.

"This will hurt you so much worse than it was supposed to hurt me."

Cassandra propelled every bullet forward at once. They peppered Deputy Palmer in the neck, chest, and arms. The tremors finally stopped, and his now empty eyes gaped at her. Cassandra calmly walked forward and picked up the radio.

"Cancel that request, Deputy Leeds." Her voice changed to mimic Deputy Palmer's voice as if it were her natural one. "I got everything under control here."

Both Eric and Max stood cemented to the floor while everything unfolded, too terrified to move. Eric suddenly realized not fleeing was a huge mistake on their part. Cassandra turned toward the living room and flashed a devilish grin.

"I guess I need to do more than put some fear into you this time."

She marched toward the doorway. Both boys screamed. They instantly heard voices again near the stairs. Eric and Max both took off on a dead sprint toward the voices. The two boys soon came face-to-face with Ron, Christina, and Casey.

All three teens remained cocooned in the vines.

"Eric? What are you doing here?" Ron shouted. "I told you stay away from here."

"Good thing I didn't listen."

"How is it good?"

"Now someone's here to rescue you."

Eric and Max pulled out the steak knives. They started sawing through the vines enveloping Christina at the foot of the stairs. As soon as they got an arm free, Christina squeezed the end of a vine between her fingers and closed her eyes.

"Wither from my sight, cursed vine, back to the place from where you sprang."

A soft glow emanated from her emerald pendant. It spread down through Christina and anywhere a vine wrapped around her skin, the plant shrank and dried up like an aging flower.

"NO!"

Cassandra unleashed an unholy scream after passing through the doorway when she saw vines no longer held Christina captive.

"Cut them loose," Christina said, pointing to Ron and Casey. "I'll deal with her."

25

Pure rage flashed through Cassandra's eyes as she approached Christina. She raised her hands high above her head. Both ceiling and walls started to shake. Cracks formed in the floor and started to widen. Eric and Max both stumbled and landed on the stairs as they climbed toward Casey and Ron.

"I will bring this entire house down on you!" Cassandra hissed.

Christina's eyes widened and darted from wall to wall looking for a means to stop her. Cassandra continued moving forward in an unbroken stride. When she neared the front door, a light clicked on inside Christina's head. She raised her fist in the air and snapped her wrist back toward her arm three times.

Bolts rose on all three door hinges. One by one each bolt popped out. The heavy oak door swayed and tipped backward.

Crash.

The heavy door knocked Cassandra down and pinned her arms to the floor. Tremors ceased and cracks stopped widening.

Christina closed her eyes and clutched her pendant with one hand. She held the other out in front of her, palm down, and pressed it downward. The front door pressed down on Cassandra's body. She screamed and gnashed her teeth.

"You all need to work fast." Christina kept her eyes pinched shut, trying not to break her concentration. "I can't hold her here forever."

Eric and Max rose to their feet and reached Ron and Casey. They pulled out their steak knives again and hacked through vines with zeal. Max freed Casey first and then Eric cut Ron loose a few seconds later. Ron stood up and brushed himself off. Every vine seemed to be gradually withering in the same manner as the ones that cocooned Christina earlier.

"It feels good not to be a human lettuce wrap," Ron said, letting out a relieved sigh.

"You owe me one, bro," Eric replied.

Ron slapped his back and smirked at him.

"It always seems that way, doesn't it?"

They charged up the rest of the stairs. Christina's eyes popped open. She gasped. Her hand let go of the pendant and it dropped down to its former spot against her chest. Cassandra shifted under the front door until she freed an arm. A second later, the door flew straight up into the air. Cassandra jumped to her feet. The front door launched forward and blasted through the doorway like a projectile. It smashed through the windshield of Deputy Palmer's truck and landed right in front of the steering wheel.

Christina stared at the truck and grimaced. Sweat rolled off her forehead and down her cheeks. She breathed with the same intensity as a marathon runner who hadn't yet caught their second wind.

"It's so draining, isn't it?" Cassandra faced Christina again. "I became infused with powerful dark magics, hundreds of years before you even existed. You are not equipped to handle what I can throw at you."

"I'm not afraid of you."

"You started a battle you can't win."

"You've lost before. You can lose again."

"Not by your hand."

Cassandra laughed and cupped her hands together to form a fireball for the second time.

"Who shall I incinerate first? Ron? Casey? I'm going to destroy every last person you hold dear, right before your eyes."

A primal scream followed.

It didn't come from Cassandra.

Christina thrust her hands forward as far as she could extend them. Cassandra found herself thrown backward like a rag doll. She slammed against the fireplace and crashed through the protective screen. Soot shot out from behind her. The fireball dropped from between Cassandra's hands. It ignited her gown and set the carpet ablaze right in front of the fireplace.

Christina turned and raced up the stairs. The other four waited for her to join them on the landing. Eric had torn off a strip from the bottom of his shirt and wrapped it around a bleeding puncture wound in Ron's arm. The wound was a token left behind by the glass shard after Eric ripped it out.

"Where's Cassandra?" Casey asked.

"I slowed her down. Don't know for how long." Christina instinctively glanced over her shoulder, looking for any sign of the witch in pursuit. "We need to put an end to this soon."

A distinct red glow filled the hall. It spilled out from the middle bedroom, along with a red mist. Eric trailed the flashlight beam along the opposite wall. It revealed fresh vines that had not withered like the others on the stairs. He also caught a glimpse of another cocoon. Eric raised the flashlight.

Ron grabbed at his brother's arm.

"You don't really want to look. Take my word for it."

His efforts to redirect the flashlight didn't work. The beam fell on the pizza delivery boy's corpse. Eyes had sunken in now. Teeth were starting to fall out. His flesh had grown discolored and had begun to rot around the lacerations. The torn Pizza Wagon cap Ron knocked off his head the last time around still lay in the same spot on the floor.

Both Eric and Max started to scream. Casey and Ron clamped their hands over each boy's mouth to prevent them from drawing unwanted attention. Christina scrunched up her nose and quickly pinched it shut with her fingers.

"That's putrid," she said. "I think I'm gonna vomit."

As the group drew closer to the middle bedroom, red mist spilling out into the hallway grew more vivid. It hung low over the floor, clinging to walls and floorboards like a dense fog surrounding a bridge. Ron wondered what purpose it served. Judging by many other things they already encountered within the house, he knew it couldn't be a good purpose.

"Be alert, everyone." Christina's eyes trailed back and forth as they reached the doorway. "Cassandra is lurking around here. I know it. We're not in the clear yet."

"Let's split up," Eric said. "That way we can find my mom quicker.

Casey looked at him and shook his head.

"Dude, have you ever watched a slasher movie? Splitting up is a death sentence. You might as well send the killer GPS coordinates to come find you."

"We'll find Mom together," Ron said. "Strength in numbers."

"I don't think you have to worry about that."

Christina pointed to a bed inside the room. Vines encircled Emily from chest to toe and bound her to the blankets atop the bed. Her eyes were closed, and her mouth hung slightly open.

"Mom! Mom!"

Both Ron and Eric carried the same desperate tone in their voices. They charged into the room at the same time and raced over to her side. Their mother lay as still as a doll on the bed. No movement from her eyes, lips, or nose. Her skin had become slightly pale.

"Mom! Speak to me!" Ron pressed his hand against her cheek. Her skin was still warm. "Can you hear us?"

25

"Is she alive?" Christina asked.

Ron moved his fingers down to her neck. She still had a pulse. A distressingly faint one.

"I think she might be in a coma," he said.

Eric knelt by the side of the bed. He pulled out a steak knife again and started sawing through vines. One vine snapped. Another soon followed.

Midway through a third vine, Eric stopped cutting. His forearm muscles tensed up and veins started to bulge. Eric's hand rose and the knife blade started turning inward toward him.

"What are you doing?" Ron asked.

Eric glanced up at him through narrowing eyes. He gritted his teeth and then let out a small moan.

"Help me. I can't control my arm."

Ron reached out and seized Eric's wrist. Max scrambled forward and grabbed the forearm. They pushed back against it, trying to keep the limb in place. Christina and Casey exchanged glances and frowned. Their respite had met an end.

Multiple candles sprang to life at once throughout the room. Both Christina and Casey turned to face the door. Ron also glanced in that direction. Cassandra stood just inside the doorway. Her hand extended toward the group. Burnt patches peppered her gown now, but Cassandra's body remained free of a single mark from those same flames that threatened to consume her downstairs.

She planted herself in front of a dresser. The object everyone hoped to see rested on top.

An open chest.

"Read the incantation!" Casey shouted.

He ran over to the closet and grabbed several empty plastic hangers. Casey tossed the bundle of hangers at Cassandra's face. She turned and thrust her other arm toward him. The hangers froze in mid-air and then crashed down onto the wood floor.

"Not a bright idea, lover."

Cassandra started to swirl her right hand. Some of the red mist hovering over the floor gathered around Casey. It began to climb his legs and soon blanketed his jeans.

"Hear me, spirits, and dissolve this attacking mist." Christina swung her hand in a semicircle. "Return it to the place from where it came."

Once those words escaped her lips, the mist shrank from Casey's legs. It coalesced into a fine red dust and fell to the floor inert.

Eric let out a sharp cry. Ron snapped his head back to him.

"Fight it, Eric! Fight it!"

Christina also glanced back when she heard Ron's urging. Both Ron and Max showed strain on their faces while keeping Eric's arm from plunging the knife into his chest. Tears streamed down Eric's face, and he clenched his teeth as the arm crept ever closer.

Cassandra started to raise all three off the floor at once. Max screamed and started kicking his feet. Christina's eyes searched the room for some way to stop her. She spotted a radio alarm clock and a lamp sitting on a nearby desk. Christina reached out toward the desk.

Both items unplugged from the wall and flew toward her. She swung her hand toward Cassandra. Both lamp and alarm clock turned in the air and followed the same path. The clock struck the witch in her right temple. The lamp slammed against her jawbone. Those twin impacts knocked Cassandra backward into the dresser.

Ron, Eric, and Max all dropped to the floor beside the bed. Eric's arm finally relaxed, and he let the knife fall and clank against the exposed wood floor.

"Ron, read the incantation!" Christina shouted.

She reached for her copy at the same time. Ron started to dig his copy out from his pocket as well, but quickly froze.

"Look out!"

Cassandra stood up again and placed her hand over the open chest. Wisps of energy from the red glow drifted upward. Her fingers absorbed them like a sponge.

"I will erase all of you from existence."

Cassandra swung her hand around. It now possessed the same red glow as the chest.

"Oh shit! This is bad," Ron said.

Casey scooped up a pair of sneakers from the closet. He lunged forward and threw both at her. One sailed over her arm and smacked against the window. The other stayed on target. It struck her hand. Cassandra shrieked and spun to face him.

"You've been a thorn in my side long enough."

Casey started running toward the dresser.

"Read the incantation!" he said, looking back at Christina and Ron. "I can take care of the chest."

A bolt of red energy discharged from Cassandra's fingertips. It struck Casey in the neck when he was only inches from the dresser. He stopped in his tracks with the same suddenness as a car slamming on the brakes. Casey unleashed the most terrified scream Ron ever heard in his life. Skin, muscles, bones, hair, and blood all changed color. Each part of his body hardened. A moment later, he stood fixed in place — solid and motionless as a statue.

"Casey! No!"

Christina cried out and reached out her hand toward him. Cassandra threw her hand outward. The now frozen Casey slammed against the wall. His limbs, head, and torso all shattered into dozens of pieces at the same time. What remained of his body collapsed into a broken heap just below a giant dent in the bedroom wall.

Cassandra turned back and flashed a grin.

"One down. The rest soon to follow."

"You miserable bitch!" Tears streamed down Christina's face. "I'm gonna make sure you stay in that chest for eternity this time."

"Empty threats. You can't withstand me forever. My dark magic is much too ancient and much too powerful for a little girl like you."

Cassandra's taunts only stoked raw hatred welling up inside Christina. It seeped into her eyes and laced through each breath. Christina doubled her hands into fists and clenched them until each knuckle turned white. Ron had seen this level of rage from her only once before.

The playground memory.

Christina closed her eyes for a split second. When those eyes popped open again, so did her fists. She thrust her arms outward and made a sweeping motion to her right. The entire room shook from the floor to the ceiling. Ron stumbled forward and fell on his knees.

Cassandra flew toward the ceiling. Christina flung her against the closet door. It snapped in half and Cassandra landed against the back wall of the closet. Clothes flew off hangars above her, some landing on top of Cassandra and some landing on the floor around her.

Before Cassandra had a chance to stage a counterattack, she flew across the room again. Christina swept her arms left this time. It sent her adversary crashing over the desk and spilled candles onto the floor.

"Here's your chance," Ron said, turning to Eric and Max. "Hurry. Start cutting Mom loose again."

Eric and Max produced their knives once more. They grasped vines and started feverishly sawing through them one at a time.

Ron turned back to watch the unfolding battle before him. Cassandra reached her hand toward the chest to try and draw more red energy to her. Christina quickly swept her arms right again. She flung Cassandra against the closet wall a second time. Sheet rock crumbled in the impact spot.

"This is for Casey."

Christina picked up Cassandra again, suspending her in the air inside the closet. She swept her arms left a second time and pushed outward as she did so. Cassandra sped through the air like a human-sized bullet. She blasted through the curtain and the blinds and finally the bedroom window itself. Glass shattered like an eggshell and flew everywhere.

Cassandra landed on her shoulder and face and rolled across the shingles. Her momentum carried her straight off the roof. A jumbled tangle of the curtain and the blinds fell to the lawn below. Cassandra reached out with her left hand and her fingers clamped onto the edge. Her other arm dangled free along with her feet.

"Start the incantation!" Christina shouted, grasping Ron's arm.

They both produced their paper copies of the incantation. Seeing the words in a room lit with dull red light and candlelight wasn't the easiest thing. Ron grabbed Max's flashlight and positioned it so the beam fell on both papers.

They started chanting.

Invoco hodie caelum et terram

Cassandra used her hand as a springboard to propel herself back on the roof. Being flung around the bedroom took a toll. Her gown had been torn in multiple places. Cassandra's face bore purple bruises and gashes inflicted on her from multiple impacts. Blood dribbled from gashes on her forehead, her cheek, and her mouth.

signum potentiae intus

Eric and Max had severed more than half of the vines. Emily's arm and a portion of her leg were now visible.

Cassandra floated toward the shattered window with unnatural speed. She stretched out her hand to draw more red energy from the chest. Her wounds began to heal as she drew closer. Those reddish black eyes grew redder as wisps of red reached out to her like matter spiraling toward an accretion disk.

arca ad finem

Cassandra snapped her head toward Christina and Ron. Her eyes reverted to their original icy blue hue. She dropped to the floor and unleashed an inhuman glass-shattering shriek. Both Eric and Max dropped their knives and plugged their ears. Ron and Christina also covered their ears. Emily's eyes popped wide open.

Wisps of red energy retreated from Cassandra back to the chest. The red glow itself grew dimmer and faded away like cooling embers in a dying fire. A howling wind arose from inside the chest. All red dust scattered across the floor rose in the air. It swirled in a cloud and then shot toward the chest in a straight line.

Ron's eyes soon fixed on Cassandra herself. Her transformation was unlike anything he ever witnessed. Cassandra stared down at her hands as they started to fragment and dissolve into a red mist. It spread from her hands and up the entire length of her arms. The gown dissolved at the same rate. Her feet and legs also began evaporating into mist. Cassandra's chest and torso soon followed.

An unseen force pulled her head downward as the dissolution neared an end. Cassandra's face became elongated and stretched out. Her mouth froze in an expression of absolute horror. Flesh and bone crumbled until no trace of her remained. Lingering remnants of red mist spiraled into the chest until, at last, it was all inside again.

Ron walked over to the dresser. He stared at the chest for a second or two and then slammed the lid.

Christina closed her eyes and fell to her knees sobbing. Ron turned and rushed back to her side. He dropped to the floor next to Christina and swept her up in a tight embrace. Ron tenderly kissed her forehead while she buried her face in his shoulder.

Their nightmare finally met an end.

26

Emily blinked and drew a long and deep breath.

"Mom's awake!"

Excitement overtook Eric's voice. Ron and Christina rose to their feet. Max and Eric finished slicing through the last of the vines. In the absence of Cassandra, the plants began rapidly withering away. The two boys ripped remnant vines away from Emily. She sat upright on the bed. Eric immediately threw his arms around his mother. Ron rushed over to the bedside and turned it into a three-way hug.

Tears welled up in Emily's eyes while she clung to both of her sons. "Thank you for saving my life," she whispered.

Ron smiled and closed his eyes. The joy consuming him now exceeded the sheer anguish he felt only hours earlier. He still had his mom. Cassandra failed in all her plans. To Ron, bringing his mom home alive and safe marked the witch's most satisfying failure of all.

He helped his mom to her feet. Her legs wobbled a bit from being pinned to the bed so long. Ron caught his mom by the shoulder to keep her from falling backward.

"I guess my legs aren't fully awake," Emily said.

"We're just happy you're safe." The tone in Christina's voice matched the physical and emotional drain gripping her. "We've all been worried sick about you all night."

Emily offered a weary smile and grasped her forearm.

"I'm so happy you all found me. And stopped that awful girl."

"Christina deserves the credit for that," Ron said, helping his mom take her first steps forward. "She kept Cassandra from destroying us."

"Christina?"

Emily looked at her thoughtfully. Recognition washed over her face as she connected the name with what Eric told her earlier in the evening.

"Thank you for all you've done tonight," she said. "Ron is lucky to have such a caring friend like you."

"Actually, Mom, Christina is my girlfriend."

Christina slipped her hand into his free hand and gave it a gentle squeeze after he said the word girlfriend. Ron did not need magic to discern her thoughts. He knew she loved him as much as he loved her.

"Girlfriend?"

Emily responded to her son's revelation with a little half-smile.

Once circulation returned to his mother's legs enough for her to walk on her own, Ron returned to the dresser. He snatched the chest off the dresser top and pushed the clasp against the lock plate. A thick chain still lay on the dresser top. Ron found a lock snipped by bolt cutters on the floor near the foot of the dresser. He passed the chest off to Christina. Ron wrapped the chain around the outside, while she held it in her arms.

"This won't work." Ron held up both pieces of the cut lock. "We'll have to search around here for a new one."

Christina stared at the lock and shook her head.

"That's not a good option for us. I don't want anything to delay us from sealing up this chest and burying it deep in the ground again."

She passed the chest back to Ron and took the broken lock from his hands. Christina pinched the two pieces together between her fingers and thumb. When she released her hand again, the lock had been restored to its original uncut state. Christina attached it to its former spot on the chest and locked the chains in place.

"That was unexpected." Emily's eyes were glued to the restored lock. "How did you do that?"

"I'll explain later," Ron replied.

They snatched a candle off the floor. Christina ignited the wick with one snap of her fingers, earning another curious look from Emily. The tiny flame didn't do much to illuminate the darkened hallway and stairs. No other candles remained lit anywhere in the house. Ron guessed each one got extinguished when they sealed Cassandra inside the chest again.

Ron turned and took in the full scope of the house's destruction for the first time when the group reached the front yard. It looked as bad as the old high school did in those photos he uncovered with Christina. Dean had the right idea all along. They had to take every necessary step to keep anyone else from uncovering Cassandra's chest and unleashing her once more.

"We've got survivors!"

Ron glanced over to see Deputy Leeds climbing through the broken living room window. He turned around and noticed a pair of vehicles with flashing lights. Both vehicles were parked directly behind Deputy Palmer's truck. Ron also noticed the front door jutting out from the broken windshield of that truck and gave a low whistle.

"I'm so glad no one was inside that thing," he told the others in a quiet voice.

"What happened here?" Deputy Leeds walked up to the group on the front lawn. "I have a dead deputy in that house, and I need answers."

Ron, Christina, Emily, Eric, and Max all exchanged nervous glances. Nobody was exactly sure what to tell him about the events that unfolded.

"I've known Deputy Palmer for nine years. He was a close friend. I need know why his dead body is pinned on a wall inside."

"He died trying to do the same thing we were doing," Ron said.

"And what's that?"

"Stopping a witch from destroying this town," Christina said.

Deputy Leeds started to shake his head.

"I don't believe this."

"Believe it." The tone in Christina's voice grew fiercer. "She also took the life of one of the closest friends I'll ever have. We've all suffered because of things Cassandra did."

"If you don't believe us, you can find your proof upstairs," Eric said, while turning and pointing to the house. "You'll finally see the dead body of that pizza delivery boy."

Deputy Leeds gave him a wary look. He radioed another deputy and told them to go check upstairs for a dead body. Confirmation of what Eric told him came across the radio a minute later. Deputy Leeds' eyes widened, and he stared hard at the group.

"A witch, huh? We're going to have to work out a different story to share when word of what happened here leaks out."

"What do you mean?" Emily scrunched up her face when he said these words. "People have a right to know what went on here tonight."

"People will panic. Deer Falls can't handle the fallout. We're going to put a lid on it just like we've done with all the other incidents."

"Other incidents?"

Ron glanced over at Christina. She answered with a sad nod. Casey's conspiracy theories had more merit than Ron originally thought.

"I wouldn't go spreading crazy stories around town, if I were you." Deputy Leeds cast a stern look at the whole group. "Life in Deer Falls will go much smoother for all of you if you play ball."

Ron finally understood how marginalized Christina and Casey felt when he first met them in detention. Many Deer Falls residents turned a blind eye to supernatural events on purpose. When the cops eventually cleared everyone to go home after some more questioning,

Ron couldn't help feeling frustrated knowing what they did to save the town would be ignored and forgotten.

* * *

Finding a suitable spot for concealing the chest meant going outside Deer Falls town limits. Ron and Christina agreed that putting it back in the same vacant lot Dean once guarded would not work. They needed to find a different place where the chest had a greater chance of remaining undisturbed.

They drove until reaching a trail head at the border of the national forest. Ron parked the car at the trail head. He grabbed a pair of shovels and a flashlight while Christina secured the chest. They walked up the trail a short distance until coming to a grouping of four pine trees that formed a semicircle.

"This is a good spot," Christina said. "Let's dig here."

They broke up hardened topsoil with their shovels. A mound piled up beside them as they dug out scoop after scoop of dirt and loose rock. Ron's muscles in his arms and shoulders felt tight and sore, but he attacked it with all the vigor he could muster. When they finally created a hole that reached his waist, Ron and Christina tossed their shovels aside.

"I hope this is deep enough," he said.

Ron knelt along the edge and carefully placed the chest down in the bottom of the fresh hole. They grabbed their shovels again and started tossing dirt and rock back on top the chest. Once Ron and Christina filled in the hole again, he rested himself and his shovel against a nearby tree. Christina cast her shovel aside and continued to stand in front of the burial spot. She clasped her emerald pendant and closed her eyes.

"Bind this chest and its inhabitant to this mountain soil." Her pendant glowed as she recited each word. "From the ground this evil came. To the ground it shall return. Never to rise again while this mountain and this forest stand."

Christina unhooked her pendant and touched the emerald to the burial spot. Soil surrounding the pendant took on the same glow until that energy finally seeped deeper into the broken ground and vanished. She lifted her pendant from the ground and strung it around her neck again.

"It's done. She can't return."

Christina frowned and stared at the burial spot. Her reaction wasn't exactly what Ron expected to see.

"What's on your mind?"

"I'm scared." She closed her eyes and drew a sharp breath. "I'm scared of what I could become."

Ron scrambled away from his resting place against the tree and put his arm around her.

"What makes you say that?"

She gradually opened her eyes again and gazed into his face.

"I tapped into a rage I didn't think I possessed when I fought Cassandra. When she murdered Casey, darkness consumed me. Only for a moment. But that moment was more than enough."

"We couldn't have defeated her without you."

"I would have ripped her apart from head to toe if I could have done it. I wanted to murder her."

Christina turned to face Ron. He grasped her shoulders and looked deep into her eyes.

"What Cassandra did to Casey and all of those other people is unforgivable. No one could be in our situation and not be overcome with anger."

"Uncovering her true nature frightens me." Christina turned away and focused her attention on the burial spot again. "I saw a darkness within Cassandra I see, in part, within myself."

"I don't see it."

"Malevolence ruled her heart. She embraced darkness and used magic as a weapon for murder and destruction."

"Some people are just bad seeds."

"What drives a person to such an extreme?" Christina walked over to the tree where Ron rested earlier. She leaned against the trunk. "Could something similar happen to me? Once you cross into darkness with magic, it's tough to remain in the light."

Ron joined her underneath the tree and wrapped Christina up in a warm embrace.

"You are not Cassandra. You will never be her."

She rested her head against his shoulder.

"What makes you so certain?"

"Love. I see it in how you use your magic. You're unselfish. You focus on helping others. I never saw those qualities in Cassandra."

"Is it really that simple?"

"It is for me. I have seen enough to know I have no reason to fear you and every reason to love you."

"I have every reason to love you too."

Christina gazed into his eyes and tenderly kissed him on the lips. Another kiss followed deeper than the first as his lips clung to hers. They slid down the trunk and cuddled up at the base of the tree to watch the sunrise together. Ron smiled as he and Christina stared up at a cloudless sky painted with brilliant streaks of yellow and orange from rays of sunlight peeking over the horizon.

Life in Deer Falls was going to be good after all.

THE END

About the Author

Being a storyteller is second nature to John Coon. Ever since John typed up his first stories on his parents' typewriter at age 12, he has possessed a thirst for creating stories and sharing those tales with others. John graduated from the University of Utah in 2004 and has carved out a successful career as an author and journalist since that time. His byline has appeared in dozens of major publications across the world.

Pandora Reborn is his debut novel. Since first publishing it 2018, John has published many other popular novels, novellas, and short stories — highlighted by the bestselling *Alien People Chronicles* science fiction adventure series.

John lives in Sandy, Utah. Bookmark his official author page, john-coon.net, for all the latest news related to his past, present, and future stories. Subscribe to his weekly author newsletter *Strange New Worlds* (http://johncoon.net/subscribe) for original short fiction, poems, and articles.

Also by John Coon

Check out these other popular stories from John Coon available at major booksellers worldwide.

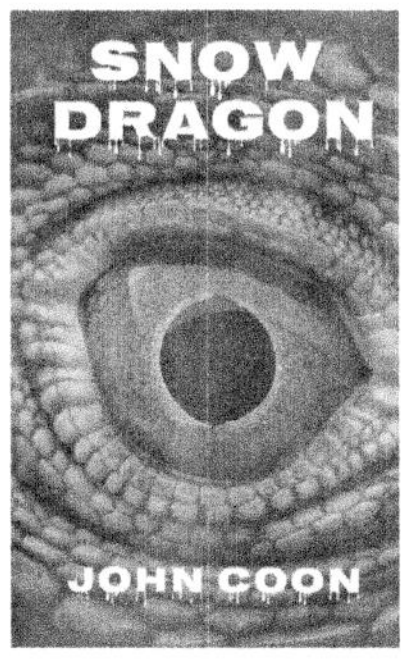

Snow Dragon

A mythical monster has awakened beneath Deer Falls following a major earthquake. Can the Duggan family destroy this vicious and lethal predator before it drives their sleepy Colorado town to extinction?

A prequel to the *Deer Falls* small town horror series.

The Crimson Reaper

Consumed by a thirst to unlock powerful dark magic, a sadistic killer stalks Deer Falls. Can Eric Olson overcome past trauma to save himself and the rest of the town from destruction?

Book no. 2 in the *Deer Falls* small town horror series.

Alien People

Discovering a distant probe bearing a message of peace inspires alien explorers to journey to a mysterious planet called Earth. Will first contact bring new understanding ... or take a deadly turn?

Book no. 1 in the *Alien People Chronicles* science fiction adventure series.

Dark Metamorphosis

A brutal abduction reveals a dark plot to destroy survivors of the Earth expedition. Can they fight deceit and evade assassins to reveal the dreadful truth?

Book no. 2 in the *Alien People Chronicles* science fiction adventure series.

Among Hidden Stars

A tyrannical ruler seeks an ancient relic that imparts god-like powers to use as a world-conquering weapon. Will a rebel couple find the hidden relic first and finally defeat their oppressor's reign?

Book no. 3 in the *Alien People Chronicles* science fiction adventure series.

Under a Fallen Sun

A small Texas town has fallen under siege from an alien menace. Four college students are trapped inside the town, battling for their lives. Can they defeat invaders who seek to conquer Earth?

A science fiction thriller novel set in the *Alien People Chronicles* universe.

Hollow Planet

A barren planet holds a startling secret tied to its distant past. Will uncovering evidence of an ancient alien race forge a new alliance? Or will discovery exact a deadly cost for these explorers?

A short science fiction story set in the *Alien People Chronicles* universe.

In Hell's Shadow

Trapped in an unfamiliar place far from home, Kate must confront a once-buried nightmare anew. Will this dark secret from her past lead her to certain destruction?

A paranormal horror short story set in the Deer Falls universe.

Hiding From Shadows

Every night is a personal battle to survive until morning for Ellen. An unseen menace lurks in the shadows outside her home. Will it strike without mercy once she lets her guard down?

A paranormal horror short story set in the Deer Falls universe.

Printed in Great Britain
by Amazon

57837597R00142